Wild Cat

Tyndale House Publishers, Inc. • Carol Stream, Illinois

STARLIGHT

3

Animal Rescue

Wild Cat

DANDI DALEY MACKALL

Visit Tyndale online at www.tyndale.com.

You can contact Dandi Daley Mackall through her website at www.dandibooks.com.

Wild Cat

Designed by Jacqueline L. Nuñez

Edited by Stephanie Rische

For manufacturing information regarding this product, please call 1-800-323-9400.

ISBN 978-1-4143-1270-5

Printed in the United States of America

17
8 7 6

FOR VERONICA,
my new horse-loving friend in Italy

One

I WISH ANIMALS COULD TALK.

This is what I'm thinking, watching Hank and Dakota unload eight horses they rescued from Happy Horsey Trail Rides.

Happy Horsey? There's nothing happy about these horses. They're skinny, scarred, scraggly, and scared. If they could talk, their stories would probably tear my heart into little pieces.

"Hank! Can I help?" I shout at him. He's trying to get a spotted mare to back down the trailer ramp. She stomps one back leg like she's squishing a snake, then lunges toward the trailer. Her flank is so scabbed over it looks like rough leather.

Hank gets the horse to back halfway down the ramp. I'm about to ask him again if I can help when he yells at me. "Kat! Stay back!"

I don't usually get to help with the horses. I'm in charge of cats. But I've been hoping Hank would make an exception this time. I really want to help these poor horses.

The mare bolts up the ramp again. Hank smooth-talks her. "Come on, gal," he coaxes. My brother–well, he'll officially be my brother as soon as my adoption is final–is 16. If that stubborn horse were a junior high or high school girl instead of a horse, she'd come thundering down the ramp fast as you please to follow Hank. Every girl I know in Nice, Illinois, has a crush on Hank.

Midway on the Pinto's bony rump is a deep brand: HH. Happy Horsey. A jagged scar streaks under the brand like a ghostly underline. I try not to think about how it got there. I wish I could do something to help.

"Quit daydreaming, will you?" Hank shouts. "You're going to get hurt." He and the spotted mare match step for step down the ramp, trotting backward when they touch ground. Then they jog off to the pasture, leaving me in a puff of dust.

I move into the barn. It's a great barn, with stalls in back and a round pen out front that takes up half of the sawdust floor. Everything smells fresh, like the forest. If I were a horse, I'd love it here. In this very barn I touched my first horse, kissed my first cat, and got my first dog bite.

My cat, Kitten, climbs my leg, claws up my back, and settles onto my shoulders, where she curls her scraggly self around my neck. I'm sweaty, so Kitten's shaggy white fur sticks to me. I don't mind. Kitten and I go way back. I found her half-dead in a ditch. She was my first rescue.

Kitten rubs her face against my ear. She purrs, and it sounds like a swarm of locusts. Then, just like that, she digs her claws into my shoulder and springs off.

"Kitten!" I scold. But she's long gone.

Dakota teases me about *Kitten* not being the most creative name in cat history. But since my nickname is Kat, I think "Kitten" is the perfect name for my first rescued cat at Starlight Animal Rescue.

"Look out!" Dakota shouts.

I turn, and I'm nose-to-nose with a scrawny chestnut pony. A wide, raised scar runs the length of his head, splitting it in two. His eyelids sag, and he's bone thin all over.

"Move, Kat! I'm not kidding!" Dakota tugs on the pony's lead rope. But she's leading another horse too, a skinny gray mare who wants to return to the trailer.

I take a couple of steps back from the pony. "Sorry. I just wanted to help."

"Right now you can help by staying out of the way," Dakota says. "You could get hurt." Dakota's 16, like Hank. She could probably pass for Cherokee–she's that exotic looking. I love Dakota like a sister, but she worries about me too much. She freaks out if I break a fingernail. Once people learn I've got cancer, they treat me like I'm made of glass.

I watch Dakota struggle to keep both horses behind her as she leads them through the barn. "The pony's limping," I call to her.

"What?" She starts to turn around. The gray mare tugs sideways, pulling Dakota with her. The poor pony's nearly jerked off his feet.

Hooves. Not feet.

Okay. So I'm not exactly a horsewoman. But neither was Dakota when Ms. Bean, the social worker, dropped her off at Starlight Animal Rescue. That was only a couple of months ago. Now Hank says he couldn't get on without her.

I wonder what that would feel like, to know people couldn't get on without you.

The whole Coolidge family is like one big hall of fame. A doctor, a firefighter, an expert dog trainer, two horse whisperers . . . and me.

"You guys are going to need help with all those horses, you know." I have to shout so Dakota can hear me. She's still making her way to the stalls with both horses.

I tag along. "That pony's favoring his right foreleg, Dakota," I try again.

"I know. We think it's a bowed tendon. The vet examined all the horses before we picked them up. Doc Jim said we'll need to give this one some bute–Butazolodine–until his leg heals." Dakota has control of the horses again. She frowns at me. "Not so close, Kat."

I'm trying to study the pony's forelegs. "His leg doesn't look bowed to me. Are you sure–?"

"Not now. Okay?" Dakota begs.

"You know," I say, hustling to keep up with her, "this is the first time we've taken on so many horses at once."

"You and your first times," Dakota says, shaking her head.

It's true that I love firsts. First snow of the year. First leaf to turn in autumn. (It hasn't happened yet.) First robin in spring. The first time Hank called me "little sis." The first time Kitten purred for me.

Yesterday I heard three cats purr at the same time. I wrote Catman, Hank's cat-loving cousin, about it. Catman knows more about cats than anybody in the whole world. He's even making a movie about cats, a documentary. He and Winnie the Horse Gentler run a pet helpline on the Web. I still haven't met them, even though they're just a couple of states away, in Ohio. But it's hard for people with animals to leave home.

"Kat! Did you hear me?" Dakota yells. She's standing in front of an empty stall, a horse on each side, pulling her in opposite directions. "Will you open the stall door? Please?"

"Oops. Sorry." I slip in front of her and unlatch the door.

"Thanks." Dakota leads the gray mare into the stall. The pony tries to follow. "Stay!" Dakota commands.

"Let me take the pony," I beg.

She hesitates. "I don't know. You could get stepped on."

"By the pony? Poor thing's so skinny, I wouldn't even feel it if he did step on me," I joke. "Besides, I won't get stepped on. Please, Dakota. I really want to help you guys." I reach over to stroke the pony. His neck twitches like a fly's landed on it. He sidesteps.

That's enough for Dakota. "Maybe later. You better ask Popeye and Annie first." Popeye is my dad, Chester Coolidge, and Annie is my mom. Dakota and I are both fosters, but she doesn't call them Mom and Dad like I do.

Dakota unsnaps the lead from the gray horse's halter. The snap startles the pony. He jerks and backs away fast. The rope slips out of Dakota's hand.

Without thinking, I lunge for the pony's lead rope, grabbing it in both fists.

The pony bolts. My hands stay glued to the rope. I jerk forward. My feet fly out from under me. The pony takes off up the stallway.

"Kat!" Dakota screams.

I hit the ground hard. My stomach's a sled as I'm dragged over sawdust.

I hear Dakota's cries behind me. "Kat! Let go of the rope!"

I see my hands on the rope. But they don't belong to me. They won't let go. The pony's tail slaps my arm. I bounce over something. Dirt sprays my face. I barely feel it. I'm numb. I can't see. I close my eyes and wonder if I'll ever see again.

I've heard your whole life flashes before you at a time like this. But my life isn't even a flash. More like a spark. A fizzle. I haven't done anything with my life.

Fear shoots through my bloodstream. I feel it like the cold ink they inject in me before X-rays.

X-rays. IVs. Tests. Cancer. That's how I'm supposed to die.

Not like this.

TWO

"WHOA! WHOA, BOY!"

I slide to a stop, inches from the pony's back hooves. My eyes sting when I open them. I shut them fast. The world is spinning as I wait for the pain to catch up with me.

"That's a good boy." It's Hank's voice I hear, coming from miles away. "Kat, are you okay? Let go of the rope."

I uncurl my fingers and roll to my side. Fetal position.

It hurts to breathe. I cough. It hurts even more. Everywhere.

Dakota drops to her knees beside me.

"Kat? Can you hear me? I'm sorry! I didn't . . . Are you . . . ?" She's crying hard.

I want to tell her I'm okay. *Am I?*

"She's bleeding, Hank!" Dakota screams.

"Where's she bleeding?" Hank demands.

That's what *I* want to know. I think of opening my eyes and seeing for myself. But I don't.

"I think it's just her arms," Dakota answers. "Or her hands." She sneezes. *Achoo!*

I smell sawdust. I feel it in my nostrils. *Please don't let me sneeze.* The thought of it makes my sides ache.

Dakota sneezes again.

"Bless you," I whisper. I'm not sure if I've said it out loud or not.

"Kat!" Dakota falls on top of me, hugging me. Then she scoots away, like I'm glass again. "Hank, she blessed my sneeze." Dakota breaks down into sobs.

Is this the first time I've seen her cry?

"Don't move." Hank runs toward the stalls, leading the pony behind him. In seconds he's back. I open my eyes enough to see the tips of his scuffed boots.

"Kat?" Hank says. He squats beside me.

My eyes are watering so much that Hank and Dakota look blurry. "I think I'm okay."

"Don't move till you're sure," Hank warns. "Can you feel your legs?"

I wiggle one. Then the other.

"Does that mean they're not broken?" Dakota asks. She wipes her eyes with the back of her hand. Mud smears her cheeks.

Hank doesn't answer. He keeps staring at me. "You're lucky you had jeans on. Try moving your arms."

I do. My elbows are killing me. Blood trickles down my arms and mixes with sawdust and dirt.

Dakota touches my shoulder. I feel her trembling.

Hank shakes his head. "You just about gave me a heart attack."

"Sorry," I say.

"I think we should get you inside." He slides his arms under me.

Dakota gets to her feet. "Hank, are you sure it's okay to move her?"

Again, Hank ignores her and talks to me. "Let me know if anything hurts too much. Okay?"

I nod. When I do, my hair–my wig–slides to the ground. Dakota picks it up, shakes it out, and sticks it back on. She doesn't look at me when she does it. They've seen me without my wig before, but I can tell we all feel weird about it anyway. Hank acts like he doesn't see. Chemo doesn't turn everybody bald, but it did me.

Hank picks me up like I'm a feather.

"I can walk, Hank." My voice comes out a whisper. Not real convincing.

"Am I carrying you?" Hank asks, striding out of the barn. "You're so light, I wasn't sure."

Hank's kidding, but he's not that far off. My kind of cancer messes with my stomach and appetite. I'll be starting junior high next week, but I still have to shop for clothes in the girls' department.

Hank hollers over his shoulder, "Dakota, will you put the last horse in the pasture? Give them all grain. And hay for the ones in the barn."

"No problem," Dakota says, jogging back to the trailer.

I wanted to help them with the horses.

Instead, as usual, I've made things harder on everybody.

"Kat!" Dad barrels out of the house and runs at us, faster than I've ever seen him move. "Kat! Kat!" he screams.

"Tell him I'm okay." I know I can't yell loud enough.

"Dad, she's okay!" Hank shouts. "She didn't faint. She just fell in the barn." He adds under his breath, "And was dragged a few yards."

I elbow him. It hurts. Me, not him.

Dad lumbers up to us. He's panting so hard that I'm afraid he'll have a heart attack. Dad's a head shorter than Hank and probably 50 pounds heavier. "What happened? How did she fall? I should have been there." He glances up at the sky and mutters, "Father, thank You for being there." Then he looks at me, and his eyes double in size. "Your arm!"

Maybe I look worse than I thought. I've never seen Dad this upset. Not even when I had that bad reaction to a new medicine. Not even when I threw up all over him in the Nice grocery store the first week I moved here.

"Dad, I'm okay. Really."

"She can move her arms and legs," Hank

says. He starts walking toward the house again.

"But what happened? How did you fall? Where'd you fall from? Does your head hurt?" Dad's short legs shuffle alongside us. He reaches out like he wants to carry me himself.

"Dad, I've got her," Hank says, stopping at the house. "Could you get the door?"

"Of course. Yes. The door." Dad fumbles with the latch. It takes him three tries to get the screen open for us.

"It looks worse than it is," I tell him. "My elbows are scraped."

Two of Wes's rescued dogs slip outside when we come in. Mustard and Ketchup, two of my rescued cats, sneak inside with us.

"Take her upstairs," Dad says. "I'll call my Annie."

"Don't call Mom," I beg over Hank's shoulder, as he takes the stairs two at a time with me. "I'll be fine until she gets home from the hospital."

But Dad's already disappeared into the kitchen to call her.

My mom is an oncologist, a cancer doctor at Nice Hospital. That's where I saw her for the first time. I was only seven, but I was already collecting firsts. The social worker brought me in for my first radiation treatment. "This is Dr. Annie Coolidge," she said. I remember thinking that I'd never seen hair that curly. She was short and stout, and she kept losing her pencil. She didn't look anything like a doctor, but I trusted her from the first minute I saw her.

Hank shoves open my bedroom door and lays me down on the bed, on top of my cat bedspread. "What should I get you? Want some water? Should I turn on your fan?"

I think about asking him to take me off the spread so I don't get it dirty, but it's too late anyway. "I'm okay. Thanks, Hank."

Kitten hops onto the bed and curls up beside me. Her purring motor starts right up.

Dad's voice rises with the sound of his heavy footsteps on the stairs. "Now, now, my Annie. We can keep Kat comfortable until . . . Of course. . . . I promise. . . . Darling, I said I promise."

Still holding the phone to his ear, Dad stumbles into my room. "I'm here with her right now. Hank's taking good care of her and . . . Well, yes, if you want, but . . ." He glances at me. "Your mother would like to talk to you."

"Sure." I reach for the phone. "Ouch!" My elbow stings. Dad puts the phone to my ear.

"Kat? Are you okay? Your head. Did you hit your head?" Mom sounds panicked. "What hurts?"

"Mom, I'm okay. Really. I scraped my elbows. It was a stupid accident."

"I'm leaving the hospital right now. Getting into the van." I hear the door open. The alarm goes off. "Oh, dear. What did I do?"

I turn to Dad. "Mom set off the alarm again. You better take it."

Dad takes back the phone and walks Mom through the steps to disarm the alarm system. They were made for each other. I've been with Dad when *he* had to call Mom to walk him through this same process.

Dad and Hank do their best to clean up my face and arms. But they're so afraid of hurting me that they quit the second Dakota joins us.

"Horses are all pastured, stabled, and fed," Dakota says.

"Thanks, Dakota. Here," Hank says, tossing her his washcloth. "You take over."

"Me?" Dakota catches the rag and acts like it's poison.

"Good idea," Dad agrees. He sets down his bowl and washcloth and kisses my forehead. "Dakota can help you get out of those jeans. Your mother should be here in a little while. She'll know what to do. Are you sure you're not in pain? Are you telling us everything, Kat? Because you–"

"My arms hurt. My hands burn. My knees don't feel so good. But I'm okay, Dad."

Hank and Dad close the door after them, and Dakota gets out a nightgown. It takes us 11 minutes to get me into it. I know because I have a cat-shaped clock on my wall next to my cat calendar.

When we're done, I lie down again, and Dakota sits on the bed with me. She picks up my wig from the floor, where I guess it fell during my struggle with the nightgown.

"Just put it on the bedpost," I tell her. I've never been able to sleep in the thing.

Dakota sets my wig on the bedpost at the foot of my bed and straightens the long blonde hairs. She looks like she's the one who was dragged behind a horse. Her face is streaked with dirt, and her black hair springs around her head in long, wet clumps.

"I can't believe your legs aren't more banged up," she says. "Your knee's purple, though. That's got to hurt." She touches my right knee.

"Ow!" My whole leg throbs with pain.

"I'm sorry!" Dakota cries, scooting away.

"That's okay. Guess I banged it up pretty good."

"You could have been killed."

My mind flashes back to the barn, to the moment when I thought I was going to die. I wasn't ready. I didn't want to die. Not because I'm scared of dying. I don't think I am. How can I be scared of being in a place where I can talk to God without other things getting in the way? Whatever heaven's like, I know it's better than here. And here is pretty great.

But I know I'm not ready because I haven't done anything with my life. That's what I learned in that barn today. I need to do something with my life, like Mom and Dad and Hank do all the time. And I need to do it now.

Knock! Knock!

"Kat! Can I come in?" Dad calls through the door.

"Come in," I holler back.

He bursts in, waving an envelope. Mustard and Ketchup prance into the room behind him. They don't jump up on my bed, not with Kitten there.

"Look what came in the–" He stops when his gaze reaches my knees. "Your knee is purple." He walks closer. "I can't stand thinking about how much that must hurt." His eyes fill with tears.

"It's not so bad," I say quickly. "You know I bruise easily." That part's true. I think it's because of one of the meds I'm on.

A horn honks outside. Brakes squeal.

"Sounds like Mom's home," I say.

Dad runs outside to meet her. In seconds they're racing up the stairs.

Dakota moves out of the way.

Mom rushes to my bed. "Kat, Kat, Kat," she mutters, kissing my forehead and cheeks.

"I'm okay," I manage.

"We'll just see about that." She turns to Dad and Dakota. "Everybody out."

Mom shoos them from my room, then

transforms from mother into Dr. Coolidge, oncologist. She opens her doctor's bag and, for the next 17 minutes, by the cat clock, examines me head to toe.

When she's done, she sits on the foot of my bed and drops her head into her hands. I know she's praying. I just hope it's a thank-You-God prayer and not a how-could-You-let-Kat-be-in-such-bad-shape prayer.

When she looks up, her eyes are red. "God had you in His palm, Kat," she says quietly.

I grin. I'm thinking of that psalm that talks about stumbling but not falling because God holds your hand. I've always pictured a parent holding a little kid's hand and not letting go when the kid's feet fly out from under him.

"You know I've never been all that fond of horses," Mom says.

Mom loves all animals, just like the rest of us. She can't stand to see one suffering or homeless. She patches up cats, dogs, and horses if the vet can't get here in time. She even brought home a bird with a broken wing once and nursed it back to health.

"When I think of what could have happened to you . . ." Her voice trails off.

I put my hand on her arm. She's wrapped my right hand in bandages so it looks like I'm a one-gloved boxer. "I'm okay, right?"

She sighs. "Nothing's broken," she admits.

Footsteps thunder up the stairs.

"Come on in," Mom hollers.

Dad enters, and I catch the look he and Mom exchange, full of meaning, like only they can pull off. I think Dad's asking if I'm really okay and Mom's saying I am but she was really scared, and now she's just thanking God it wasn't worse and Dad's agreeing with her. But they don't say anything out loud, and the look lasts only a couple of seconds, by the cat clock.

Then Dad waves his envelope over his head and shouts, "It came!"

"It came?" Mom jumps up from the bed and reaches for the envelope. She opens it and looks inside. "Where's the letter?"

"Not there?" Dad peeks in for himself. "I must have left it downstairs."

"Left what downstairs?" I ask.

"I'll go down and get it." Dad turns to leave.

"Don't you dare!" Mom says. "Chester

Coolidge, you come back here right this minute and tell me what they said."

"Two weeks from Saturday," he declares.

Mom grabs him and dances him around the room.

They're making even less sense than usual. Maybe I did hit my head after all.

Dakota and Hank appear in the doorway.

"What's going on?" Dakota demands.

"Two weeks!" Dad answers.

"Two weeks?" Hank glances at me, and I shrug.

"Kat's adoption . . . ," Mom begins.

". . . will be final in two weeks!" Dad finishes.

Hank lets out a whoop.

Dad grabs Mom for another dance around the room.

Dakota runs up to high-five me but stops when she sees the bandages on my hand.

I want to whoop or dance or high-five too. But something won't let me. And it's not the bandages.

Ever since I became a foster child of Annie and Chester Coolidge, I've dreamed of the day I'd be adopted, officially, by them. They're so good. They help everybody. Mom saves lives at the hospital. Dad saves lives working for the fire department.

And now *I'm* about to be a Coolidge too.

But I haven't done anything.

Three

"KAT COOLIDGE," Dakota says, grinning at me. "Katharine Coolidge. Has a nice ring to it."

I try to return her grin. But all I can think is that now I have only two weeks to do something that could make me worth calling myself a Coolidge. I can't become a doctor or join the fire department. Even Wes has turned into somebody people need. The old people at the assisted-living home couldn't get along without the dogs he's trained for them.

I know I can't train horses like Hank and Dakota. But there should be something I can do, some way to help. Maybe if I had another chance with that pony . . .

"Kat?" Mom touches my forehead with the back of her hand. "Honey, are you feeling okay? You're so quiet."

"I'm fine. I guess I'm just tired."

Dad walks up behind Mom and puts his arm around her. "Say, maybe this will help. Kat, what's a cat's favorite song?"

Mom gives him a fake punch. "Chester Coolidge, one of your jokes will most certainly not help."

Hank and Dakota trip over each other in a rush to get out of the room. Dad's pretty famous for his bad jokes and riddles. But I know how much he loves telling them, so I play along. "I don't know, Dad. What's a cat's favorite song?"

"'Three Blind Mice'!" He barely gets it out before he starts cracking up.

"I didn't hear that!" Dakota shouts from the stairs.

"Time to go now," Mom says, gently pushing Dad toward the door.

He obeys but turns back and shouts, "What's a cat's favorite car?"

"Chester!" Mom cries, shoving him with both arms now.

"What's a cat's favorite car, Dad?" I ask.

Mom has him out the door and out of sight. But I hear him shout, "A CAT-illac! Get it, Kat? Cadillac, *Cat*illac?" His voice fades on the stairs.

I close my eyes. I think it's just for a couple of minutes.

When I open my eyes again, I can feel someone watching me. I look to the door, and Wes is standing there.

Wes has been at Starlight Animal Rescue just over a year. He's small for 14, but when he frowns, like he is now, he looks older. Until a couple of weeks ago, Wes was the angriest person I'd ever met. I know he misses his mother, who's back in Chicago, bouncing between jail and rehab. But God's been working overtime on Wes.

"Hey." My voice is gravelly from all the sawdust I swallowed.

Wes doesn't move from the doorway, but Rex, his German shepherd, trots up to my bed and sticks his nose in my face. Kitten shifts from my pillow to my feet. She's not a big Rex fan. I think the other two cats might be hiding under the bed.

"Good dog, Rex," I say. "Come on in, Wes."

He steps into the room like it's booby-trapped. "They said you were okay. You don't look okay."

I wave my bandaged hand at him. "This is way overkill. Mom says I can take it off tomorrow. I'm just scratched and bruised." I scoot up so I'm sitting in bed. It's tough to get comfortable. "You can come closer."

Rex's tail thumps the floor.

Wes stops a couple of feet from my bed. "Hank never should have let you near the barn."

"I wanted to help."

"Dakota should have known better too," he says, like he hasn't heard me.

Rex barks once. It's a warning. Dad calls Wes's dog his "anger-meter." Rex knows when Wes is getting mad before Wes does.

"It wasn't their fault," I explain. "It was a stupid accident. If I hadn't grabbed the pony's lead rope, I wouldn't have gotten hurt."

"But you did!" Wes snaps. "And look at you now."

Rex barks louder.

Wes opens his mouth like he's going to yell at Rex. Then he presses his lips together and leans down to pet his dog. Rex stops barking. I think we're going to be okay.

"Lucky for you there's a doctor in the house," Wes says. His shoulders relax as he keeps stroking Rex's head. I've read somewhere that animals can lower blood pressure. I'll bet it's true with Wes and Rex.

We're quiet for a minute. Then he asks, "Does it hurt?"

"Only when I laugh."

A closed-lips grin tugs at the corners of his mouth. "I'll tell Popeye to keep his jokes to himself then."

I don't remember when Wes started calling Dad "Popeye." Dad doesn't mind. I think he kind of likes it. Plus, it fits. He's bald, stocky, strong, and pretty much a hero.

"Tell me what's going on at the nursing home," I beg.

Wes comes to life. "You should see Munch. I admit that dog won't win any beauty contests, but Miss Golf brings her in to work with her, and Munch can push Buddy's wheelchair now! Bag barks at Rose when her phone's ringing and she can't hear it. And little Moxie's learned to pick up books and pens and things when people drop them." He keeps going with stories from Nice Manor, filled with characters like Leon and Buddy and Moxie and Munch.

I guess I must have slipped off to sleep because all of a sudden Wes is tiptoeing out of my room. "Sorry, Wes," I say, yawning.

"Go back to sleep. You need it. I'll bring you dinner later if you're hungry." He shuts the door after him, leaving me alone with Kitten stretched across my waist like a fuzzy belt.

The next time I open my eyes, it's dark. Through the window, dozens of stars twinkle, including most of Orion and half of the Big Dipper.

I click on the lamp beside my bed and see that Mustard and Ketchup have made themselves at home on my bed, a safe distance from Kitten. Mustard is an overweight tabby I rescued from the Nice Animal Shelter. Ketchup is a sweet gray longhair I found in a ditch out front. I think the cat had been hit by a car.

She was so bloody that I thought she was red. That's why I named her Ketchup.

I need to find homes for Mustard and Ketchup, but I've been holding out for an owner who will take both of them. House rule is that I can't rescue more cats until I find homes for these. Kitten's different. Mom agreed I could keep Kitten forever.

I sit on the edge of my bed a minute before heading to the bathroom. When I stand, I'm a little dizzy. And when I walk, every part of me aches. I wonder if this is what Gram Coolidge feels like when her arthritis acts up.

"Kat!" Dakota runs into my room and puts her arm around my waist. "You should have called me. I tried to stay awake."

"I'm okay. Just stiff. Thanks." She walks me to the bathroom. "I can take it from here, Dakota."

"You sure you're all right?" she asks. I nod. "Then I'll go down and get you something to eat. You missed dinner. All they could talk about was your adoption being final. Are you hungry?"

I shrug. "I'm kinda thirsty."

"I'll bring something up."

When I come out of the bathroom, Dakota's already back with a sandwich, milk, and cookies. It's 2:17 a.m. by the cat clock.

I sit on the bed and drink half of the milk in one gulp. "Thanks, Dakota. You can go back to bed."

She sets the sandwich and cookies on my dresser. "Are you sure you're okay? I could get Annie."

"I'm okay," I tell her. "I'll finish the milk and go back to sleep."

"If you're sure," she says, yawning.

I do try to fall asleep. Only I can't. I keep thinking about my adoption being final in two weeks. That's not very long. Not if I want to do something to prove to myself that I belong in this family.

I roll over, scooting Kitten off my pillow. When I close my eyes, I see the spotted horse with scabs and scars on her flank, the gray mare with her ribs sticking out, that scared-looking sorrel. And the chestnut pony. I try to imagine how he got that limp. Or the long scar on his head.

I wish I knew more about horses. Understanding cats has always come naturally to me. I'm not as great with them as Hank's cousin Catman. But Catman's taught me a lot through our e-mails.

Suddenly, more than anything, I want to e-mail Catman Coolidge. I'm not sure why I think he'll understand. Hank calls his cousin "a man of few words," and Dad agrees. But in our e-mails, Catman has a way of saying just the right thing.

I say a quick prayer for super strength and stand up again. Mustard and Ketchup stay where they are, on the foot of my bed. Kitten curls around my feet, ready to follow. Taking a deep breath, I start the long trek downstairs to the computer.

My knees feel a stab of pain with every stair step, but the thought of writing Catman makes it worth it.

Sometimes when I can't sleep, I come downstairs and sit in the dark and soak up what I call the "Coolidgeness" of our home. I love the smell of the living room. When Dakota first moved in, she said the house smelled like rain. She meant it as a slam, but I love that smell. It's what I imagine most grandmas' houses smell like.

I never met my biological grandmother.

My bio mom gave me up when I was four. Every time I try to remember what she looked like, all I come up with are her eyes. Her eyes were tired. Tired and sad. I can almost picture her lying on an orange couch, her back to me. I think she's crying, but I don't understand why. She's wearing an orange nightgown or maybe an orange T-shirt. I see my hand reaching up to touch her shoulder, but she shakes it off. She has a cigarette between two fingers, the tip orange, like her gown.

I hope she's quit smoking.

Without meaning to, I reach for the two scars on the inside of my left arm. They're rough and soft at the same time, like tiny stones the ocean hasn't finished smoothing yet. My old doctor, the one I had before I met Mom, told us they were scars from a cigarette.

But they're not. I think I'd remember a thing like that.

I'm not sure how long I've been standing at the foot of the stairs, staring into the darkness. Kitten rubs against my bare legs like she's on duty. Back and forth, back and forth. I pick her up and turn on the light. "Come on, Kitten," I whisper. "Let's write Catman."

I pour myself another glass of milk, then settle in at the computer. The screen sits on the little desk between the kitchen and living room. Mom and Dad like to keep an eye on where we go on the Internet. The screen saver flashes pictures while I drink my milk: Dakota on her horse, Blackfire. Hank riding Starlight, the first animal rescued here. Hank's horse is blind, but you'd never guess it if you saw them galloping down the road together, like they are in this picture.

Wes and Rex come up next. Wes is holding his hand in front of his face, but he wasn't quite quick enough to get out of the picture. His fingers are calloused and dark–Wes is African American–and they stretch across his whole face, like he's about to change masks.

Then the old photos cycle in, and my favorite one of all time comes on the screen. It's a picture of Hank and Catman in front of Gram Coolidge's roses. They can't be more than six or seven years old, and even then you could tell how different they are. It's not just that Hank has dark hair and Catman's is long and blond. Hank's standing straight, focused on the camera. You get the feeling that he's just mowed the lawn, organized the garage, and walked a dozen old ladies across the street. On the ground in front of Hank sits Catman, cross-legged, his right hand raised in a peace sign. And on his lap is a big black cat.

I move the mouse to wake up the computer. In a few seconds, I'm logging on to my e-mail with one hand. I'm a hunt-and-peck, two-finger typer anyway.

While I wait for my in-box to fill, my thoughts start running wild again. In two weeks I'm supposed to go before a judge and declare that I want to be a Coolidge forever. Ms. Bean, my social worker, explained it all to me. It's like a marriage, where we all get one last chance to say "I do."

I do. Of course, *I* do. Who wouldn't want to be the daughter of Annie and Chester Coolidge?

But what about them?

Why would they want someone like me to have their name? The name of Hank Coolidge. Catman Coolidge. They deserve the name *Coolidge.*

But me?

My spam filter kicks in and snaps up most

of the messages heading for my in-box. A few pieces of junk get through. Then I see I've got an e-mail from Catman. I go straight to it.

Hey, Cool Kat!

Man, I dig your last list of firsts. Three cats purring in sync? Groovy, Kat!

Far out, seeing Uncle Chester petting Kitten for the first time. That cat's coming around. So's Kitten. (You dig?)

Standing by for more Kat firsts. Lay 'em on me, man!

Stay cool,

The Catman

It feels better, imagining Catman at the other end of cyberspace. Since Catman graduated from high school last year, he's been on the road, off and on, filming his "cat-umentary" on cats in rural America. But he's never failed to answer my e-mails. I hit Reply and type back:

Dear Catman,

Thanks for writing. You have no idea how much I needed to find you here. Kind of like one of the prayers I didn't even ask and God answered it anyway.

It's been quite a day. But I do have a lot of firsts to report.

I sit back in the chair. Typing with one hand is taking me longer than I thought it would. Plus, I'm feeling a little sick to my stomach, the way I feel a lot of mornings. I wanted to type a big list of firsts I've been keeping in my head for the Catman. But I'm not sure how long I can stay up.

I cut to the chase.

Kat's Firsts for Today:

* Today I rode a pony for the first time. Only thing is, I always thought my first horse ride would actually be ON the horse.

I stop typing and stare at the screen so long that it powers down. My mind is powering down too. I need to get upstairs and back to bed.

I maneuver the mouse and hit Send.

For a minute, I stay where I am, gathering courage to tackle the stairs again. Going up is bound to be harder than coming down.

The computer slips into screen saver mode, triggering the slide show of photos back into action. The first picture that comes up is of me. I'm sitting on the lowest branch of the big oak tree out front. I look like a ghost. Pale face, my long blonde wig uncombed, white shorts and white T-shirt.

Just sitting there. Like now.

Just sitting there. Not doing a thing for anybody.

Just sitting there. Not looking anything at all like a real Coolidge.

Four

The rest of the night is filled with fitful dreams and flashes of sleep. Each time I wake up, there's a second of panic before I make myself think of that psalm and picture God holding my hand. Then I drift back to sleep until it happens all over again.

A couple of times I sense people checking in on me. But it's too hard to open my eyes.

It's totally bright and sunshiny before I drag myself out of bed. Even the cats have bailed on me.

"You're up at last." Mom shuffles into my room in lime green tights and an oversize plaid shirt that fits snug around her middle. She's still wearing her fuzzy red bedroom slippers.

"You look Christmassy," I say, yawning in the general direction of her slippers.

"Do I?" She sounds pleased.

I squint at the cat clock and can't believe the cat's paws are at two again, only it's two in the afternoon this time.

"Feeling any better?" Mom asks, hovering over me. "You need to get fluids in you, Kat."

"My little Kat." Dad rushes in and kisses the top of my head. I feel it, which means I don't have my wig on. "One day closer to your adoption being final," Dad announces. "Hungry? Which reminds me . . . Do you know what cats eat for breakfast?"

Mom elbows him, but she's laughing already.

"What *do* cats eat for breakfast, Dad?" I ask.

"*Mice* Krispies! Get it?" He laughs so hard that he breaks into a coughing fit.

Mom slaps him on the back until he's back to normal. "Come on. We'll help Kat downstairs."

"You guys go ahead. I can get downstairs on my own."

"Don't we know it," Dad says.

Mom explains, "Your father played detective this morning. He deduced that you got up in the wee hours, drank some milk, and read your e-mail."

"Not bad," I admit.

"You have five new e-mails from Catman, by the way," Dad says.

"Catman's mother called this morning to make sure you were all right. We filled them in on your accident." Mom pulls a curler out of her hair, letting the curl bounce across her forehead. "Your aunt Claire is quite a character. She was so upset I could hardly understand her. Bart had to take the phone from her. He said Catman had heard from you last night and was really worried."

"You think Claire's a character?" Dad laughs. "My little brother, Bart–now *there's* a character for you." Dad's only a few minutes older than his twin, but he still calls Bart his little brother. Whenever Dad talks about him, his eyes get big like his head's filling with memories. "That man tells the corniest jokes. Always has."

"I'm sure he learned everything he knows from his big brother," Mom says, hugging him from behind. Her arms don't reach around.

"Do you get to stay home today, Dad?" I ask, pulling on my wig.

"No! What time is it?" He squints at my cat clock. "Oh my. I better get going or I'll be late to the firehouse." He comes over and kisses my cheek. "You sure you'll be okay, Kat?"

I nod. "Thanks, Dad. I'm good."

"Great. Then I'm off to the firehouse. Can't wait to tell the guys the good news! In two weeks, Kat will officially join the long and distinguished line of Coolidges." He takes Mom's hand. "Walk me to the car, my Annie?"

Mom leaves with Dad. By the time I get myself cleaned up and dressed, I feel like going back to bed.

"Hey, Kat," Dakota calls when I finally make it downstairs. "I was just heading out to the barn." She has one hand on the screen door. Dogs and cats circle her feet, waiting for their chance to bolt.

"Hang on, Dakota." I make my way toward her and try not to walk like a robot. "I wanted to ask you something about that pony."

She lets go of the screen and meets me halfway. "I know. I'm sorry about that crazy animal. I never should have let you near that pony."

"No. I wanted to help. It wasn't your fault. Or his. That's what I wanted to talk to you about. Do you think I could help with him? I know I could handle him."

Dakota lets out a sharp laugh that's not really a laugh at all. "You're kidding, right? You want to *handle* the pony that dragged you across the barn?"

"That won't happen again."

"You bet it won't. You're not getting near that horse, Kat." Dakota's brown eyes narrow to dark slits.

Hank walks in. "What's going on?"

"Hank, make her listen," I plead. "Yesterday wasn't that pony's fault."

He turns to Dakota. "Kat's right. I think the chestnut's pretty good-natured from what I can see."

"Me too." I'm relieved to have an ally.

"Fine," Dakota says. "The chestnut is a peach of a pony. Kat's still not riding it."

"What?" Hank wheels on me. "You want to ride that horse?"

"I didn't say that." But I *would* love to ride him. "I just want to help with the pony. Is it so crazy to think I might be able to help you guys?"

"Yeah. It's crazy," Dakota says.

I take a deep breath and try again in a calmer voice. "Isn't there anything I can do?" I stare into Hank's blue eyes, counting on the fact that he has trouble saying no to people.

Hank tilts his head toward Dakota. "We do have our hands full."

"I don't believe this." She sounds disgusted. "If you need me, I'll be in the barn." Wes's three-legged Pomeranian slips out behind her before the screen door slams.

I grin at Hank. "I'll do anything, Hank. I just want to help. And I promise I won't do anything stupid like grabbing that lead rope."

But Hank's not looking at me. He's staring over my head.

I turn to see Mom standing there. She's frowning like she's overheard everything.

"Mom, I didn't know you were still here," I admit.

"I noticed," she answers.

"I'm not asking to work with the horses

or ride them. I just want to help." I think about trying to explain to her why this is so important to me. But I'm not even sure I understand it myself. I know it's tied up with becoming a real Coolidge. But I can't say that.

Hank speaks up first. "That chestnut pony is lame. We're going to have to keep him in the stall for a few days at least. Kat wouldn't have to set foot in the pasture."

I could hug Hank for being on my side.

"Hank," Mom says, "Kat wasn't in the pasture yesterday, was she? When that horse dragged her around the barn? There's plenty of room to get hurt in a stall."

"But I won't–"

Hank cuts me off. "Then she'll stay out of the stalls, too," he says.

"Hank!" I protest. "If I can't even get near the pony, how am I supposed to help him?"

"Well," Mom says, completely ignoring me, "I suppose if she doesn't get in the stalls, she'll be safe."

"I'll keep her out of the stall," Hank promises.

"Hello? I'm right here. What can I do without getting into the stall?"

Hank grins. "You can give the pony his medicine, Kat. The vet says we have to give the Butazolodine twice a day. With everything else I've got to do around here, plus the extra horses, not to mention the fact that school starts Monday, I don't need another chore. If you can take over this one, it would be one less thing I'd have to do."

"Really, Hank?" I'm trying to read him. "You're not just making this up so I'll feel better?"

His forehead wrinkles exactly like Dad's does when he's paying bills. "Making what up? The horse needs meds. I hate that job. And I'm too busy to add one more thing."

"And you *promise* Kat won't get inside the stall with that horse?" Mom demands.

"She'll just bute the pony in his feed twice a day so I won't have to," Hank explains.

"Please, Mom?" I beg.

Mom walks up to me and starts unwrapping the bandages from my hand. "Do you promise to keep a stall between you and that horse?"

"Promise."

"Okay," Mom finally agrees.

I hug her. Then I hug Hank. “When do I start?”

“No time like the present,” Hank says. “You up for it?”

Truth is, all I’m up for is going back to bed. But I’m not about to tell them that. “Lead on.”

FIVE

"HANK?" He's halfway to the barn before I can even clear the front porch.

"Sorry, Kat." Hank jogs back. He sticks out his arm, and I take hold. His arms are thicker than my legs. "I've been trying to figure out what to do with the old sorrel. She's been used up on the trails. I'd love to let her pasture with some yearlings. She's got great manners in spite of everything. That gray mare is still a mystery to me. Not sure what's going on with her. And the Pinto's so scared that I'll probably have to imprint her, start her all over again like a colt."

I like that he's talking to me about the horses as if we're in this together. "If anybody can help these horses, Hank, it's you. Or Winnie, of course."

Hank grins. "Of course. Did I tell you Uncle Bart and Aunt Claire and Catman might come out here for Thanksgiving?"

"That would be great!"

"Yeah. Gram goes there every Thanksgiving. It's time for them to come up here. Catman always acts like his cats couldn't get along for a few days without him."

"You're the same way with your horses, and you know it," I say.

We reach the barn. Seeing the sawdust brings back everything that happened yesterday. I look away and follow Hank to the tack room.

"I'll show you where I keep the meds," Hank says. "You can dump feed into the pony's trough from the stallway."

"I wish I could do more," I say, half to myself.

"I'm not kidding when I tell you this helps, Kat. It's a hassle to remember to give a horse medicine. I'll be too busy with the other horses.

The faster I get them fattened up and gentled again, the better chance we'll have of finding good homes for them. It's going to be tougher once school starts too."

The tack room is about the size of my bedroom. Feed bins line one wall. Bridles hang on the opposite wall. A bunch of different kinds of saddles are stacked up on sawhorses. Gram Coolidge is always bringing over tack she's picked up at an auction or at a barn sale.

Hank lifts the lid on a wooden box that's sitting in the far corner. "You don't have to refrigerate bute. Just keep it in here with the syringes."

Syringes? "This stuff comes in pills, right? No shots?"

Hank laughs. "No shots." He pulls out a large white envelope and shakes a giant pill into his palm.

I can't believe how big the pill is. Bigger than a quarter and three times as thick. "Hank, how can you expect that poor little pony to swallow *that*?"

He bites his lip like he's trying not to laugh. "We'll crush it up first, Kat."

"Crush it up," I repeat. "Good call."

He glances around the tack room, spots an empty coffee can, and sets it on the old school desk Gram Coolidge found last fall at a garage sale. "You can crush it up in this." He hands me the pill and the can, then stands back.

I try to break the pill in half. It won't break.

Hank takes the pill back. He gets a pair of pliers from the toolbox. Then he holds the pill over the coffee can. "This will be easier for you. Pinch off pieces all the way around, like this."

Snip, snip, snip. Pieces of the pill drop into the coffee can. "There." He sets the pliers down. "You can do the other pill. Two pills in the morning. Two in the evening. Got it?"

I stare at the white, chalky dust in the bottom of the can. "Won't it taste horrible?"

"I never tried one, but it probably does," Hank admits. "Which is why you mix it with oats. Okay?" He nods and starts to leave.

"How much oats?" I know I'm bugging him with too many questions. But I don't want to do it wrong.

Hank's about as patient as they come, but he sighs. "Two of the scoops, Kat. They're in the green bin with the oats. And leave the scoop in the bin when you're done. Okay?"

"Okay. Thanks."

Hank heads for the door, but he turns back. "Second thoughts?"

"Not on your life, cowboy." I pick up the pliers and wave good-bye to him.

Once he's gone, I shake out the second pill. I position the pliers just like Hank did, hold the pill over the can, and squeeze.

Nothing happens.

I try again. I squeeze harder. And harder. My hand aches. My shoulder hurts.

"I can do this," I mutter. I use both hands and every bit of muscle.

Dakota sticks her head into the tack room. She's got her horse, Blackfire, by the reins. "Everything okay in here?"

"Great. Thanks, Dakota."

She doesn't look like she buys it, but she leaves.

This is ridiculous. I try everything, including beating the stupid white pill with the pliers. It doesn't even crack.

How can I be so useless? I can't even break a pill.

God, I don't suppose You'd like to have lightning strike this pill? Or a tiny earthquake, maybe?

Nothing happens.

Didn't think so.

Then I get an idea. Hank has hammers hanging on the wall, neatly organized by size. I pull one down and raise it over the pill. "Great idea, Kat," I mutter, "if you really want to splatter medicine all over the tack room."

But if I had a plastic bag . . .

I check to make sure Dakota and Hank are in the pasture. Then I make my way to the house and get a box of plastic sandwich bags. Back in the tack room, I drop the evil pill into the bag, sealing it and then double-bagging it to be safe.

"Here goes." I lift the hammer with both hands and bring it crashing down on the pill. It breaks into several pieces, all of them staying inside the bag. "Gotcha!" I exclaim.

A few more well-placed whacks, and that pill is dust. I empty the bag into the coffee can with the pill Hank crushed. Then I dump in oats and shake it up. The white powder blends in with the oats, making it look like cookie mix before you put the butter in. The whole thing smells too familiar. Not like cookie dough, though. More like the hospital. I sure hope horses don't have a great sense of smell.

Holding out my precious bute mixture, I walk to the stalls. When Hank and Dad started Starlight Animal Rescue, they rebuilt the whole barn, designing the stalls so horses could see out as much as possible. The top of the stall-way door is always open so horses can see us coming. The back of the stalls on this side of the barn open into the pasture.

The pony's back stall door is shut on the bottom, but the top is open. Through it, I see Hank cantering Starlight in the pasture, the Paint's tail flowing behind her. Dakota and Blackfire are trotting after them, with the gray mare on a lead behind her.

The pony is standing alone and silent in his stall, his neck so low his nose almost touches the straw bedding. I want to go in and put my arms around his neck. But I won't.

"We have to get you well so you can play with the other horses, Pony. And I can't keep calling you Pony, either. You need a name."

Kitten climbs the gate, then pounces on

my shoulders. She rubs her face against my cheek and purrs.

"I love you too, Kitten. Help me think of a name for this skinny pony." It hurts to see his ribs poking out from his dull coat. I know there's a beautiful chestnut under that dusty brown. "Chestnut." I roll the name around in my mouth. "What do you think, Kitten?"

Kitten kneads my shoulder with her paws. Her sharp claws hurt a little, but I know she only does it because she loves me.

"It's settled, then. We'll call you Chestnut."

I shake the coffee can to get the powder off the bottom. Chestnut's ears perk forward at the rattle of oats in the can.

I reach in and dump the whole oat mixture into the trough. "Come and get it."

He doesn't.

I step back in case it's me he's afraid of. "Come on, boy."

Chestnut steps cautiously to the trough and lowers his head. His nostrils flare. He lips at the mixture. Then he snorts. White powder flies everywhere. Chestnut jerks up his head and backs away.

"You have to eat it." I try mixing the oats again and hiding the white powder in the trough. It can't be done.

Chestnut stays at the rear of the stall. He won't even try. And I know he's hungry.

"Kitten, I am a complete and total failure." I must have done something wrong, or he would have eaten the oats. I wish I knew more about horses. The last thing I want to do is ask Hank and make him come in from the pasture to do my little job.

"Winnie!" That's it! If anybody in the world could help me with this, it's Winnie the Horse Gentler.

Kitten jumps off my shoulders as I head for the house. My brain's spinning. I could call Winnie. But I don't know her number, and I don't want to ask anybody for it. I could e-mail her. But what if she doesn't check her e-mail for hours? Chestnut needs his medicine now.

Then I remember. It's Saturday. Catman is probably on the road, filming his cat-umentary. But Winnie and Eddy Barker should be at the pet store right now, answering questions on the Pet Helpline. If I hurry, I could still catch Winnie.

Six

HANK HAS THE PET HELPLINE bookmarked, and it takes me only a few seconds to get there. Postings are going on live, so I jump in:

KoolKat: Sorry to interrupt, everybody. But this is an emergency.

Just like that, a response comes. In seconds, Winnie and I exit the helpline and enter a private chat room:

WinnieTheHorseGentler: Kat! How are you? Catman told us what happened. Your mom said you were okay—but bruised and scraped, right?

KoolKat: I'm fine. Tell Catman I'll write him later. Sorry I left him hanging.

Catman: Chill, Kat. I'm here. All is groovy. So what's the emergency, man?

KoolKat: Great. Okay. Here goes. Chestnut, one of the abused horses Hank rescued, needs Butazolodine. I volunteered to give it to him. I got the pills crushed and mixed with oats. But the pony won't touch it.

Catman: Get my cousin on the case, dude. You shouldn't have to do it.

KoolKat: I want to do it. Hank and Dakota are so busy with the new horses. This is the least I could do . . . and I can't even do this.

WinnieTheHorseGentler: No problem, Kat. Molasses.

KoolKat: Molasses? That sticky stuff that looks like syrup?

WinnieTheHorseGentler: That's the one. Mix it with the oats and bute. Chestnut will eat it.

KoolKat: Winnie, thanks! I knew you'd know what to do.

WinnieTheHorseGentler: Let me know how everything turns out.

KoolKat: Thanks, Winnie! Thanks, Catman! You'll never know what this means to me.

It takes me a few minutes to find the jar of molasses behind the cereal boxes. My head is buzzing, so I know I'm overdoing it. But I can't stop now. I race to the barn, holding the jar up in front of me like it's the Olympic torch.

Dakota and Hank are still out in the pasture with the horses. Chestnut's feed trough is just like I left it. It's a wooden trough, long enough to hold a salt block and grain.

"You just wait, Chestnut," I tell him. He sniffs the air while I dump in a glob of molasses. "You're going to love this. Winnie promised." There's nothing to stir with, so I use my fingers and mix the powdery oats with the sticky molasses. "This feels pretty gross," I admit, "but the smell's not bad."

When it's all mixed, I stand over the trough and bow my head. My fingers are sticky and disgusting. "Father, Chestnut and I thank You for this delicious food before us. Please use it to make Chestnut well again. Amen."

I look up at Chestnut. His ears rotate back, then forward. His nostrils twitch like a rabbit's. "Come on, boy. You know you want it."

He's not going for it. The memory of the awful white powder must be too fresh in his mind. Hank told me once that horses put elephants to shame when it comes to good memories. An old mare could be frightened her whole life because of something that happened when she was a filly.

Chestnut hovers by the stall door, refusing to take a single step toward the trough. I have to wonder what's happened to this poor pony to make him so cautious.

"Please trust me, Chestnut," I whisper. I dig my hand into the sticky, gooey mixture and come up with a handful of gunk. Then I start singing: "'Amazing grace . . .'" I keep it soft. I'm a pretty bad singer. With my arm out straight, I edge toward the stall door.

Chestnut watches as I stick my hand into the stall. My elbow aches, but I keep my arm stiff and my hand flat. Hank says it's a bad habit to let a horse eat from your hand, but I see him do it all the time.

Chestnut's ears twitch. Then he takes one step toward me.

"Good, Chestnut," I coo. I'm done with "Amazing Grace," so I make up a song. "Chestnut, the snub-nosed horsey–" he takes a step closer–"had a very shiny nose." Chestnut stretches out his neck as far as he can. "And if you ever saw him–" his lips barely reach my fingertips–"you would ask for one of those." His lips tickle my hand. "All of the other horseys . . ." He nuzzles the molasses mixture, getting most of it into his mouth, until all that's left in my hand is a sticky mess.

"Way to go, Chestnut," I whisper. I ease back to the trough and get another handful. We replay the hand-feeding scene. Then I take a third handful, but I don't go to Chestnut this time. Instead, I stretch my hand over the feed trough and wait.

It takes about five minutes and two songs–"Chestnut galloping in an open field. Jack Frost nipping at his hooves . . ." and "O Chestnut tree, O Chestnut tree, how lovely are your brown eyes . . ."–but he comes around. Finally the pony munches straight from his feed trough.

When the last powdery oat is gone, I feel like I've invented ice cream or duct tape. I could list a dozen firsts, including the first time I've been on the doctoring end of giving meds.

I'm still glowing when I hear a *clip-clop, clip-clop* crossing the barn.

Dakota walks in, leading two of the abused geldings. "You still here? Everything okay?"

"Yep. I was just chatting with Chestnut."

She grins. "Chestnut?"

"Like it?" I ask.

"Not bad," she admits.

Hank rides in on the gray mare. "Did that pony get the bute down, Kat?" He dismounts and unbuckles the mare's saddle.

"His name is Chestnut," I explain. "And he downed every last bite of the medicine. But he didn't at first. So I mixed it with molasses."

"Good job," Hank says. He pulls off the heavy Western saddle like it's no heavier than a washcloth. "It's a big help. Thanks."

As I leave the barn, Hank's words stay with me. *Good job. Thanks. Big help.*

Maybe I'll make a good Coolidge after all.

★ ★ ★

"Okay!" Dad shouts over the clang of silverware around the dinner table. Mom cooked a roast, and it's taking a lot of work to cut it. "Where does a cat go when it loses its tail?"

Wes groans. Dakota looks like she's trying not to smile.

I start to repeat Dad's riddle question for him, but Mom beats me to it. "Chester, sweetheart, where *does* a cat go when it loses its tail?"

Dad sets his knife on his plate. "To the *retail* store! Get it? Re-*tail*?" He's laughing so hard he can barely get the words out. "And what is the cat's favorite color in the retail store?"

"I don't know, my love," Mom says, still laughing hard from the last joke.

"What's the cat's favorite color?" Dad repeats. "*Purrrrrrr*-ple!"

"Funny," Dakota says, not laughing.

Hank's chuckling, but I'm pretty sure it's got more to do with Mom and Dad than with the joke. They're clinging to each other so they won't fall out of their chairs.

Wes is the only one who's managed to finish his meat, although I caught Lion, his three-legged Pomeranian, snatching a table scrap from him. Wes clears his throat. "All right." He says this like we've all been begging him to say something and he's only now given in. "What's up when you hear '*meow* . . . *splat* . . . *woof* . . . *splat* . . . *meow* . . . *splat* . . . *arf* . . . *splat*'?"

We're all so shocked that Wes would tell a joke or riddle that nobody speaks. He stares from one person to the next. Wes telling a riddle? Now there's a first for my list. I can't wait to write Catman.

Hank comes to his senses first. "Um . . . okay. What's going on when you hear, well, *that*?"

Wes is quiet for so long I'm afraid he doesn't have a punch line. Then he says, "It's raining cats and dogs."

We howl. Mom and Dad fall into each other's arms. Dakota's eyes have tears, she's laughing so hard.

And then it hits. The nausea. It's like an ocean wave rolling over me while my back's turned. I never saw it coming.

I bite my cheek and hope it passes. But I know better. Already the room wobbles. My head feels like it could float off my body.

I push my chair back and stand. The floor is an ocean, and I'm trying to stand on it. I grab the edge of the table to steady myself.

Hank's watching me. The others are still lost in laughter. Hank whispers across the table, "Kat? Need help?"

I shake my head. The room shakes with it. My forehead breaks into a cold sweat.

I dash to the little bathroom off the kitchen. I'm steadier when I'm moving fast. I make it. Close the bathroom door behind me. Drop to my knees.

And hurl.

Vomit.

Puke.

We have a thousand names for it in my house. I'm never sure if it's the cancer or the medicine or what both have done to my kidneys. But throwing up is as much a part of life around here as riddles.

"Everything okay?" Mom asks through the bathroom door. I'm guessing she's been there all along.

I'm still sitting on the cool tile. "I'm okay." I pull myself up and splash water on my face.

"That's good. I'm sliding a pill, a Zofran, under the door. You holler if you need us or anything." Mom's voice is cheery. I love that she does her best to keep things normal. They all do. They try to keep everything as normal as it can be.

I take the pill. Then I check the mirror before walking back to the table. Strands of my wig are stuck to my forehead. My pupils are huge.

I open the door and step out. My head is light, but I think I'm done being sick. Maybe.

"Hey, Kat," Hank calls. "I was just telling them about the pony. We'll keep him on bute for a week."

Dakota says, "I'm getting pretty close to that gray mare. Don't suppose we could keep all eight of the new horses?"

"I hope you're joking," Mom says. "So, who wants dessert?"

"Mom?" As soon as I talk, they all get quiet. "Would you save my dessert for later? I think I'll go upstairs and set out something to wear to church tomorrow."

"Need any help?" Dad asks. He stands.

"No thanks." I try to hurry to the stairs and out of sight. I know they're all watching me, even though little conversations are springing up. I'm so tired that my bony legs feel like redwood trunks as I drag upstairs.

I walk into my bedroom and am greeted by Mustard and Kitten, who fight over me. I don't think the Zofran's helping my nausea.

Another wave of dizziness slaps me. I dash for the bathroom.

I barf.

Upchuck.

Kneel before the porcelain throne.

Make my white-bowl deposit.

And wish I didn't have to be such a burden.

Seven

Sunday morning I don't wake up until everybody has gone to church. Everybody except Dad. I hear him humming hymns in the kitchen. Poor Dad loves church, and he had to miss it so he could keep an eye on me.

I don't feel like getting out of bed. I roll over and face my window, where a tiny breeze moves the cat curtains. I hear a cardinal. To me, they always sound like they're saying, "Birdie, birdie."

Then I see him, a bright red male on the tree limb outside my window. He's close enough to touch if I were at the ledge. But the most amazing thing is that on the limb directly above the cardinal sits a bluebird. We don't see many bluebirds, and this is the first time I've seen both birds at once. It feels like a gift.

I sit up in bed and try to remember Bible verses about animals. I know there are some great ones. I take my Bible off the bedside table and read a few. They're easy to find because those pages are dog-eared. Psalm 104 is one of my favorites: *"The earth is full of your creatures. . . . You open your hand to feed them, and they are richly satisfied."*

I flip back to Deuteronomy 33:26: *"There is no one like the God of Israel. He rides across the heavens to help you, across the skies in majestic splendor."*

I try to imagine God galloping across the heavens to help me.

Galloping.

"Chestnut!" I slam the Bible shut and jump out of bed. I forgot all about the pony. It must be noon by now, and he won't have been fed yet. He needs that medicine.

I pull jeans on over my nightgown and get downstairs just as Mom walks in with Dakota and Hank, followed by Wes.

Dad greets me, then runs to Mom and hugs her like she's been gone a year instead of a morning.

"Kat, you're up," Mom says.

"Sorry I missed church." I brush past them to get outside. But my shoes aren't by the door. "Dakota, have you seen my shoes?"

"Nope," she answers, heading for the fridge.

There must be two dozen shoes out here on the porch, and none of them are mine. "Where could they be? I know I put my sandals out here yesterday." I toss shoe after shoe, searching.

"Why do you need shoes?" Dad asks.

"Yeah," Mom agrees. "Where are you going?"

"To the barn to feed Chestnut." Frustrated, I give up and slip on an old pair of Dakota's boots. They're a few sizes too big, but I don't care.

"That's okay," Hank says. He takes a long swig of ice water as he stands over the sink, then refills his glass. "I fed Chestnut for you. I had to feed the others anyway."

I stop at the screen door, my back to

everybody. Hank fed Chestnut? "That was my job," I mutter.

"What did you say?" Hank asks.

I don't turn around, but I raise my voice. "It was *my* job to feed and bute Chestnut."

"I'm sorry," Hank says. I hear him coming over to me. "If I'd known you'd be . . . up . . . by now, I wouldn't have fed the pony."

"It only took him, like, two minutes, Kat," Dakota says. "No big deal."

I turn to face them and hope my smile looks less fake than it feels. "You're right. Chestnut shouldn't have to go hungry because I slept in. He's supposed to get that medicine the same time every day. That's the way it is with my meds. So, thanks, Hank."

It's all true. I make so much sense, I almost believe myself.

I excuse myself from Dad's Sunday dinner and go back to bed.

The next time I wake up, it's dark. Outside I hear the faint voices of my family and know it's a moon check. On any given night, any one of us can call for a moon check, and the rest of us have to go along. We sit or lie down under the stars. Dad points out constellations and tells the stories that go with them. Hank's almost as good as Dad at picking out planets and constellations. I call for more moon checks than anybody.

The screen slams downstairs. I hear footsteps coming up, then a tap on my door. Wes steps in with a bottle of water. "You awake, Kat?"

"I'm awake." But for somebody who's slept most of the last 48 hours, I don't feel all that awake.

"Good. Annie said you need to drink." He shoves the cold water bottle at me. "You missed old Mrs. Coolidge."

"Gram was here?" I take a big drink. Maybe too big. "Wes, do you know if Hank fed Chestnut for me tonight?"

Wes shrugs. "Probably. I was out walking Rex and Lion, but I saw him go to the barn."

"Well, will you ask Hank just to be sure? Make sure Chestnut got his second dose of bute."

"Sure."

"And tell him I'll take care of the pony myself tomorrow. Before school."

"You sure you're ready for school?" Wes asks.

"I'm not missing the first day of junior high," I insist. I motion for Wes to sit on the bed.

He sits on the rug instead. Rex immediately curls next to him and puts his big head in Wes's lap. "Junior high." Wes says it like he doesn't approve. "Nobody has junior high anymore. Hasn't Nice heard about middle schools?"

I shrug. Wes is going to be a freshman.

"You could stay home if you wanted to," Wes says. "*I* sure would if Annie would let me."

Wes had a rough time in school last year. I think Nice Junior High turned out to be a whole different world from the school he went to in Chicago. "Things will be better this year, Wes. *You're* better. And you'll know kids already."

"Which will be such a bonus, since they all loved me so much last year." Wes can't match Dakota in the sarcasm department, but he's got his share of it.

"Okay. Here's what I do. When you walk into school alone, or into a classroom, imagine you're holding God's hand. So you're not really alone, right?"

Wes laughs, almost. "You know you're the only person who can get away with saying stuff like that, don't you?"

"Has Dakota said anything to you about starting school here? She hasn't said anything at all about it to me."

"Me either." Wes gets to his feet. "Except she hasn't let up complaining about Hank being a junior and her being a sophomore when they're the same age."

They were both born on July 4, 16 years ago, in totally different worlds. "At least they're in the same building. Hank can be there for backup."

"When he's not fending off girls who throw themselves at him," Wes says.

"True." I start to laugh. Only here it comes again, that wave. It hits my head and moves to my stomach.

I press my hand to my mouth and race to the bathroom, making it just in time. There's not much in me, but it all comes out anyway. I heave until my sides ache.

When I walk out of the bathroom, Wes is standing there, studying his shoelaces. "Honking."

I wipe my mouth with the back of my hand. "What?"

"Honking. That's what they call hurling in Scotland."

"Good to know," I say, making my way back to bed. "Don't tell them I *honked* again, okay, Wes? I want them to enjoy the moon check without worrying about me."

He nods. "See you in the morning."

☆ ☆ ☆

In the morning, I'm up by 5:10 on the cat clock. It's a good thing, too. By the time I let out the cats and feed them, then go back upstairs and shower, then get dressed, I hear Mom and Dad having breakfast in the kitchen.

I check myself in the full-length mirror I stash in the corner of my room. I'm not crazy about mirrors, but I need to check out my first-day-of-school outfit. A couple of weeks ago, Gram Coolidge bought me a new shirt and cool tan capris for my first day. Now, sizing myself up in the full-length mirror, I can see that my new clothes are way too big on me.

I change into old jeans that still fit and a

white shirt. Not exactly a fashion statement, but at least I don't look like I'm playing dress-up. And the long sleeves hide my scraped elbows.

I've put on my blonde wig. It's long and straight, but this morning it looks all wrong. I try the short red wig. Too Orphan Annie. I settle on the long black wig and work on the side part.

Before I go downstairs, I have to sit on the bed to catch my breath. I feel like I've already put in a full day.

Kitten weaves between my sandaled feet on every step as I walk downstairs. "Morning, Mom and Dad," I call.

"Kat?" Mom walks to the bottom of the staircase and peers at me. "We thought we heard you getting dressed up there. You look wonderful." She's not as convincing as she probably thinks she is. "I did think you might do better starting later in the week, honey."

Dad joins her. "Nothing much goes on the first day, right?"

My legs are wobbly, so I hurry around them and sit at the table. But the smell of eggs makes something rise in my throat.

"Hey!" Dad shouts, checking something in the oven. "Here's a math question to get you ready for school. Ten cats were in a boat. One jumped overboard. How many were left in the boat?"

I'm afraid to answer. My head's light. I press my lips together to keep everything in.

Mom picks up the slack. "Um . . . how many cats were left in the boat, dear? Wouldn't it be nine?"

"Nope," Dad says, not very heartily. He's sneaking glances at me. "None. They were all copycats."

I get up. "I'm going to the barn." I run outside and honk so hard I think I'll never stop.

Eight

I stay doubled over outside, leaning against the house until my heart quits racing. The sun is already shining brightly in a clear blue sky. A light breeze rustles the leaves on the trees and cools the morning. Geese fly in a crooked V. A mourning dove's soulful cry comes from behind the barn. It's a perfect, glorious day for my first day of junior high.

Only I won't be there.

I feel Dad's arm slide around my shoulder. "We'll get 'em tomorrow, Tiger Kat."

I let him walk me back to bed. The second I shut my eyes, I'm out.

When I open my eyes, Gram Coolidge is standing over me. She's taller than Dad, with a long face and stylish blonde hair that would look great on somebody my age.

"Good! It's about time." Gram sits on my bed, shoving Kitten off. "Now, I've been working on your birthday party, Kat."

"Gram, I already had my birthday. Remember?" I pull myself up to a sitting position. Nobody should face Gram Coolidge lying down.

"Ah, but this is your Coolidge birthday. We must celebrate your official adoption. I think the best time will be right after you leave the courthouse."

"What courthouse?" I ask. Then I remember what the social worker said about going before a judge to say, "I do." I just didn't picture it all happening in a courthouse.

"The Nice Courthouse, of course," Gram answers. "We can have the party at my house. I'll invite the bridge club. You're welcome to bring any of your little friends, of course."

"Gram, wait." My head is too foggy to keep up with her. My stomach is knotting.

"Too much? Your mother thought you'd

say that. Oh, all right. We'll go to the Made-Rite in town, just like we did for your birthday. Will that do?"

Mom sticks her head into the bedroom. "There you are, George." She's the only person who can call Georgette Coolidge "George." She walks over and takes my pulse. "Need anything before I head to the hospital, Kat?"

"No thanks. I think I'm still sleepy," I admit.

I rest most of the morning, but I can't sleep. I keep imagining what's going on at school without me.

In the afternoon, I make myself eat crackers and drink ginger ale, and I start feeling better again. While I wait for everybody to get home from school, I watch Mustard and Ketchup play with their ball of yarn. They don't play together, just side by side. It reminds me of the way it is at school, where I always seem to be more side by side than *with* anybody. It's not that Nice kids aren't "nice." But sometimes it feels like they're afraid they'll catch cancer from me if they get too close.

By about three o'clock I can't wait any

longer, and I go out to the barn to see Chestnut. Rex tags along. I know he misses Wes.

"Good to see you up, Kat," Dad calls. He's digging a garden on the west side of the house, and he puts down his little shovel.

"Hi, Dad. I'm going to check on Chestnut."

He nods and acts like he's going back to digging. But I can see him peeking at me. He's a terrible pretender, but I appreciate the effort.

Kitten prances toward me when I walk into the barn. Her tail is high, waving slowly. "What are you up to, Kitten?" I ask her. She eyes Rex, who knows enough to keep his distance.

I head for the tack room and pound up two bute tablets, dump them into the coffee can, and mix it with molasses and oats. When I deliver the mix to Chestnut, Kitten is sitting on the pony's back. She's curled up, with her paws under her. I wish I had a camera.

"Hey, Chestnut." I pour the molasses mixture into the feed trough. "Looks like you got yourself a new friend."

Chestnut dives in and cleans his trough.

"Did you see that, Rex?" I bend down to pet the dog's soft head. "I did good." It's crazy to feel this proud about feeding the pony, but I do.

I'm about to go inside when the van drives up. Mom stops under the oak tree, and Wes and Dakota get out. I don't see Hank. And anyway, I thought he took the pickup.

I walk toward the van. "Where's Hank?"

Wes stomps by me. "You'd have to ask Hank. He's too popular to be bothered with us. And I'm not riding with Annie again. I'll tell you that. I'll walk first. Or take the stupid bus." He storms into the house, hollering, "You think I need people seeing me get picked up by my mommy?"

Dakota shrugs. She and Mom and I walk inside together.

Wes has already gone upstairs. Mom pours two glasses of lemonade and heads up after him. Dakota pours herself a big glass of lemonade and collapses onto the couch. I take the other corner of the couch and start pumping her about her day.

"Did you get to know anybody in your classes?" I ask. "Do you have any classes with Alicia?" Alicia and Dakota know each other from church.

"I didn't see her," Dakota answers.

"What about lunch?" I ask. "Who did you eat with?"

"I thought this girl, Charlotte something, was being really cool asking me to sit with her and her friend at their table. She introduced me to everybody. Then she started asking me questions."

"That's good, right?"

"Wrong," Dakota says.

Outside I hear the crunch of gravel. It's probably Hank, but I don't want to get up and look. I think Dakota needs to talk. "What kind of questions did she ask you?"

"Let's see," Dakota begins, and I know this isn't going to be good. "'Are you really Hank's foster sister?' And 'What's Hank really like? What kind of music does he like? Is Hank going out for football? Is he dating anyone?'"

"Ah," I say, understanding why she's so mad. "Sorry, Dakota."

"Yeah. Whatever." She gets up from the couch and starts for the stairs. "Anyway, thanks for listening, Kat. Glad you're feeling better. You were white as a ghost this morning."

Mom comes down the stairs as Dakota

goes up. She kicks off her shoes and collapses in the big chair.

"Did Hank and Wes have a fight?" I ask her.

"No. Not really. Hank was going out with some friends after school, so I said I'd pick up Wes and Dakota. I didn't think about how Wes would feel."

I pull back the curtain and see Hank's truck parked by the barn. But there's no sign of Hank.

Then I get a horrible feeling. What if he's doing chores? What if he feeds Chestnut . . . again?

I dash to the door.

"Kat? What's the matter?" Mom calls.

"Nothing! Be right back." Chestnut's had all the medicine he can have today. Hank can't give him any more. I don't stop running until I'm in the barn, even though my chest heaves and I feel like hurling. "Hank!" I stumble, pick myself up, and stagger to the stallway.

"Kat?" Hank's in front of Chestnut's stall, inches from the feed trough. He's holding the coffee can.

Nine

"STOP, HANK!" I scream. "Don't feed Chestnut!" I'm panting so hard I have to bend over to catch my breath.

"Kat? What's wrong with you? Should I get Mom?"

I shake my head. I still can't breathe right, and my voice comes in puffs. "I just . . . had to stop you. You can't feed Chestnut."

"Look," Hank says, "I don't mind. Honest." He shakes the coffee can.

"No!" I cry. I lunge for him and grab for the can. Only I miss. The can sails out of Hank's hands and smashes into his chest, sending oats, bute, and molasses all over the new shirt Gram gave him.

"What's the matter with you?" he shouts. He tries to brush off the sticky mixture, but it smears all over him.

"You can't feed Chestnut . . . because I already did." Tears are coming now, and I can't stop them.

I watch his face as it sinks in. "I almost gave him two more pills," Hank says. "I would have overdosed that pony."

"I know," I whisper. I'm shaking all over.

Hank starts to say something, then stops. He takes a deep breath. I have the feeling he's praying, even though his eyes are wide-open. "Listen, Kat. This could have been bad."

I nod. I know it could have been bad. I can't even think what might have happened if Chestnut had gotten four pills so close together.

Hank is staring into the empty coffee can. I think we're both imagining what could have happened, what almost did happen.

"It's supposed to be my job," I snap.

"I had no way of knowing you already fed Chestnut." His voice is steady–kind even.

And it makes me feel worse. He's right. I'm not mad at Hank. I'm mad at me. What was I thinking? That Hank could read my mind and know when I've fed the horse and when I haven't?

"Maybe we better rethink this."

"No!" I protest. "I can do it!"

"I know. And you did a great job. I've been using your molasses trick. Works like a charm." He's quiet a few seconds, then goes on. "But it's too risky to leave it like this. I don't know how else to handle it. I'm just saying that until you're sure you're better, maybe we shouldn't both be feeding Chestnut the bute. We could get mixed up again."

I start to argue. But he's right. I can't guarantee that I won't be too sick to help. Then what?

Chestnut has to come first.

Tuesday I don't even bother getting dressed until noon. I spend the first hour of daylight hurling into the toilet. Each round feels like I'm being pushed further and further away from becoming a Coolidge, from doing anything that would make me worth being a Coolidge.

Mom goes to the hospital, and Dad stays home with me. Nobody's in the house when I finally come downstairs. I check my e-mail and find one from Winnie.

Hi, Kat!

Good to hear the molasses worked for you and Chestnut. And I'm sorry about the problem with the feeding schedules. I've been thinking of another way you could help Hank with the horses, though.

The best thing you can do with horses is watch them. Sounds simple, right? But it's how I learned about horses. My mom and I used to observe mustangs in the wild a long time ago, before she died and Dad moved Lizzy and me to Ohio. Most of what I know about horses I've learned from watching them. Why don't you watch the new horses, Kat? Take notes. Run them by me if you want to. You'll end up helping Dakota and Hank more than you can imagine. How about it? Up for a Kat Horse Clinic?

Love, Winnie

I write her back and thank her. I don't know if I can help the way Winnie thinks I can, but I'm definitely up for trying.

I figure I have at least an hour before everybody gets home from school. Outside, Dad's crouched over the riding lawn mower. Pieces of metal and mower lie scattered in the long grass. "Dad, I'm going to hang out with the horses for a while," I tell him.

His head jerks up. Grease smudges cover his face. "The horses? Is your mother all right with that, Kat?"

"I promise I won't get into the stalls or the pasture. I'm just going to watch."

"That's nice," Dad says, fiddling with the mower again. He pulls out a thin black belt from the overturned engine and acts like he's just delivered a baby. "Ta-da! It's a belt!"

"Congratulations, Dad. I'm off." I head toward the pasture because Hank turned out all the horses except Chestnut this morning.

"Wait! Kat!" Dad calls after me. "Come back!"

I trudge back, ready to do battle if he's changed his mind about letting me hang out with the horses. "What?"

"Why do you always find your cat in the last place you look for him?"

A joke? That's why Dad called me back? I'm so relieved that I feel like laughing. But I'll wait for the punch line. "I don't know, Dad."

"Why do you always find your cat in the last place you look for him? Because after you find him, you stop looking!" Dad and I both laugh so loud that Rex and Lion trot over to see if we're okay.

I leave the dogs and Dad with the lawn mower and head toward the pasture again, hoping that Winnie's right and I can help these horses simply by observing them.

For almost an hour, I observe and take notes. At first, I feel pretty silly.

The gray mare takes two steps. The buckskin's ears go back. The sorrel lifts her head.

But after a while, I see more and start to pick up on interactions. All the buckskin has to do is turn her head, and the others stop grazing. There's a pecking order going on too. I think the Pinto is at the bottom rung.

She takes the bits of pasture the others leave behind.

But what if I'm wrong? I'm afraid Hank and Dakota are going to come home any minute and ask me what I'm doing. I don't know enough about what I've observed to tell them. I need to run everything past Winnie.

It's Tuesday, and I'm pretty sure Winnie mans the Pet Helpline after school. So, armed with pages of notes, I retreat to the house and log on.

KoolKat: Winnie, I don't know if I noticed what I should have, but here goes. The gray mare and the Paint greeted each other by rubbing noses. Maybe they didn't rub, but they did something with their noses. What's that about?

WinnieTheHorseGentler: Great observation, Kat! They probably blew into each other's nostrils. It's a friendly greeting. You should try it sometime. Not with people, but with that pony, Chestnut. If he blows back, you've got yourself a friend.

KoolKat: Wow! I'll try it. Maybe I should try it on the gray mare. I thought she was warming up to me. She seemed to be waiting for me, sticking her head over the fence. But when I walked up to her and reached for her, she backed off fast like she was afraid I'd hit her. I felt horrible.

WinnieTheHorseGentler: She may have been hit at some time. If that's the case, it will take time for her to warm up to you. But it might help to think like she does. Horses have the biggest eyes of any land mammal. They can see all around themselves except right in front and right in back. So when you stand in front of her, she can't see you, and she gets nervous. Try standing to the side of her.

KoolKat: Okay. Sounds good. I observed the bay and the sorrel together. They're so cute. It's a case of I'll-scratch-your-back-and-you-scratch-mine. They used their teeth, but it seemed like they loved it. Not sure what to take away from that, but there you have it.

WinnieTheHorseGentler: Terrific! Horses love to be scratched by people, too. They'd much rather be scratched than patted.

KoolKat: Makes sense. And this is really helping me. But I was kind of hoping I'd come up with something that would help Dakota and Hank get through to these horses. I'm the most worried about the buckskin. She grazes, but she's always watching. When the others get close, her ears go back. If she lifts her head, the other horses keep their distance.

WinnieTheHorseGentler: That's great info. The buckskin is probably your dominant mare. You guys can use that in training!

"Kat? Are you writing Catman?" Hank asks.

He and Dakota are standing behind me at the computer. I can't believe I didn't hear them come in. "You guys scared me half to death." I don't usually use that expression, "half to death," and I can tell by Dakota's face she doesn't like it.

"You're writing Winnie?" Dakota asks.

"About *our* horses?" Hank moves in closer. "Good idea."

"Yeah, really," Dakota agrees.

They're both hunched in front of the screen, one on each side of me. I want to exit from the helpline or cover the screen with my hands or tell them that this is *my* conversation, *my* horse clinic.

"Winnie's right!" Hank says. "That buckskin must be the dominant mare. I was thinking it was the gray."

"So she's the boss?" Dakota asks.

"Yeah," Hank says, still reading. "That's why the others watch her all the time. She's the key, Dakota."

"So we should get her on our side, you mean?" Dakota asks.

They're talking over my head, literally.

"She'll be the one they'll all follow when they're in a pack," Hank explains. "They'll try to please *her*."

"Ah," Dakota says, "kind of like Guinevere in the pack of girls I tried to eat with today?"

Hank laughs. "Ask Winnie how she thinks we should use the buckskin to get the others on our side. Tell her I've ridden the buckskin, and I think she's pretty teachable."

I start typing, using my two-finger method. I'm slower than usual because my hands are shaky. I'm not nervous. I just haven't eaten much today.

WinnieTheHorseGentler: Kat? Are you still there? Where'd you go?

KoolKat: Sorry about that. Hank and Dakota walked in. They're pretty excited about your advice.

"Go on and ask her about using the dominant mare thing," Dakota says. She pulls over a stool and settles in.

"And tell her what I said about riding the buckskin," Hank adds.

I start to. Then I can't exactly remember the questions. A throbbing starts in my left temple and moves across the top of my head.

"Kat?" Hank sounds impatient.

"Want me to type?" Dakota asks.

I don't. But I don't think I can keep up. I scoot my chair back and stand. "Go for it, Dakota."

"You sure?" She takes the desk chair.

"Thanks, Kat," Hank says. He's staring at the screen. "Huh. Ride the sorrel with the buckskin. We could do that this afternoon."

As I walk away, I hear the computer keys whizzing, Hank's and Dakota's voices, and the buzzing that means I'm in for a king-size headache.

Ten

"KAT, HONEY? Are you okay in there?" Mom shouts. When I don't answer right away, she knocks on the bathroom door.

It's Friday morning and the first time since Monday that I've gotten dressed for school. I refuse to miss the whole first week of junior high. I wipe my mouth, flush the toilet, and splash cold water on my face. "I'm fine," I call back.

"Hank needs to know if you're riding with him, honey. He and Dakota are leaving in a minute. Wes took the bus. I could drive you later, if you feel up to it." She pauses. "Or maybe you should stay home today and–"

I open the bathroom door and hope I don't look like I feel. "Good to go."

Her eyes narrow. Like it's not hard enough to fool a mom, I have to convince a mom who's also my doctor. "You don't look fine."

"Thanks, Mom. Just the vote of confidence I need to start seventh grade." I move past her and get my book bag. "I'm good. Really."

She doesn't move. "Kat, you don't have to do this."

"Please," I beg. "I don't want to miss any more school."

She sighs, but when I head downstairs, she follows. "Promise to call me if you . . . if you need to come home? I'll keep my pager on. And I'll make sure your dad has his cell on him. I've signed in your meds with the school nurse. So if you need anything for nausea or a headache, just go there."

"I know. Thanks." I really do feel better.

"Hey! Look who's up." Hank takes my pack and slings it over his shoulder. "Riding with me?"

"Yep," I answer.

"Cool hair," Dakota says. "Good choice."

"Thanks." I've gone with the black wig, but it looks brown next to Dakota's hair. I'd love a wig exactly like her hair–curly, thick, black. She looks beautiful in her jeans and a sleeveless T-shirt.

"Let's hit it," I say. "I'd hate to be late for class. Four days late is probably late enough." I kiss Mom good-bye. "Where's Dad?"

At that exact moment, Dad comes running in, panting. "Phone. Mother. Wouldn't let me hang up." He takes a deep breath. "Your grandmother says good luck on your first day at Nice Junior High. She also said to call her if anyone gives you trouble."

I love Gram Coolidge.

We're out the door when Dad hollers, "Wait!"

Dakota rolls her eyes. Hank checks his watch. We all know what's coming.

Dad catches us at the truck. "What do you call a cat who keeps the grass short?"

I've already figured this one out. But I can never leave him hanging. "I don't know, Dad. What *do* you call a cat who keeps the grass short?"

"A lawn *meow*-er! Get it? Lawn meower?"

Dakota groans. She opens the driver's door. "I'll drive."

"Think again," Hank says, dangling the truck key. Dakota's only had her license a week.

I take the front seat without arguing when she climbs in back. Better odds of me not getting carsick if I ride in front. We all know this, but we don't say it. I wish Wes had waited for us. I can't believe he'd rather ride the bus.

Hank starts the truck on the first try. Thinking of that first makes me realize another. "Do you realize this is the first time I've ridden to school with my sister?"

"You and your first times," Dakota mutters.

"Seat belt, Dakota," Hank orders, adjusting his mirrors before backing out.

Dakota buckles up. I'm already buckled. "Listen, Kat," she says, "if you get sick, call me at the high school. I can take the truck and come get you."

"What about me?" Hank asks.

"You can get one of the girls in your fan club to drive you home," Dakota suggests.

Hank laughs. "Fan club? So, are you a member?"

Dakota gives him her "yeah, right" look.

I don't think Hank has an official fan club, but it wouldn't surprise me.

Dakota stares out the window. "Anyway, if I cut classes, it's no big loss." Something in her voice tells me she's not joking anymore.

I glance at Hank. He flashes me a secret-code look. Translated, it means Dakota's not exactly the dominant mare at Nice High.

Dakota's life in Chicago gave her defenses that don't work in our little town. She can come off pretty tough. She and I have gotten along since the day she came to live at Starlight Animal Rescue. But I've seen her A+ sarcasm in action against Wes and Hank. If she felt cornered or put down by people in her classes, I don't think she'd take it in stride. She'd make them wish they'd never opened their mouths.

"Things will get better, Dakota," I say. She's still staring out the window. We've left the rural outskirts of town and turned onto the main drag of Nice. We'll be at the junior high in a minute.

"You know what I hate?" She doesn't wait for an answer. "Hand holding."

"You hate hand holding?" Hank repeats. "Okay."

"Don't get me wrong," she says. "I can be as romantic as the next girl. But please. Like the halls aren't crowded enough? Puppy love has to hold hands so nobody can get by?"

Hank laughs. "Didn't realize you were so anti–hand holding."

But I think I get it. When you don't have a best friend or a boyfriend, it can hurt to watch people who do. Maybe Dakota wishes she had someone.

I know better than to say that to her though.

The picture of a father holding his kid's hand flashes to my mind. "Dakota, I'm giving you a verse for today–a verse about hand holding."

"See? I always thought you had a verse for everything. Now I'm sure." She grins at me, waiting.

"It's from Psalm 37. 'Though they stumble, they will never fall, for the Lord holds them by the hand.'"

Dakota stares at me, her eyes narrowed to slits. For a second, I'm afraid I'm about to be on the receiving end of Dakota's sarcasm . . . for the first time. It's one first I'm not looking forward to. Then, like sunlight bursting out of clouds, she smiles. "Kat, you always know exactly the right thing to say. Do you come in a pocket version? I'd like to take you with me."

"You don't think she's pocket-size already?" Hank says, sounding relieved. He pulls up to the junior high loading zone. Groups of girls huddle all across the lawn. A guy and girl walk by holding hands. Three girls hop out of the car in front of us. Everybody looks high school to me. I was the smallest kid in sixth grade, and I haven't grown much. I probably look like I missed the elementary school bus.

We don't say anything as we sit in the loading zone. Nice Junior High and Nice High School are side by side. The cafeterias overlap even, with a shared central kitchen in the middle. Still, I know it's two different worlds. I don't know what Dakota and Hank are thinking as we sit in the truck, but I'm thinking that all I want is to make it through this school day without getting sick.

My mind kicks into pray-without-ceasing mode, and I open the door.

“Show ’em who’s the dominant mare in this school, Kat!” Dakota calls as I climb out.

Hank honks the horn and turns in to the parking lot.

My elbow hurts when I wave, but I keep it up until the truck disappears into the mass of cars trying to park in the student lot. I wonder if Wes is here yet.

I hate the minutes in the hall before that first class begins. Having cancer makes you a bad choice for small talk. Like people are afraid they’ll ask me how I’m doing and I’ll answer, “Oh, I’m dying, thanks. And you?”

When the first bell rings, I take my time getting to room 121, my first-hour social studies class. I know where it is because Mom and Dad and I met with my teachers during the summer to work out a system for me to make up work when I’m absent.

I stand outside the classroom, listening to the buzz of voices. Their words crash against each other like waves. But the waves are all part of the same ocean. And I’m just passing through their ocean.

My stomach flutters, but I think it’s nerves. I sure hope so. The last thing I need is to puke all over the classroom on my first day. I hike up my book bag, walk in, and look around for an empty seat.

"Take your places, ladies and gentlemen!" Ms. Buffenmyer shouts. She's younger than Mom, taller, and a lot thinner. Her brown hair is caught up in a banana clip.

I edge to the middle of the room. Desks to the left, desks to the right. Makes me think of the parting of the Red Sea.

Ms. Buffenmyer is messing with her briefcase, so I don't think she's seen me yet. But everybody else has. I know most of them from elementary school. A couple of kids from church smile at me, and I smile back, but their row is full. Across the aisle, a whole row of girls stare at me. When I smile at them, their heads swivel away in unison, like they're on the synchronized stare team.

Maybe I have a big letter *C*, for "cancer," on my forehead today and didn't notice.

I need a seat. My legs twitch. They shake, like they're not going to stand here another minute. If I don't get a chair, I'm going to collapse in the middle of this classroom.

ELEVEN

FIONA MORRIS STANDS AND WAVES at me from the front of the room. "There's a seat up here, Katharine!" she shouts. "Come sit by me."

I'm surprised she knows my name, even though we had gym together last year. I mostly sat out.

"Katharine!" Ms. Buffenmyer sees me now. "Welcome. Glad you could make it. I mean, it's good to see you."

I walk to the front and take a seat next to Fiona. She's wearing a skirt with a green V-necked top. Her shirt matches her eyes. Her auburn hair flows straight to her shoulders and tucks under perfectly, like those expensive wigs in catalogs. I think she's lived in Nice only a couple of years, but she was the most popular girl in elementary school last year.

"Thanks, Fiona," I whisper.

She pats my hand. "I don't mind," she whispers. "Really, I don't."

I'm not sure why, but having her say she doesn't mind makes me feel like maybe she does. Then she flashes me a smile, and I know I'm imagining things. I'd still be standing in the aisle if she hadn't flagged me down.

Cassie's on the other side of Fiona. I can't believe how much she's changed over the summer. She's streaked her hair, and it looks great. Maybe it's her low-slung jeans and low-cut top, but she could pass for 18.

"Hey, Cassie," I whisper. "I love your hair."

"Thanks. You too." She smiles, but her gaze is stuck on my wig and stays there a few seconds too long. Makes me wish I'd picked the blonde wig instead.

Alex leans up from the seat behind me. He's in my youth group at church, when I feel well enough to go. "Hey, Kat. Cool hair. New?"

I whisper back at him, "Kind of. Thanks, Alex." I could hug the guy for liking my hair. My stomach unclenches. I reach into my book bag for a notebook.

Fiona leans over. "Don't pay any attention to Alex. Boys can be so rude."

I ease back into my seat, clutching my notebook like it will keep me from falling off the earth.

"All right," Ms. Buffenmyer says, "let's get down to business, people. Now, I'm going to need something in writing from you by the end of the hour. You've had a week to think about your social studies project."

As if she's just remembered that I haven't been here all week, our teacher turns to me. "Um, Katharine, we're doing projects in teams of two. Each team has to come up with a civic service project. Teams set goals together, draw up a plan, and do some kind of service for the community. The whole project will be worth a fourth of your grade." A shadow passes over her face, and she steps closer to my desk. "Since you're coming in on this late, maybe you and I can come up with an alternate project, something you can do at home if you want to. A report, maybe?"

I know she's trying to be helpful, but the last thing I want is special treatment. "I'd like to do the civic service project." My voice cracks, so I clear my throat. "It sounds great. Fun. I really want to do it."

"Well . . ." Ms. Buffenmyer draws out the word like she's trying to string thoughts together. "That's a problem. We're doing the work in pairs–partners. I . . . I don't think we have anyone for you to work with."

I hate the silence that follows. They knew I was coming. Why didn't they put me on a team?

"JP, you don't have a partner, do you? I mean, since Ian got his schedule changed?" Meagan Reed announces this from the back of the room. Meagan is probably the smartest person in seventh grade.

JP turns and glares at her, like she's ratted him out. He's wearing a Chicago Bears T-shirt and gray sweatpants. His legs are sprawled out, and his big feet rest on the chair in front of him. JP lives football. It's the only thing I've ever heard him talk about, although he wasn't talking to me. I don't think he's said two words to me in the last two years. In sixth grade, if we heard snoring in class, we all looked at JP.

"I'm doing my own project," JP says.

"And what might that be, Mr. Peterson?" Ms. Buffenmyer asks.

"Football," he answers. He slumps down even farther.

A few chuckles ripple across the room.

"I'm not sure you've quite grasped the assignment, Mr. Peterson," Ms. Buffenmyer says.

"Will you just call me JP? I keep thinking my dad's walked in or something."

"Well, JP," Ms. Buffenmyer says, "you need a partner. And a better idea than football."

"Better than football?" JP whines. "Man, junior high is as tough as my brothers said it was."

More laughs follow. I hate this. Everybody sees that JP and I should make a team. They also see that JP doesn't want *me* for a partner.

"I have an idea, Ms. Buffenmyer," Fiona says. We all look to her like she's the teacher now. "Cassie and I were going to be partners. But, well . . ." She puts her hand on my arm. "Maybe Cassie could team up with JP, and Kat and I could work together."

"Hey!" Cassie objects. "You and I already have our project."

Fiona turns to her friend. "You and JP can do that one. Sounds like JP needs a new project anyway. *And* a new partner. Kat and I will come up with something else."

"That's okay," I tell her, even though I'd love to be her partner. "You don't need to switch partners because of me."

"It's not a problem," Fiona says.

"Cassie really doesn't want to," I whisper.

Fiona whispers back, "Don't kid yourself. Cassie's got a monster crush on JP. She's going to thank both of us later."

"Cassie?" Ms. Buffenmyer says. "What do you say?"

"Well, I guess it might work," Cassie says. She turns around and smiles at JP. "You game, JP?"

He shrugs. "I still think football was a cool idea."

Cassie's already out of her seat and moving in on JP. "Make room, guys. I need to sit by my new partner."

"Good. Now get busy, people." Ms. Buffenmyer strolls toward us. "Thanks, Ms. Morris."

"Glad to help," Fiona says.

"For this to work, though," Ms. Buffenmyer says, "you girls will have to come up with your project by the end of class today. We don't have time for an extension."

"No sweat," Fiona says.

I'm sweating already. I don't want to wreck Fiona's grade. "What were you and Cassie doing for a project?" I ask.

"Nothing terrific," Fiona says. "Her dad owns Nice Pizza in town."

"I didn't know that." We've eaten there a couple of times, but we're too far out in the country for delivery.

Fiona studies her fingernails. They're amazing–long and this bronze color that goes great with her hair. "Cassie and I were going to make up a new specialty pizza with tons of cheese, all kinds of cheeses. We thought we'd promote it for a week and see if we could make a profit. Then we'd give the profit to poor kids or something. Or use the profit to feed poor people. Something like that."

"That's pretty cool," I say.

Fiona shrugs. Her hair swishes, like in those silky shampoo commercials.

Two guys from the second row are trying to get Fiona's attention. When she looks at them, they're pointing to themselves, trying to elbow each other out of the way. "Be on *my* team, Fiona!" one of them whispers. But his whisper is so loud that Ms. Buffenmyer walks over to them.

Fiona shakes her head. Again, her hair flows from side to side.

As I watch her, I can't help wondering what it would feel like to be Fiona Morris. And if I *were* Fiona Morris, I wonder how much I'd regret pairing up with me.

Twelve

"I GUESS WE BETTER get going on this, huh?" I suggest. "I'm afraid I don't have anything we could sell."

"We don't have to sell anything," Fiona says. Her eyes dart around the room while she talks. "It could be a do-gooder project or a service or something." She waves at a guy I don't recognize. He waves back.

Behind us, Alex and Michael are getting pretty loud. Alex scoots up and asks, "Hey, Katharine. You still like being called Kat?"

I nod. I'm too surprised he's talking to me, and not Fiona, to say anything.

"Are you still running that animal rescue out in the country?" he asks.

"Yep." This is crazy. I've never had trouble talking to Alex before. Last year in youth group we were partners for a scavenger hunt. I puked halfway through the hunt. We lost.

"How'd you like another cat?" Alex asks.

"*I* would. I always want another cat. But I promised I wouldn't take on any more until I find homes for the ones we have."

What I don't tell him is that I know Mom made this rule because I've been sick so much I haven't kept up my end of the work, even with the cats, especially the barn cats. Dakota has had to cover for me. That's why I didn't try to fight the ruling. I hate making extra work for anybody.

"Too bad," Alex says.

"Why?"

"We've got the stupidest cat in the whole world. My mom's going to make me get rid of it if it doesn't come around."

"No way," Fiona says. "*I've* got the stupidest cat in the world."

"I'm serious," Alex insists. "This cat, Bozo–he isn't normal, even for a cat. He pukes all over the furniture. Mom's convinced he does it on purpose."

"He wouldn't do it on purpose," I assure him. "What do you feed Bozo?"

"I don't know. Milk. He likes eggs."

"Well, there you go," I say. "Cats like a lot of things that aren't good for them."

"Just like us girls," Fiona chimes in.

"Milk's not good for a cat?" Alex asks.

I shake my head. "Milk can make a lot of cats sick. Try not giving Bozo milk or eggs. I'll bet he stops puking on the furniture."

"That's great, Kat," Alex says. "But Bozo's got worse problems than that. Like, he licks us all the time." He shudders. "Gives me the creeps."

"Eew," Fiona says, shuddering too.

"You should be flattered, Alex," I assure him. "Do you ever watch cats together? Our barn cats won't let anybody near them except for me. But they lick each other all the time. It's part grooming and part bonding. That's why they lick people, too."

"So Alex's cat thinks he needs to be groomed?" Fiona says, giggling.

"More like his cat really likes him."

"Well, our cat hates us," Fiona says.

"Are you talking about the cat you think is dumber than my cat?" Alex asks.

"Oh, she's dumber all right. I guarantee it." Fiona tugs a strand of her hair. "Mom and I picked out this cat for my little sister for her birthday. It was the prettiest cat in the pet store–long white hair and big blue eyes. That's why we got it."

"So what's wrong with her?" Alex asks.

"She won't listen. She's too stupid to get out of the way of the car. Dad almost ran over the thing twice. Oh, and she gets lost. What kind of a cat gets lost when it goes outside? And we have to carry her to her food dish. She never comes when we call her. We phoned the pet store and complained. The guy finally admitted the cat's already been returned twice! They won't take her back again."

"There's got to be a reason your cat acts like that," I suggest.

"Yeah," Fiona says. "There is. She's dumb as dirt. I'll bet even Catman couldn't help this cat."

"You know Catman?" I can't imagine Fiona and Catman together. I'm not sure why that is.

"I've never met him. But I know he's

Hank's cousin, and he's supposed to be great with cats." A big smile passes over her face. "So how *is* Hank, anyway?"

"Fine, I think." I glance at the clock and know we're running out of time. I don't have time to talk about Hank. And I shouldn't be using up time talking about cats either. But I worry when people don't like their cats. I'm already wondering if Mom would change her mind and let me take on these two cats.

"Your sister loves her cat though, doesn't she?" I ask Fiona.

"Are you kidding? She hates it. She and Mom are taking the thing to the animal shelter over the weekend."

"You can't, Fiona!"

"Why not?" Alex asks. "We're thinking of doing the same thing. Maybe they can find a family the cat will like better than us."

I wheel on him. "Alex, don't let them take your cat there," I plead. "The shelter's overloaded. They'll never find a home for your cat. Seventy percent of the cats that go into shelters don't come out."

"Man, I didn't know that." Alex taps his pencil on his desk like he's thinking it over. "Maybe I can talk Mom out of it. Do you think you could train Bozo not to claw the furniture? That's the other thing that drives Mom over the edge."

"I don't know." Catman says you don't train cats. You train people. But I did get Ketchup to quit scratching the table legs. I just got him hooked on a scratching post. "Maybe."

"Five minutes left, people," Ms. Buffenmyer announces.

"Fiona, what are we going to do?" I can't believe we haven't even come up with a single idea.

"Your guess is as good as mine." She doesn't sound panicked though. "I could sure use an A in this class. My parents are expecting me to be on the honor roll again."

Alex and Michael get busy writing down their ideas for their project. From what I can hear, it's a garage sale.

Ms. Buffenmyer is making her way toward us. I get the feeling she's been watching us the whole time. "You girls certainly did a lot of talking with the boys this hour. I hope it was about your project."

"Of course, Ms. Buffenmyer," Fiona says. "Alex and I were discussing our projects."

Ms. Buffenmyer raises an eyebrow. It's a skill they must train teachers in teacher school. Every teacher I've had could do it. "Katharine, have you come up with a good idea for your project then?"

"Not really," I admit.

Alex interrupts. "Sorry. My bad. I kept bugging Kat for advice."

"Advice?" Ms. Buffenmyer asks.

"About my cat."

"Your cat?" Ms. Buffenmyer sounds unimpressed.

"Yeah," Alex says. He grins at me. "Kat's a terrific cat shrink."

"I'm sure that's really helpful," Ms. Buffenmyer says, "but not in social studies." She turns to Fiona. "So, Fiona, would you like to tell me what you meant when you assured me you and Alex were talking about your social studies project, when you were actually discussing his *cat*?"

I hear Alex gulp.

But Fiona doesn't miss a beat. "Of course, Ms. Buffenmyer. Because Alex's cat is part of our project. Kat and I will be putting on a cat clinic."

THIRTEEN

"I HAVE NO IDEA how I pulled that off," Fiona brags to the lunch table full of girls.

I'm sitting across from Fiona. I'm not totally sure how I ended up here. I walked into the cafeteria alone. The smell of hot dogs and pizza, mixed with sweat, made me turn to leave. But Fiona was there. And I guess I got swept along with her.

"Seriously," she continues. "Buffenmyer had me, back to the wall, for goofing off with Alex the whole hour. We were talking about his crazy cat and my stupid cat. So when she pressed me for a project, there it was. Cats!

Stroke of genius." Fiona glances at my plate. "Kat, you haven't touched your lunch. Eat up, girl! We need our strength to pull off the best project in junior high, right?"

"Guess I'm not that hungry." I poke my fork at the pork and beans on my plate. The thought of eating this stuff makes my stomach flip.

"You need ketchup?" Fiona tears open a tiny packet from her tray and squirts red on my untouched hot dog. She tears off one end of the dog that's wrapped in a soggy bun and hands it to me. "There. Eat."

I take a bite and try to smile while I chew. I know better. The smells here are enough to make me sick. The hot dog tastes like rubber.

"That's better." She turns back to her friends. They've waited through the entire hot dog scene. "Anyway, nobody else will have a cat clinic, right? I think we might even ace this thing. My parents would love that. Don't you think it sounds sweet?"

The heads at the table nod like those bobblehead dolls. I think they'd agree with anything Fiona said. Not that I'm complaining. Most of the girls in this room, even the eighth graders, would love to sit at Fiona's table.

Chew, chew, chew. My stomach's shouting at me, warning me not to send this stuff down there.

Fiona turns to me. "I hope you've got tomorrow free."

I nod. And swallow. And swallow again. Chewed-up dog lodges in my throat. "I need to go to the bathroom."

Fiona puts her hand on my arm. "You're a big girl now. You can wait until we're done."

I'm done. She could stick that whole dog in my mouth and I wouldn't eat it. But I don't leave. This is the first time–*first*–I've been asked to sit at a table filled with girls from my class.

My forehead breaks into a cold sweat. The room tilts. The taste of hot dog rises from my stomach and pushes through my nostrils. My head's light. The table spins.

"Kat?"

I look up. "Wes?" I can't believe he's talking to me. Not that Wes doesn't love me, but high schoolers don't want to be caught dead with the junior high kids. Especially not seventh graders who are about to lose their lunch. I'm not even sure it's okay for him to cross over into our side of the cafeteria. But, man, I'm glad he did.

"You've got a call," he says.

"A call?" My heart speeds up. "Why didn't they call my cell?"

"Don't make 'em wait," he warns.

I stand. "Is something wrong?"

"Nothing's wrong. Everybody's fine. Are you going to take the call or not?"

"I'm coming." I scurry from the table and hurry to catch Wes, who's halfway out of the cafeteria already. When I'm in range, I call out, "Wes, who is it?"

"There's no call," he says. "And the closest bathroom is right down there." He points down the hall.

"Thanks, Wes." I dash to the girls' bathroom and make it in the nick of time. I'm loud, retching and retching, the echo four times as loud as at home in my own bathroom, thanks to these gray cement walls.

"Let's get out of here." Footsteps of two or three girls shuffle out. They can't get away fast enough. I can't blame them.

I'm sick again. I can't believe there's anything left inside me. After another minute, I leave the stall and splash water on my face. I lean on the sink, careful not to look in the mirror.

When I finally come out, Wes is at the drinking fountain.

"You're still here?" I can't believe I'm this glad to see him.

Wes wipes his mouth with the back of his hand. "Good thing you came out when you did. If I drank any more water from this fountain, I'd have to run in there and hurl myself."

I laugh a little. "How did you know, Wes?"

"Good guess. That's all."

"It could have gotten pretty ugly in the cafeteria if you hadn't come to my rescue like that," I admit.

He shrugs. "Don't mention it. *Please* don't mention it. You want me to call Popeye to come get you? Or Hank?"

I shake my head. "No. Please don't tell them. It wouldn't help anything."

"Maybe. But you're looking whiter than usual, Kat," he says.

"All I want is to get through the whole day. I can do it. I know I can."

"What do you have next hour?"

"English. Wes, what if I hurl in English class?" I picture it, and the thought almost makes me want to run back to the bathroom.

"Then you give them an English lesson," Wes says.

"An English lesson?"

"Sure. Vocabulary. Vomit vocab. I guarantee you know more words for *vomit* than anybody in that class, including your teacher."

I laugh, but my laugh cuts off when the bell rings.

Wes heads back toward the high school. The halls fill with students pouring in from every classroom door.

"Thanks!" I yell. I can't see him any longer. He's not tall in this crowd.

Then I see a dark-skinned arm rise above the masses, and Wes gives me the thumbs-up sign. Wes may not have the Coolidge name, but he's a Coolidge through and through.

I let myself be swept through the hall to the stairs. Then I make my way to my English classroom.

"Do you have English now?"

I turn to see Alex. He's a lot taller than I thought he was when he was sitting in social studies. Man, that kid has grown. "Yeah. English. Do you?"

He nods. "I've heard Rice is cool."

"Rice? Our English teacher?"

"No. Rice, our lunch." He grins, and I'm pretty sure he's not laughing at me. In fact, I like that he's treating me like a regular person. "So, you going in or watching from out here?"

"I'm going in. And taking *your* seat." It's not that clever, but he laughs anyway.

"Yo! Alexandro! This way!" Michael waves Alex toward an empty seat near the back of the room.

Alex shrugs and takes off to sit with his buddies.

I glance around the room. The good seats, close to the door, are taken. I have to go to the far side of the room and crawl over three kids.

Rice calls roll and dives straight into the romantic poets.

I'm taking notes as fast as I can when the room dips. I look up, half expecting everybody else to be holding on to desks or at least trying to figure out what's happening to us. But they're all writing in notebooks as if nothing's happened.

The wave comes again, bringing full-blown nausea with it. I shove my fist into my mouth and bite.

I have to get out of here.

Rice is writing on the board. "Pay attention to new words in the sonnets. We'll be learning specialized vocabulary. Vocabulary tests will make up 10 percent of your grade."

I need fresh air. Or a toilet.

I get to my feet and start shoving my way out of the row. Then I remember my book bag. I go back for it and climb over desks and people again to get out to the aisle. My head is so light I can't see well. I'm wobbling.

I am not going to make it.

Bile rises to my throat. I burp it back.

"What's the matter with her?" someone asks.

I go down to my knees before I fall. And still my stomach lurches. Frantically I reach into my book bag. My can. I can't find my emergency can. It's got to be here.

I dump my bag out in the middle of the aisle. Chairs near me squeak as people scoot back. Away from me. The can's right there in front of me. The empty coffee can I take with me everywhere. For emergencies. Like this.

No time to be embarrassed. I pull off the lid and stick my mouth over the can. Then I hurl. The sound echoes in the metal can.

"Gross!"

"Eew!"

Groans and disgusted noises surround me.

And still I hurl. And hurl. Everything disappears except the spasms in my stomach. And in my throat. My shoulders heave. My hands shake. I couldn't stand up if I wanted to. And it keeps going until I empty my stomach, my guts, and my heart.

Fourteen

When I'm sure I'm done, when there's nothing left inside of me, I still keep my head down, hanging over my coffee can. It helps the dizziness stay away.

Besides, I can't bear to look up. The classroom is silent. I know they're staring.

"Are you okay?" Alex kneels beside me, but somehow he's still towering over me.

"Oh, man," I mutter. I feel in my bag for a tissue and wipe my mouth. *I'm disgusting.*

"Is she okay, Alex?" Rice asks, still at the board. "Katharine, can we call someone?"

"Tell him I'm okay," I whisper, still not looking up.

"She's all right," Alex relays.

"Thanks," I whisper. "I don't want to leave class." I put the lid on the coffee can. For all that noise and effort, there's not much in it.

Alex takes the can from me. Then he gets to his feet and helps me up. I see that he's already repacked my book bag. "She was just kidding. She didn't really hurl. She's trying out for the theater."

There's a little laughter from somewhere.

"Oh, she hurled, all right," Cassie says. Her chair is the closest to me. She scoots it even farther away than she already had. "Trust me. She hurled."

Father, You promised that when I'm weak, You're strong. Well, I'm weak now.

I stand up straight and look at Cassie. "*Hurl*? That's the best you can come up with?"

"What are you talking about?" Cassie frowns at me, then makes a face to the guy next to her, like I'm a lunatic.

Maybe I am. But Wes's idea is making its way into my brain, and I've got nothing to lose.

"I'm talking about *hurling*, since that seems to be the only word you have for it."

"What? You want another word for . . . for what you did? Fine. *Puke.* Like that?" Cassie looks to the guy next to her for support. He shrugs.

"That's all you got?" I ask, like I'm disappointed.

She doesn't answer.

I turn to the rest of the class. "Anybody? What's another word for *hurl* and *puke*?"

Nobody says anything.

For a second, I think about running out of the room and never coming back. *When I'm weak, You're strong.*

"Um . . . *vomit*?" Alex offers.

I smile at him and hope he knows how grateful I am for that answer. "We're getting there."

I walk toward the front of the classroom. My legs tremble, but I don't think it shows. "Mr. Rice, do you suppose I could take a few minutes and share some specialized vocabulary with the class?"

He grins. It's a great grin, like his whole body relaxes into it. "It would be the greatest of pleasures." He hands me a marker for the board. "The floor is yours." He takes a seat on the edge of his desk and waves me to the board.

All or nothing, I think. In big letters, I print: *VOMIT VOCABULARY.*

Laughter ripples across the room.

"Yeah, man!" someone says.

Under my heading, I write *vomit, hurl,* and *puke.*

"Hey, I'm starting to like seventh grade!" somebody shouts.

A girl's voice asks, "Mr. Rice, will this be on the test?"

He quiets the class, and I turn around. "What else? Who knows another way to say *vomit*?"

"Does *throwing up* count?" Margaret asks. I almost didn't recognize her because she cut her hair really short over the summer.

"You bet, Margaret."

She looks surprised that I know her name. We were in fourth grade together.

"Don't want to neglect the obvious," I say while I write *throw up* on the board. "Come on. Don't tell me this is it for you guys?"

"*Blowing chunks*!" somebody shouts from the back. Everybody groans.

"I know. *Barf*!" hollers a girl named Sarah. "That's what my dad calls it."

I write the words on the board, and they keep 'em coming.

"*Lose your lunch*?"

"*Retch*."

I'm caught up writing, so I wait. "Are you done?" I ask.

"Oooh! Oooh! *Upchuck*!" Danita shouts. She laughs, then adds. "Sounds like rap, don't you think? *Oooh! Oooh! Upchuck!*" The way she says it, it does sound like rap.

This time when I ask for more, I'm met with silence. I wait a minute longer. Then it's my turn. "Not bad. But as you might imagine after today's performance, my family and I know many ways to vomit."

This is met with nervous laughter from a few kids.

"So, first, let me take this opportunity to apologize to the class for not quite making it to drive the porcelain bus."

"The what?" Rice asks.

But a few of the kids are cracking up.

"Porcelain bus, get it?" Michael shouts. "Like, as in the toilet? *Driving* the porcelain bus?"

"Gross!" Cassie says. But it's a different "gross" than the one she said a few minutes ago.

I press on, writing as I go. "Then we've got *hugging the porcelain nurse*, *bowing at the porcelain throne*, *talking to Ralph and Bertha on the porcelain phone*. And so on. Eventually you can even make up your own vocabulary."

"Which," Rice chimes in, "is how our language expands. Proceed."

"I believe we forgot *spew*, a concise vocabulary word, for you guys still taking notes."

There's real laughter for that one.

"*Doing the bulimic boogaloo*, which sounds funny but isn't. So don't do it."

The bell rings. A couple of people say, "Aw," like they're disappointed.

I turn to face them. "I'll leave you with a few words to help when you travel. In England, particularly in Birmingham, you will be *currying cufflinks* or maybe *giving a technicolour yawn*. And finally I'll close with a word you can use on your next trip to Scotland, especially if you get seasick. If you're hanging over the side of your boat, grossing out the other passengers, you're probably *honking*."

When school's over, kids are still coming up to congratulate me on my terrific vomit vocab. I wait in the loading zone for Hank, and I replay the instant Alex came to the rescue after the coffee can disaster and the moment I asked God to be strong because I was so weak.

It's hot in the sun, but I smell rain waiting behind gray, bottom-heavy clouds. What a day. I'll have volumes of firsts to write Catman about. First time teaching. Maybe the first time anybody ever has taught vomit vocab.

I watch cars back out of spots in the parking lot and pace the loading zone. I don't see how Hank will ever get through this parking lot mess to pick me up.

"I caught you." Fiona walks up. I think her ride must be here waiting on her because a black car honks, and she holds up a wait-one-minute finger.

"Hey, Fiona." I wonder if she's heard about

English class. I wish she'd been there to see it-not the hurling incident but the vocab lesson.

"Waiting on your ride?" she asks.

"Yeah. I think it will be a while. Parking lot's crazy."

"I wanted to touch base on our project," she says. The black car honks again. So does the car behind it. Fiona shouts, "Be right there!" Then she says to me, "Just so you know, I don't like cats. You're going to have to do the training thing without me."

"People can't actually *train* cats," I explain.

"Whatever." Her gaze darts around the parking lot. "I'll write things up and give the final class presentation and everything. But you've got to do all the cat stuff."

This is sounding better and better to me. "Great. So you really think it's going to work?"

"Better than that," she says. "That pizza sale idea of Cassie's was like half the projects in our class. Make money and give it somewhere. Big deal. But this project? I think it could be the best one if we do it right. Listen, Kat, are you busy tomorrow? 'Cause we ought to get going on this. I could come out to the Rescue."

"*Our* Rescue? Starlight Animal Rescue?"

She laughs. "Makes sense, doesn't it. We're going to *rescue* all the cats, right?"

"Sure." I know I should check with Mom and Dad first. At least, I think I should. I've never had a friend come over before.

Fiona stands on tiptoes and gazes across the parking lot. It's thinning out some. The black car honks. Other cars pull around it and pick up their passengers. Fiona ignores all of them. "So, will Hank be there tomorrow?"

"Yeah. Probably. He rescued eight horses from a trail ride place that got shut down because they abused the animals. I'm sure he'll be working with them all day tomorrow."

"Poor Hank," Fiona says.

"He'll be okay. He's really good with horses."

"He must be a great guy. You're so lucky, Kat."

"I know."

"And his parents must be really nice people too. I mean, how many people take on problem kids and fosters like that? Extra work when you've already got so much to do? You'd think they'd at least get kids who could help out with the Rescue."

I want to tell her that we help, that we all help. Only *not* helping is what's been nagging at me ever since we got the final court adoption date. Fiona isn't saying anything I haven't been saying to myself.

"And Hank's willing to drop you off and pick you up every day. That's pretty cool of him. Not everybody would do that."

The black car's horn honks again, loud and long. This time, Fiona strolls over to it and gets in.

By the time Hank drives up, all I want to do is get home as fast as possible. Hank and Dakota fire questions at me about my first day in junior high, but I'm too tired to go into details. Besides, there doesn't seem to be much to tell. My big "success" in English class feels about as dumb as my big "success" giving the pony his medicine. Neither one amounted to anything worth mentioning.

FIFTEEN

SATURDAY MORNING I sleep in. I don't get out of bed until I hear the dogs going crazy downstairs. The night before, Dad kept talking about the big court date, and Mom spent the evening on the phone with Gram, planning the "Kat Coolidge birthday party."

The whole time, I watched Lion hop on three legs around the kitchen. The dog does fine. Wes rescued the three-legged Pomeranian from Nice Animal Shelter, but he couldn't find a home for him. Now he's saving Lion for his mom, when she gets out of rehab and has a place of her own.

But what I thought as I watched the little dog was how he'd been tossed from home to home, returned because he was too much trouble. And I know that's what would have happened to me if the Coolidges weren't the kind of people they are. *I'd* be the one returned to sender.

The dogs are still barking downstairs. I walk to the banister and peer down. *Fiona!* She and Hank are standing on the front porch.

I dash back to my room and pull on clothes and my wig, brush my teeth, and get downstairs as fast as I can.

"Kat!" Mom calls from the kitchen. "I was just coming to get you. Your friend's out on the front porch with Hank."

I can see them talking, so I slip around to the kitchen. "Sorry I didn't ask if Fiona could come over, Mom. I kind of forgot. I was so tired after school."

"Nonsense. I'm thrilled you have a friend to invite over." Mom smooths my hair. It's the black wig again.

When I walk out to the porch, Fiona's laughing at something Hank said. "Hank, I had no idea you were so funny."

Then I see she's holding a beautiful white cat. "Fiona, hi. Is this your cat?"

"My sister's cat," Fiona answers.

"Where's Wes?" Hank asks. "He should take these dogs on another walk. Maybe they'd stop barking at this poor cat."

"Princess doesn't care," Fiona says, holding out the cat for me to take.

"Anyway," Hank says, one hand on the screen door, "nice to see you again, Fiona. I've got to get back to the barn."

Fiona watches Hank leave, then brushes off her blue silk shirt. "That cat sheds."

"She's beautiful." I stroke her where Kitten loves to be scratched. The cat doesn't make a sound. "How do you get her to purr?"

"Are you kidding?" Fiona says. "That cat hasn't purred since we got it. She doesn't do anything. I told you."

"Doesn't she meow when she's hungry?" I ask, thinking that this cat's eyes are the bluest I've ever seen.

"Nope. My sister has to pick her up and carry her to the food dish. That's how stupid this cat is. You'll see. All she does is sleep." Fiona walks past me into the living room. "Shouldn't we get to work?" Her head rotates as she takes in what she can see of our house. "You guys sure like animals," she observes.

I try to see the room through Fiona's eyes. Cat throws on the big chair. Dog throws on the couch. Horse wallpaper, cat curtains. "You can come in and sit down."

"Would you girls like something to eat? Or a milk shake?" Mom asks.

"No thanks, Mrs. Coolidge," Fiona answers.

"I better go get dressed," Mom says, not correcting Fiona for calling her "Mrs." instead of "Dr." Mom's probably been up for hours, but she's still in her fuzzy blue robe and red slippers. "I'm driving out to check on Mrs. Wilson. See how she's faring after her surgery. You girls have fun."

We sit at the table and Fiona pulls out a notebook. Princess settles on my lap. "I've already drawn up a plan," Fiona begins, opening her notebook. "Basically, Princess here will be your main client. It would be great if you could train her to do something. Anything. You know, like come when we call her, even. Or a trick?"

I still don't like the idea of "training" cats, but I don't want to be negative. Fiona's already put in a lot of work on this project, and I'm lucky to have her as a partner. It's my fault we're getting such a late start on it.

"I don't know how much I can do in one day," I explain.

"You can keep Princess all week. That's all the time we have, remember? So during the week you can have cat shrink appointments. Then we'll have, like, this fantastic grand finale at my house. People will bring their cured cats. And you can tell them more about cats or whatever. And show them what Princess can do and everything. My mother's ordered cat-shaped cakes, and we'll get cat plates and napkins. I'm inviting Buffenmyer for that part so we get credit."

"When?" I have a million questions, but this is the first one that pops out.

"Saturday."

"I'm not sure how much I can do in a week," I admit.

"I thought you'd be excited about this, Kat. I've put in a lot of work on it already." Fiona sounds crushed.

"It's a great plan, Fiona. Thanks for working on it without me. It's just . . . well, whose cats am I supposed to work with?" I stroke Princess, who's been sleeping so soundly on my lap that I check her pulse and make sure she's still breathing.

Fiona doesn't answer. She's staring out the window. I stare too. Hank gets something–a halter, I think–out of the truck and walks back to the barn.

"Where do we find problem cats?" I ask again, trying not to sound desperate.

"The cats? I don't know. The humane society? That shelter where Alex got his? They're loaded with cats. You said so yourself. We could take them back when we're finished with them."

"We can't do that!"

"Fine," she says. "Then you come up with the cats. I'm doing everything else."

I'd love to use cats from the shelter. But no way I'm working with cats and sending them back. And I could never find homes for them that fast. "Okay. We've got Princess."

"Big deal," Fiona says, still staring out the window. "One cat won't get us an A."

She's right. "Alex is having trouble with his cat. Maybe he could bring his." I'm thinking as I talk. "You know, I'll bet a lot of kids in our class have cats. I think Meagan does. The Brewsters have two cats. Don't the Thompsons have a tabby who just had kittens?"

"How should I know?" Fiona says.

"I'm just saying, I'll bet there are plenty of cat owners in seventh grade who wish their cats were better behaved. Maybe we could ask them to bring their cats."

"Works for me," Fiona says, finally facing me again. "You could set up cat appointments after school every day next week. I can work on the big finale for Saturday."

I feel bad that the excitement is gone from her voice. I know it's my fault. "Sure. Good idea."

"On second thought," she says, "I should be the one to set up the appointments. I know more people in our class than you do. They won't tell *me* no. I know. I'll let them bring the cats to *my* house. That'll get them to come for sure. You could come home with me after school and do the cat stuff there. Everybody knows where I live. We can't expect them to drive way out here anyway."

"Would your mother mind having people and cats in her house?" I ask.

"We have tons of room. You could use one of the screened-in porches. But seriously, Kat, you can't miss school. And you'll need to stay in town every day after school too. All week. Monday through Friday. Can you do that?" She stares at me like she's trying to see for herself if I could last all week.

"Sure. Not a problem. I can stay in town after school." I'm trying to sound confident, but problems are crushing in at tiger-force. I have to stay well. And if I pull that off, I still need to find a way home. I can't ask Hank to wait around for me. Not when he's got the horses to see to.

"I can bring you home with me when you're done, Kat," Mom says from the kitchen, like she's been reading my mind. Or eavesdropping. She's dressed in her khaki pants and a white shirt.

Fiona's expression says Mom's been eavesdropping, and Fiona doesn't like it.

"Thanks, Mom," I call.

"Well, I'm off," Mom says. "Your dad's outside playing with that lawn mower. Fair warning. He's got a fistful of new jokes about cats." She searches for her purse. Then her keys. Then she kisses me good-bye and leaves.

Fiona waits until Mom and Dad say their good-byes and Mom drives off. Then she asks, "Is your foster mother really a doctor?"

I nod. I'm not sure I've ever thought of Mom as my foster mother. But that's the reality.

Thinking about this brings back my determination to do something that will make me feel like I'm a good fit in the Coolidge family. Maybe this whole cat clinic is what I've been waiting for. Maybe this is the way to finally be helpful instead of being the one who always needs help.

Kitten scratches at my pant leg, then climbs up the back of the chair until she's on my shoulders. From there, she stares at Princess and hisses at the intruder.

"Be nice, Kitten," I say, trying to pet them both. Kitten keeps hissing. But Princess barely looks at my cat.

"I've written everything down in here,

Kat," Fiona says, standing. "Just read through it. You really don't need me anymore. Why don't I leave you with Princess? You can get started working on her." She moves toward the door. "Dad won't be back for me for another hour. Maybe Hank can show me how he trains horses."

Fiona leaves, and I don't see her until her dad's car drives up and honks. I recognize the black car from the loading zone yesterday.

After a couple more honks, Fiona strolls out of the barn, turning backward twice to wave at Hank.

"Bye, Fiona!" I shout out the window.

But I guess she doesn't hear me because she doesn't tell Princess or me good-bye.

SIXTEEN

I SPEND THE REST of the weekend getting to know Princess. She's a sweet cat and loves to sit on my lap. The minute I set her down, she goes to sleep at my feet. In my room she curls up on my cat rug and sleeps all night.

During the day, I watch her inside and outside. She seems fearless. Or unimpressed. Lion yaps at her, and she doesn't even blink. No matter what Mustard and Ketchup do, Princess has no interest. She doesn't even wake up when Rex and Wes storm in for lunch.

Fiona's right about one thing. This cat is very, very strange.

Sunday afternoon it rains, so Dad declares family movie time, and everyone settles in by the TV. Dakota and I are on the couch with Mom. I've got Kitten in my lap, and Princess has curled up in Dakota's, surprising both of us.

Dad stands in front of the TV, his chosen DVD behind his back. "Ready? Ta-da!" He whips out his favorite movie, *Old Yeller.*

"Not again, Dad," Hank pleads.

"Didn't we just watch this the last time it rained?" Dakota asks.

"No," Mom corrects, "we watched it the last time it snowed. But Wes didn't watch it with us then."

Wes gets off the floor and checks out the DVD cover. "Man, this is an oldie. Did you guys see the date on this?"

"It's a classic, Wes," Dad says.

"Yeah? Well, not where I come from. I've never heard of it."

Dad's eyes get big. "Are you telling me you've never seen *Old Yeller*? Never ever?"

"So?" Wes challenges.

Rex lets out a little whine to warn Wes he's getting close to anger.

"So, my fortunate, doubly blessed Wes,"

Dad exclaims, "you are in for the treat of your life!"

Wes shakes his head. "Thanks. I think I'll pass. Again."

"There are dogs in it, Wes," I say. I want us all to do this together. Rain pounds the roof. Wind rattles the windows. It's a perfect day for a family movie.

"I don't know, Kat," Dakota says. "Wes would probably cry."

"Yeah, right," Wes says.

"Bet you tonight's chores you can't make it through the whole movie without tears," Hank says.

"Are you kidding? You're on." Wes and Rex scoot back on the floor so Wes can lean against the couch. Hank takes the other side, and Dad sits at Mom's feet, even though there's a recliner empty at the other end of the couch.

When the movie's over, Hank's won his bet easily, although Wes claimed he had something in his eye that made him tear up like that. He can't get outside fast enough. "I'll grain your horses anyway," he calls back.

Hank jogs out after him. "I'll do the pony,

Wes. Besides, I want to see Starlight, and she'll want to see me."

Hank always says that, even though his horse can't see.

His horse can't see. Can't see . . .

Something's stirring in my brain. What if . . . ?

"Kat?" Dakota whispers. "I need to get up, but I don't want to disturb this cat. I can't believe she sat on my lap the whole movie."

"Wait," I whisper back. I slide to the floor in front of Dakota and Princess. I'm kneeling, facing them, inches from Princess's face. "Now jiggle."

"Excuse me?"

"Jiggle Princess awake."

Dakota moves her knees up and down, jiggles her legs, and jostles Princess until she opens her eyes. The cat shows no surprise seeing me in front of her. "Now what?" Dakota asks.

I raise my hands, making cat claws in front of Princess.

"What are you trying to do? Scare the poor thing?" Dakota asks.

"Something like that," I answer. I back up a foot. "Go ahead and set her down."

Dakota sets Princess on the carpet. The cat stretches, then starts to walk away. I move in directly behind her and clap my hands. "Scat!" I yell.

"Kat!" Dakota shouts.

Again I clap and yell inches from Princess's tail. "Shoo! Scat!"

The cat stops and stretches again.

"Want to tell me what's wrong with you?" Dakota asks.

I sigh. Tears push at the backs of my eyes. I turn to Dakota. "Nothing's wrong with *me*." I lie down beside Princess and stroke her long fur. She can't purr because she's never learned how. She's never *heard* purring. She's never even *seen* another cat. "Dakota, this cat is blind and deaf."

That night I e-mail Catman about Princess. I'm pretty sure I'm right about this cat, but I want to hear it from the Catman himself. Even though he can't study Princess in person, I know he'll be able to help me. I tell him everything I know about the cat, including what Fiona said about other families returning the cat to the pet store because they thought she was dumb.

I keep checking my e-mail until I get an answer an hour later:

Hey, Kat!

Sorry I wasn't here. I needed some follow-up footage of a Persian cat in Polk, Ohio. Far out, man!

Anyway. To cat business. Way to nail this one, Kat! You're right on, man. Your Princess cat's seeing no evil and hearing no evil.

You said Princess has long white hair, right? No dark fur anywhere? There's your proof. Like half of all totally white cats are totally deaf. It's a genetics thing, man. Like calico cats being chicks. (Okay, officially one in 3,000 calicos could be a guy.) Bet Princess has blue eyes too. Go figure, the gold or green-eyed cats have a better shot at hearing.

Come back at me if you're online.

The Catman

As soon as I see Catman's message, I start typing:

Thanks! Sad to know, but good to understand this cat. Poor thing's been bounced around like a tennis ball. At least now we know why she's so weird.

I've got another problem, Catman. For the cat clinic I told you about yesterday (and thanks for the vote of confidence), I'm supposed to teach this blind and deaf cat something, like a trick. Any ideas what I could teach a blind and deaf cat to do . . . in just a week?

Freaking out,

Kat

Catman's answer comes back in seconds:

Teach Princess how to use the john.

Seventeen

Monday morning Fiona grabs me in the hall and drags me into Ms. Buffenmyer's classroom before school starts. "Good. You're early for once. We have six clients signed up already, and I haven't even made the problem-cat announcement yet."

"Wow! That's great, Fiona."

"I guess." She doesn't sound enthused. "It's just that I'm hearing about these other do-gooder projects, like starting a soup kitchen–"

"Somebody's starting a soup kitchen? That's amazing."

"Right. And we're training cats. I'm

starting to think we blew it, going with this cat thing."

I'm catching her disappointment like it's the flu. "So what do we do?"

"It's too late to change now."

Fiona and I plop into the same seats we had Friday. I was sick around five this morning, but I'm pretty good now. And I'm *not* going to miss school, not this week anyway.

She sighs. "We're stuck with cats. Some social project. We'll probably get a lousy grade. We're not helping *people.* Just their stupid cats. I should have stuck with pizza. At least that would end up getting money for the poor. We won't make a dime on this project."

I can't believe how fast she switched from loving the idea to hating it. She's probably right, though. We're supposed to help people. I lean back in my chair and wonder why I ever thought I could help people or cats.

"Anyway," Fiona continues, "we're stuck. We'll have to make the best of it. Alex is bringing his cat to my house after school. And Cassie wants to bring hers today too."

"I didn't know Cassie had a cat."

Fiona shrugs. "Me either. She probably

bought one so she wouldn't be left out. Before I knew what a waste this cat thing was going to be, I told her about the big finale at my house Saturday." Fiona glances around the room until she sees someone and waves. She gets up. "I'm going to go sit with Cassie and Brett. If we don't bump into each other before school's out, be in the loading zone, okay? My mom will pick us up."

I don't get a chance to talk to Fiona the rest of the day, although several kids tell me they're signed up for "cat therapy." Fiona's lunch table is filled when I walk into the lunchroom. And anyway, the second I step into the cafeteria, I lose my appetite.

After school, we meet up in the loading zone. Her mom is first in line, but I wait until Fiona comes out. I've met Mrs. Morris before, but I don't think she recognizes me.

We get in, and her mother introduces herself. "I guess we'll be seeing a lot of you this week."

"It's nice of you to let us do this at your

house, Mrs. Morris," I say, still hunting for my seat belt. "Thanks."

"It's nothing, dear. I'm sure your mother wants you to get an A as much as I want Fiona to. It may seem like college is a long way off to you girls, but it's right around the corner."

"Brett's coming over later," Fiona tells her mother.

"Does he have a cat?" I ask.

Fiona laughs. "Brett? A cat? He's trying to get rid of his little brother. I can't imagine him with a pet. He's coming to hang out with me." She checks her notebook. "Alex will probably get there before we do. He's walking. Then you've got Matt, who's been trying since fifth grade to get me to go out with him. And Cassie."

I thought I might have one or two cats to see. Not three. I've been praying for a second burst of energy–and a third and a fourth–since noon. Plus, I want to get back for another toilet-training session with Princess. I'm not mentioning that to Fiona. It will be a surprise if it works. And I won't have to let her down if it doesn't.

Fiona flips down the car visor and puts on pink lip gloss. "Watch the bumps, will you, Mother?"

"Sorry," Mrs. Morris replies.

Fiona's house is one of the newer homes in Nice–white brick, sprawled over two lots. I've been by it dozens of times. It's right up the street from Nice Elementary. Fancy-shaped evergreens don't quite hide it from the road.

"Your house is so nice," I say. "I mean, beautiful." When you live in Nice, you try not to use the word *nice*, even when it fits.

"Thank you, Katrina." Mrs. Morris says my name wrong. I wait for Fiona to correct her, but she doesn't. "The house is a mess right now. We're rebuilding the pool. Workmen track in day and night. But you and the cats should be safe and private on the east porch. Isn't that what you were thinking, Fiona?"

Fiona is already out of the car and halfway up the long drive. "This way, Kat!" she calls without turning around.

Fiona's sister, Arianna, is watching what looks like a soap opera when we walk in. She doesn't turn around.

"Arianna, you know Katrina, don't you?" Mrs. Morris says.

"It's Katharine," I tell Mrs. Morris. "You can

call me Kat if you want. Hey, Arianna. How's sixth grade? Do you have Mrs. Albertson?"

"Hey," she calls without taking her gaze from the TV, where a man and a woman are arguing.

I wait a few seconds, but she doesn't answer the school questions. And she doesn't ask about her cat, Princess.

"Kat?" Fiona calls.

I follow the sound of Fiona's voice and find her in a sunny porch off a room that looks like a library. "This is perfect." I step down onto tiled floor. The room forms a circle with windows all the way around. Outside, workmen are painting an empty pool. The doorbell rings, and chimes echo through the house–some classical song I should probably know.

"That's Brett," Fiona announces. She starts for the door, then turns back. "I'll send the cat people to you when they come, okay?" She tosses the notebook with the names of the cats and their owners in my direction.

I grab it and nod. I'd give just about anything to have Catman here with me. Again I picture the image in that psalm, the kid holding

Dad's hand. Only I picture me holding God's hand. And I'm holding a cat. It helps.

Seconds later, Alex walks in with a big, fat tabby cat. "Man, you could get lost in this house."

"Hey, Alex. And this must be Bozo."

I sit in the chair closest to the couch, and Alex takes the couch. The tabby hangs over his arm like a towel. "So this is cat therapy," he says, glancing around the porch. "I feel like I should lie down on the couch and tell you all my troubles, doc." He fakes lying back. We both laugh.

"Why on earth did you name this sweet cat Bozo?" I ask, scratching the tabby behind the ears.

"Pretty bad, huh? I mean, how smart is anybody going to be if he starts out life as Bozo, right?"

I shrug because I agree with him.

"My dad's crazy about that old clown Bozo who used to be on TV. I'm just lucky they didn't name *me* after that clown."

Neither of us says anything for a minute.

Then Alex says, "Oh yeah. I almost forgot. Your magic's working already."

"No magic here," I interrupt. "I just watch cats."

"I know. I'm just kidding. But what you said about Bozo puking? We stopped giving him milk and eggs, although I think Dad still sneaks him scraps when we're not looking. Anyway, the cat stopped puking. Or should I say doing the technicolor yawn?"

"That's great, Alex." We smile kind of lamely at each other. "Thanks again for helping me out in English."

"Anytime," he says. "I mean, not that you'll do that again anytime. Not that you couldn't if you wanted to. I mean, needed to."

I think Alex is having as much trouble talking to me as I am to him. I wish Fiona were here to help keep the conversation rolling.

Bozo is still hanging over Alex's arm.

"Um . . . what's the biggest problem you need help with?" I ask. "For Bozo, that is. Is it the licking? Didn't you say your cat licks you guys and it creeps you out?"

Alex grins, showing straight, white teeth that make me want to hide my not-so-straight, not-so-white teeth. "Everybody's okay with the licking thing since I convinced them it was

Bozo's way of kissing. Dad claims Bozo likes him best because he's the most licked."

"That's good, then."

"Yeah. But Bozo's still scratching furniture. He loves Mom's best chair. And her great-grandmother's tea table. We've got to get Bozo to stop scratching."

Scratching furniture was one of the first problems I had to learn to handle when I started rescuing cats. "I think I can help Bozo with that one."

"Cool." He hands over the cat. "Be my guest."

I take Bozo from Alex. "You are one big boy," I mutter.

"Thank you," Alex says. He laughs. "Seriously, Kat, why does Bozo scratch Mom's furniture?"

"Cats have sweat glands between their paw pads." I hold up Bozo's paw and show him. "Scratching lets him leave his scent around. So he's saying, 'This couch? That's mine. This expensive table? Mine. This guy named Alex? Mine.'"

He laughs again. "You're right. He scratches us, too. Mom thinks if we're going to keep Bozo, we should declaw him."

I shake my head. "Terrible idea. Cats need their claws. It's their best defense."

"Yeah, but we don't let him outside. Even Mom knows that wouldn't be fair, sending him into the world without his weapons."

"Even inside, Bozo *thinks* he needs those claws. If he doesn't have that clawing defense, he'll probably start biting."

"Not good," Alex admits.

"Declawing cats is illegal in England because it's so cruel," I explain.

"So how do we teach him not to scratch?" Alex asks.

"We don't. Cats *have* to scratch. It's their nature. What we can do, though, is teach Bozo *what* to scratch."

For the rest of the time, I give Alex ideas on how to get Bozo not to scratch the furniture. "I wish we were at my house so you could see some of the things Dad and I have rigged up for our cats. Dad made a scratching post by covering a box with carpet. Ketchup, one of our rescues, loves that thing. Mustard, on the other hand, prefers this log we set up. It's just a regular log, but that cat spends hours scratching at it."

Alex actually writes down my other tips: Dangle toys from the scratching post. Smear the post in catnip. Put the scratching post near the furniture Bozo likes to scratch but drop treats near the post to make it more tempting.

"You can put balloons on furniture you want Bozo to leave alone. It usually takes only one big pop to make a cat leave something alone forever. But you have to stay close by so you can get rid of the popped balloon before he tries to chew it."

"You guys done?" Fiona asks. She and Brett are standing in the doorway of the porch, Brett's arm around her waist. "Because, as they say in the cat shrink business, 'I'm sorry, but your time is up.'"

"I can't believe how fast that hour went," Alex says.

I stand and walk him to the door. "I hope it helped."

Fiona takes over. "And even if it didn't, please say it did." She hands him a sheet of paper. "Here's an evaluation form. Give it back to me when you're done. It's part of our project. I know this is a stupid project, Alex, but it's all we've got."

"Stupid?" Alex glances at me. "I thought it was–"

"Whatever," Fiona says. "Just fill out that evaluation. And try to say something good about how helpful this was. Blah, blah, blah." She's still giving him instructions as they disappear down the hall.

Within minutes, Fiona brings Matt back. He's carting a tiny black cat that looks like she couldn't give anybody problems. When Fiona leaves with Brett, Matt stares after her so long that I have to call him back to earth. This is definitely going to be tougher than the Alex and Bozo act.

EIGHTEEN

"I DON'T KNOW WHAT Fiona sees in that guy," Matt mutters. His cat springs out of his arms, and I don't think Matt even notices.

"Matt?" I scramble after Squirt. Twice, she squirts through my arms, making me wonder if that's how she got her name. But when I get hold of her and sit back on the couch, she purrs for me.

"Squirt is a sweetheart." The more I stroke her, the louder she purrs. "What could possibly be wrong with this cutie cat?"

Matt launches into a list of wrongs, a dozen grievances he and his whole family have against poor Squirt. "You should see what that cat does while we're gone. Mom gets home from work or I come back from practice and the whole house is a mess."

"Matt," I begin, stroking the smooth, black hair on the cat's skinny body, "what you've got here is a latchkey cat."

"You mean like a latchkey kid? When kids come home after school and lock themselves in because their parents are still at work? Kind of like my brothers and me, I guess." He cocks his head at me. "I've never heard of latchkey cats, though."

"Well, you've got one." Squirt is purring up a storm in my arms and rubbing her cheek against my hand. "This sweet kitty doesn't like being left alone. Cats are curious. If you don't leave fun things for her to get into, she'll make her own fun. And you probably won't like it."

"No kidding," Matt says. "Well, what fun could I leave her? She's got more toys than I had when I was a kid. We always leave those out for her. But she'd rather tear up the newspaper or get into the plants."

"Okay. Try this. Tomorrow, put half of the cat's toys away where she can't find them.

Leave a couple out. Then hide the rest in places she can find easily. You could put one in a paper bag. My cat could play with a paper bag all day. The next day, switch toys, bringing out the ones she hasn't seen for a while."

"Cool." Matt's nodding his head. "Kind of a lot of trouble, though."

"Cats take work. And be sure your cat can see out the window without climbing your plants. Pull a table over, or get a card table and put a pillow on it. Anything that will let Squirt watch the birds and see the outside world. She'll do that for hours, which means she won't be getting into trouble, right?"

"Yeah. But I don't know if Mom will want me moving things around. Sounds like a hassle."

I feel like giving Matt and his whole family a lecture on taking time to care for pets. "Here's one I don't think you'll feel is too much trouble. Leave your smelliest T-shirt out for Squirt when you go to school in the morning."

"I can do that," Matt promises.

When Matt leaves, I feel pretty useless, even to the cats. I'm sure Matt came for Fiona, not for his cat. Maybe Alex did too.

I'm glad to have a few minutes to myself before the last cat shows up. My throat feels sore, but I think it's because I'm so tired. When I sit down, my knee hurts, and my legs feel like they're filled with molasses.

"Here she is," Fiona says, leading Cassie into the porch. "The doctor is in."

"Aren't you staying?" Cassie demands.

"Brett and I are busy," Fiona answers. She hands Cassie an evaluation form. "Don't forget to give us a good report. I need that back by Friday."

The whole time Cassie and her cat, August, are with me, I pray that I won't have to run outside and hurl. It's hard to focus on August.

"My mother says if August keeps jumping up on her kitchen counters, she's getting rid of him. She'll do it, too," Cassie promises.

I'm grateful this is a pretty easy fix, because I have only half of my brain power for it. The other part of my brain is trying to talk my stomach out of doing what it feels like doing. "Aluminum foil," I tell her.

"Aluminum foil?" Cassie sounds like she suspects I'm crazy again.

"You cover your kitchen counters with aluminum foil for a couple of days. When August jumps up, he won't like the sound or the feel of foil. Cats hate the stuff. You should be okay to take the foil off after a day or two."

"What if my mother doesn't want to have her counters decorated with foil?" Cassie demands.

"Some people use double-sided sticky tape, but I like foil better. Or you can go with smells, if your mom doesn't want to do the foil thing. Cats hate the smell of vinegar, raw onions, lemon peel, menthol, and stinky perfumes. Put lemon peels on the counter, and your cat won't go near them."

Even thinking about lemon peels makes me want to puke. I bite the inside of my cheek because that helps. Who knows why.

Mrs. Morris comes out to the porch. "I believe your mother's here for you. Someone's honking."

Honking? I almost run to the van. We make it out of town before Mom has to pull over and let me do the honking by the side of the road.

* * *

Tuesday I stay in bed the whole day. I hate letting Fiona down, but all I can do is sleep the day away. I leave her messages, but she doesn't call back.

Wednesday morning when I come downstairs, Mom and Dad are talking about our big court date. They fill me in on everything, but I only half listen. I can't help the feeling I get whenever they talk about the adoption being final, about me being a Coolidge. There's nothing I want more, but there's nothing I deserve less.

"We can all fit in the van," Mom says. "We should drive in early, maybe stop by Nice Donuts first and–"

"Saturday morning?" I don't know why I haven't thought of this before now. "Saturday morning I've got to be at Fiona's for our project. Our teacher's going to be there and everything."

"What?" Dad sounds horrified. "But the courthouse! Our court date! It's the only time they do adoptions in this county."

"Easy, my love," Mom says. "What time is your project?"

"I'm not sure. Fiona and her mother are planning it."

"Well, I'm sure it will all work out," Mom says. "Not to worry. One of us can drive you to Fiona's and wait for you. You can meet up with us at the courthouse. It will all work out."

"You are such a level head," Dad tells her.

I ride to school with Hank and Dakota. All the way there, I stare out the window. I don't want to stand before a judge and lie about how I deserve to be a real Coolidge. I don't want to make Mom and Dad lie about it either. Maybe this project at Fiona's will be my way out.

★ ★ ★

Fiona doesn't hide her feelings about my missing school yesterday. "Kat, I asked you in the beginning if I could count on you, and you said I could." We're standing in the middle of the hall before first hour. Kids walk around us and stare.

"I know," I say. "And I'm sorry. I'll be here the rest of the week."

"Well, you better. I told yesterday's cat

owners to come back today. I had everything scheduled, and you threw it off by not showing."

"I can–"

But Fiona's too mad to hear me out. We don't talk the rest of the day until we're sitting in her mother's car after school.

"Have you set a time for Saturday's finale?" I ask.

Fiona's mom answers, "The invitations say 10:00. Fiona, didn't you give your friend an invitation?"

Fiona sighs for an answer. "She doesn't need an invitation, Mother. She's the one they're coming to hear talk about cats."

Cats file in and out of my "cat shrink" office at Fiona's all afternoon and evening. Cat problems range from a runaway cat to a cat who constantly gets underfoot. I have to phone Mom and ask her to pick me up later than planned.

My last client is Mikayla Noel, a girl who goes to our church. She brings Socrates, a sleek female Siamese.

"You know I love animals," Mikayla says. "All animals, including the birds Socrates has been killing in our backyard. I can't stand it anymore. Sometimes she leaves them on our step. Otherwise, she's such a great cat. I don't know what to do to get her to stop killing things, though."

"Cats are hunters," I tell her. "You can't change that. But we *can* make Socrates a bad hunter."

Together, Mikayla and I rig a collar with two bells and a mirror. When we're done, we put the collar on Socrates.

"There you go, Socrates," I tell her. "Now those backyard birds are going to get fair warning when you're on the prowl. Hunting is about to get a whole lot tougher."

On Thursday Mrs. Morris picks me up, but Fiona stays for cheerleading practice. I see three cats and get home earlier than usual.

Friday I ride home with Fiona, but she disappears as soon as we get to her house. I see four cats, including Berta, a short-haired gray brought in by Stephen Kirk, an eighth grader.

"I hope it's okay to come, even though I'm not in your class," Stephen says. "Alex told me you can cure any cat, and mine needs help."

I can't believe Alex told him about me. "I don't know about curing any cat, but I'll try. What's up with Berta?"

"She's an unwanted alarm clock in our house. Berta jumps on our beds at dawn and won't stop yowling until we're up."

I like the way he's holding his cat. I can see how much he cares about her. "All I can do is give you some ideas to try. Okay?"

He nods. "I'll try anything."

"Play with your cat right before you go to bed. Tire her out. Feed her later too. That way her stomach won't wake her."

"Okay," Stephen says. "Anything else?"

"If that doesn't work and you're desperate, you could have a hair dryer by the bed, or one of those little car vacuums. If your cat comes in too early, you can surprise her with a noisy blast of air. Only do it as a last resort. It shouldn't take more than once or twice.

Bottom line, Stephen: it's cool that your cat wants you up to play with her."

I actually feel pretty good watching Stephen and Berta leave . . . until I meet Fiona on my way out.

"You know he doesn't even count, don't you?" she snaps as soon as she closes the door on him. "He's not in seventh grade. I couldn't give him an evaluation."

"Sorry, Fiona," I say. But I'm not sorry I got to try to help Stephen and Berta.

"Yeah. Well, look at the bright side. After tomorrow, this whole thing will be over, one way or the other."

Nineteen

At home, my secret project with Princess is coming right along. Dakota catches me in my room before dinner. "Want to explain to me why I'm sharing the john with a cat?"

I stare at her. "No way. You're not telling me Princess used the toilet."

Dakota nods.

"Seriously? You saw her?" I can't believe it worked.

"Twice," Dakota answers. "Craziest thing I ever saw. How did you get her to do that, Kat? I mean, I saw the litter box on the toilet Monday. Then I saw when you took that away and covered the seat in plastic wrap. Gave me flashbacks to pranks in one of the foster homes I ran away from."

"Catman told me how to do it. I only had to put litter on the plastic wrap for one day."

"Yeah. That was pretty gross."

"I know. And thanks for letting me use our bathroom for Princess. Can you believe how fast she learned? Yesterday she went with just the plastic wrap on the toilet. I took that off this morning. And she's got it already? Unbelievable!"

"And all of this so you and I could have a third party share the bathroom with us?" Dakota's grinning, though. "Seriously, Kat, you're amazing. I expect Princess to be demanding her own reading material in there before long."

"Not our problem after tomorrow," I tell her. Something clenches inside every time I give up one of the rescues. I feel the same way about Princess.

"Well, you did good, kid," Dakota says.

"Princess did, anyway. And she learned all of this blind and deaf. She must be a really smart cat, Dakota. Fiona and her sister will have to see that now."

"What did Fiona say when you told her Princess was blind and deaf?" Dakota asks.

I don't answer.

"You haven't told her?"

"I was hoping I'd have some good news to go with the bad," I explain. "And now I do."

Dakota squats down to stroke Princess. "Good news, bad news, huh? That reminds me . . . Chestnut wasn't limping at all today."

"Really? That's great. He's finished the bute, too, right? So that's good news." But I can tell by her face that the bad news isn't far behind.

"Hank thinks we might have a buyer for Chestnut," she says.

Again, there's that pinching inside me. That's the way it is when you rescue. Your goal is to get the animal to a place where you can find a great home for him. And when you do, it hurts like crazy.

☆ ☆ ☆

After dinner I go out and visit Chestnut. He's in the pasture with the other horses.

Hank walks up behind me. "He looks good, doesn't he? He's not limping at all."

Chestnut comes up to the fence, and I reach in and pet him. I pull up grass and feed him. "Dakota says you might have a buyer."

"It's a family with a little girl who's crazy about horses. She's been riding at a stable for two years. It's a good home. And they've got a neighbor who might want the sorrel."

I pull up more grass and stick it through the fence. Chestnut devours it. It's the same grass he's got on his side of the fence, but it always looks greener this way. I'll miss this pony.

"You getting excited about the adoption deal? I hear Gram wanted to invite the entire state to celebrate." Hank puts his arm around my shoulders and squeezes. "You've been my sister since the day you came here. But I'm glad it will finally be official."

It's all I can do not to cry. "I can't go to the courthouse, Hank."

"Right," Hank says. When I don't chuckle with him, he asks, "You're not worried about that school thing, are you? Dad got the court date bumped to 11:00."

"I don't know if I'll be done by then." I don't look at Hank. I think I'll fall apart if I do.

"Well, *be* done! This isn't something you

can miss. What if they can't make it official unless you're there to speak for yourself or to sign the adoption papers or something? Did you think of that?"

"Yes."

Hank turns me to face him. "Kat? What are you saying? What's going on with you?"

I don't know if I can explain it. I don't know if I want to. I shrug and look away.

"Is there some reason you don't want the adoption to be final?" Hank asks. "Are you thinking about your biological parents?"

I frown at him. "Is that what you think?"

"I don't know what to think. You're blind-siding me here. But you better get it out. Are you . . . are you having second thoughts about us?" I can hear the pain in his voice.

"Hank, no. That's not it. Who wouldn't want to be adopted by your family?"

He doesn't move.

"I just . . . I don't want them to do it out of pity."

"Pity? Kat, they love you. We all love you. How can you not know that?"

"I do know that. But they can love me without giving me their name. *Your* name. It's too big of a gift. I don't want them to do it because they think they have to, because they feel sorry for me."

"Sorry for you?" Hank asks.

"Yeah, sorry for me. I'm too sick and too weak to do anything around here. You should know that better than anybody."

"Kat, this isn't you talking."

"If I could *do* something–something to make me feel like I'm not just a burden to everybody . . ."

Hank shakes his head. "Have you talked to Mom and Dad about this?"

"No. And you have to promise me *you* won't. Promise me, Hank."

He's quiet a minute. "Okay. But have you at least talked to God about it?"

That takes the wind out of me. I'm usually the one telling everybody else to talk to God about stuff.

Out in the pasture, something stirs. The gray mare squeals. One of the other horses has his ears back and looks ready to fight.

Hank leaps into action and vaults the fence. "I'm driving you to that courthouse!" he shouts. "I'm not giving up my sister that easy."

TWENTY

WHEN I COME DOWN for breakfast on Saturday, Mom and Dad are waiting, arm in arm, at the foot of the stairs.

"There she is!" Dad exclaims. "Our own Kat Coolidge."

"I wish you could ride with us to the courthouse instead of coming later with Hank," Mom says.

"Mom, I told you–," I begin.

"Not that we don't understand," Dad says.

"Because we're understanding parents," Mom adds, winking at Dad.

I've told them I don't know if I can make it there or not. But they won't hear it.

"George called me," Mom says.

"Mother called you?" Dad sounds hurt that he didn't get a call from Gram.

"We're all set for the Made-Rite as soon as we finish at the courthouse. I'm glad you kept it just family, Kat. I don't want to share you with anybody."

I hug both of them, and they hug me back. Then I push away and get Princess. "Hank, we better go."

In the truck, Hank makes small talk. "You and Dakota will be sad to see that cat go. Did you really teach it to use the toilet?"

I nod. But I know Hank's thinking about the same thing I am. "I can't go to the courthouse, Hank."

"Kat–"

"I don't want to talk about it anymore."

He pulls up at Fiona's and shuts off the engine. "I'll wait right here for you."

"Don't. I need you to go to the courthouse for me."

"You can't–"

But I don't let him finish. I know what I'm

doing, what I *have* to do. "I'm going to put on the best cat clinic anybody has ever seen. Tell Mom and Dad I'm sorry. But this is something I have to do." I climb out of the truck. Princess is still asleep in my arms.

"Kat?" Hank calls after me. "I can't just leave you here."

I turn to face him, but I keep walking backward, clinging to Princess. "You have to. If you ever want me to be ready for the adoption, you've got to let me do this." Then I turn around and don't look back.

On the front step, I ring the bell. Music is blaring from inside. Mrs. Morris opens the door, looking older, with lopsided hair and no makeup.

"It's you, Katrina." She lets me in. "You can be glad you couldn't make it to the sleepover."

"Excuse me?"

"I know you had to get your rest. Fiona said you needed to recharge before today. You wouldn't have gotten a bit of sleep here."

Nobody said a word to me about this sleepover. Couldn't Fiona have asked me, at least? A sleepover. I've never even been to one.

"I'm so proud of Fiona," Mrs. Morris says, leading me through the maze of a hall. "You know, for volunteering to be your partner in this project. She's usually very competitive."

I must have asked myself a hundred times why Fiona volunteered to be my partner. I guess I have my answer. I was her own little good-deed project.

We stop at the door to a big room I haven't seen before. Fiona and Brett are laughing together in one corner. Girls are sprawled out on the floor and couches. A couple of Fiona's cheerleading friends are still in their matching pj's.

Mrs. Morris leaves Princess and me in the doorway.

I picture myself clinging to Princess with one hand and reaching up for my Father's hand with the other. Then I walk in.

Fiona hollers at me. "Finally! Kat, come here."

I glance around and see only three cats. Alex has his Bozo. He waves at me. I wave back, then join Fiona. "Where are the rest of the cats?"

"I told people they didn't have to go home

and get their cats. Buffenmyer can't come, so she won't know anyway."

Fiona barely glances at Princess before shouting, "Hey, everybody! Let's get this over with."

A couple of girls groan. The cheerleaders don't budge from their makeshift bed on the floor. Somebody bursts out laughing from the other side of the room, where it looks like they're playing cards.

This whole thing is so lame. *I'm* lame. What did I think I could do here? The only reason I'm here at all is because Fiona had pity on me.

Fiona shoves me to the front of the room. "Go!" she whispers.

I stand in front of the stone fireplace and look out at my classmates. Only I can't remember what I was going to say.

"Kat?" Alex says. He's moving to the front. "You okay?"

"Oh, great," Cassie says. "Is she going to puke again?"

"Gross!" Arianna shouts.

I clear my throat. I'm *not* going to hurl.

"Somebody ask her a question," Fiona suggests.

"I've got one," says Melissa, a friend of Fiona's. "My cat hates me. What have you got for that?"

I stare at her. Her cat doesn't hate her. Should I say that?

"Kat?" Fiona says, like she's had it with her good-deed project.

I turn back to Melissa. "Well, try to think like your cat."

"What?" Melissa snaps. "I can't hear her."

Before Fiona can tell me to speak up, I do. "Do you pick up your cat and hold her on your lap?"

"I do that," Melissa insists. "But she won't sit and watch TV with me. She jumps off and runs away."

"Yeah. Cats don't like to be picked up unless it's their idea," I explain.

"How was I supposed to know that?" Melissa asks, like it's my fault I didn't tell her before.

"Just pet your cat where she is. And stop petting her before she's tired of it," I tell her, hoping she really wants to help her cat.

"How am I supposed to know when she's tired of being petted?" Melissa whines.

"Watch her tail," I answer.

"For real?" Melissa asks, looking kind of interested now.

"If her tail is up," I explain, "your cat loves what you're doing. If her tail's down, not so much. If she arches her back or her fur stands up, back off fast."

"Cool. What are some other clues?" Alex asks.

Thank heaven for Alex. "Ears forward means your cat's on the offense. Ears back, defense. Whiskers forward might mean your cat's ready to attack. If she's aggravated at you, watch that tail move back and forth, faster and faster."

Alex asks me another question. Then Stephen asks one. Then Mikayla.

The clock gongs. I stop talking and listen. Eleven gongs. Hank has probably already told everybody that I'm not coming. He would have gotten to the courthouse early. He's early for everything. Hank can't stand to be late. I feel like a coward for not explaining things to Mom and Dad myself. But Hank will explain it better than I could anyway.

"Look at Berta," Stephen says.

I'm glad to get my mind out of the courtroom. "What's she doing?" I ask.

Some of the kids move so they can see Stephen's cat. Berta is lying on her back, legs in the air.

"She really trusts you, Stephen," I begin. "When a cat rolls over on her back like that, she's letting herself be vulnerable to you."

"Don't go there, Berta!" Cassie yells. "Been there, done that."

Everybody laughs. I'm probably the only one who didn't know Stephen and Cassie have history.

Stephen reaches for his cat's belly.

"Don't try to rub her belly or scratch her when she's like that," I warn. "She'll remember she's vulnerable, and she might scratch *you*."

"Exactly," Cassie says.

The room cracks up.

"Okay, okay," Fiona shouts. "That's enough."

"Don't we get to tell how our cats got better after we talked to Kat?" Mikayla asks. "Mine did."

"Mine too," Alex agrees.

Fiona ignores them. "Everybody just make

sure you've turned in your evaluations. Kat, cut to the chase."

I force myself to check the time. It's 11:15. I try not to think about the courtroom and what Hank's telling everybody. Maybe without me there, they can all be honest with the judge . . . and with themselves.

"So, what about my stupid cat?" Fiona demands. "Did you teach her anything?"

"Princess is *my* stupid cat," Arianna says. "Not yours. And who are you kidding? Nobody can teach that cat anything."

I've held on to Princess the whole time, partly because I thought it would be scary for her to maneuver around so many people and partly because holding her helped keep me together. "This week I discovered a lot about Princess," I begin.

Fiona sighs.

"I suspected something was wrong with her when she didn't meow. Then I noticed she didn't care about dogs barking or birds chirping."

"I know all that already," Fiona says.

Then I blurt it out. "Princess is blind. And deaf."

Somebody says, "You're kidding!"

Someone gasps.

Somebody else says, "That's so sad."

"Well, that's just great," Fiona says. "That pet store sold us a blind and deaf cat? They're going to hear from us, believe me."

"Now they *have* to take the cat back, right?" Arianna adds. "That's, like, false advertising or something."

"You can't take her back," I object.

"Just watch me," Fiona vows.

"But there's more, Fiona," I begin.

"What's left? The cat can't see, hear, or speak," Fiona complains. "She's going back to the pet store, and you can't change our minds."

"But she's a sweet cat. She'll love your family, and she'll let *you* love *her*."

"But we won't," Fiona says.

"No kidding," Arianna agrees. "Who wants a deaf, dumb, blind, and whatever cat?"

I don't understand how they can feel that way. I stroke Princess's head. Once I tell Fiona and Arianna that Princess is probably the only cat in Illinois who can use the john, it's got to change the way they feel about her. "Your cat is so smart, you guys. Wait till you hear what she can do."

Fiona rolls her eyes. "I'm waiting. And this better be good."

"Princess learned–" I stop. *This better be good?* "Wait. Why had this better be good?"

"Because the cat's going back to the pet store–or to the pound–if it's not. That's why," Fiona says.

And what if I tell them about their toilet-trained cat? What then? Why should that earn Princess a spot in this house? "Fiona, can't you love Princess as she is, for *who* she is?"

"I knew it," Fiona says. "You couldn't teach that cat to do anything, could you?"

"That's not what I'm saying," I answer. "I'm asking you why she *has* to do anything."

Fiona glares at me. "You know, I'm still not hearing any reason to keep that cat."

I look down at Princess lying in my arms. "Just because," I whisper, more to myself than to Fiona.

"What?" Fiona demands.

"Because," I repeat. And it feels like a revelation.

"Because? That's it? That's all?" Fiona laughs.

"Yep," I tell her, getting it myself at last. "That's all. Just because. Princess should have a home because she's Princess. That's all. She doesn't have to *do* anything. And guess what. Neither do I!"

"Fine," Fiona says. "I think we're done here."

For once, Fiona and I agree. We're done. "What time is it?" I ask.

Alex answers, "Um . . . 11:30." He walks up to me. "What are you going to do with Princess?"

I look at the cat, still asleep in my arms. "She's coming with me."

"Yes!" Alex whispers.

"Don't even think about bringing that cat back here," Fiona calls after me.

I dash out of the house, prepared to run to the courthouse with Princess in my arms.

A horn honks, and Hank opens the truck door. "About time," he calls.

"You waited?" I can't believe it. It must have killed Hank to sit out here, getting later and later. I hop in. "Thanks, Hank."

Hank takes back streets to the courthouse. The lot is almost empty. The courthouse is closed on Saturdays except for when they do adoptions. We park and run inside. Security at Nice Courthouse is a chubby security guard who goes to our church. He lets us in–with Princess–without any problem. But the girl at the front desk stops us cold.

"We're looking for the adoption judge, Judge Carroll," Hank tells her.

"First door on your right," she answers. "But you can't go in there with a cat."

I stick Princess inside my jacket and head back anyway while Hank works his magic on the girl. He catches up with me at the courtroom door.

I stand on tiptoes and peek in. It's not the way I pictured a courtroom, more like a big office. On one side of the desk sits a thin man in a navy suit. On the other side, their backs to us, sit Mom, Dad, Dakota, and Wes. I reach for the doorknob, but Hank stops me.

"I know Judge Carroll," Hank says. "I called him when I knew we were going to be late. I told him what you told me, Kat."

"You promised, Hank."

"I promised I wouldn't tell Mom and Dad." He cracks the door and holds his finger over his lips. The judge looks up and nods at Hank. The others still have their backs to us.

". . . such a blessing to our family," Mom is saying. "I loved that girl from the first minute I saw her in the hospital. I thought the day we brought her to the farm was the happiest day of my life. But maybe this is. I just wish she were here with us."

"Mr. Coolidge?" the judge says.

"I second everything my Annie said," Dad answers. "I don't think I could go a day without seeing that angelic face, those eyes of hers. Sometimes I think Kat never let go of God's hand when she came down here. There's something so special about her."

I can't believe he said that, about God's hand.

The judge turns to Dakota.

"I'm not a Coolidge," she says, "so I don't get to vote or whatever you do here. But if I did, it would be a big thumbs-up for Kat. She taught me about family. And God. Kat's the reason I didn't run away from here. That kid deserves the best. And these guys are."

"What about me?" Wes snaps. "I've known Kat longer than Dakota."

"I'd love to hear from you, young man," the judge says.

"Okay. When I came to the Rescue, I was mad at everybody. Everything made me angry. Except Kat. I don't even know why. But it says something about her."

"Thank you for being so forthright, everyone. This isn't an official vote, of course. But I would like to ask you once more if you're sure you want to accept Katharine into your family, to give her the Coolidge name?"

"Yes!" They all shout it at the same time.

I can't take it any longer. I push through the door and into the arms of my family. "Me too!" I cry.

Hank joins the group hug. I think we're all crying. I look around at these people–my family. We're all holding hands: Mom, Dad, sisters, brothers . . . and God.

"Meow!"

I'd forgotten all about Princess, still stuffed inside my jacket.

"Is there a cat in my courtroom?" The judge stands up from his desk.

Princess meows again.

"Princess, you meowed!" I cry. I can hardly believe it. "You spoke!"

"It spoke?" the judge asks. "Now that's a first. And in *my* courtroom. I guess you better tell me what it said."

They're all staring at me, waiting for an answer. Then I get one. "I couldn't make out all of it, but it was something about *claw* and order."

Dad explodes in a bellow of a laugh that shakes the room. When he can speak, he beams at me. "Spoken like a true Coolidge."

Tips on Finding the Perfect Pet

- Talk with your whole family about owning a pet. Pets require a commitment from every member of the family. Your pet should be around for years–ten, fifteen, twenty, twenty-five, or thirty years, depending on the type of pet. Pets can be expensive, especially if they get sick or need medical care of any kind. Make sure you can afford to give your pet a good life for a long time.
- Think like your future pet. Would you be happy with the lifestyle in your house? Would you spend most of your time alone? Is there room for you in the house? If you're considering buying a horse, what kind of life will the horse have? Will someone be able to spend enough time caring for it?
- Study breeds and characteristics of the animal you're considering. Be prepared to spend time with your pet, bonding and training, caring and loving.
- Remember that there is no such thing as a perfect pet, just as there's no such thing as

a perfect owner. Both you and your pet will need to work to develop the best possible relationship you can have and to become lifelong best friends.

Consider Pet Adoption

- Check out animal rescue organizations, such as the humane society (www.hsus.org), local shelters, SPCA (www.spca.com), 1-800-Save-A-Pet.com (PO Box 7, Redondo Beach, CA 90277), Pets911.com (great horse adoption tips), and Petfinder.com. Adopting a pet from a shelter will save that pet's life and make room for another animal, who might also find a good home.
- Take your time. Visit the shelters and talk with the animal care handlers. Legitimate shelters will be able to provide you with documentation on the animal's health and medical records. Find out all you can. Ask questions. Who owned the pet before? How many owners were there? Why was the pet given away? Is the pet housebroken? Does it like children?

- Consider adopting an adult pet. People tend to favor "babies," but adopting a fully grown animal may be less risky. What you see is what you get. The personality, size, and manners are there for you to consider.

Rescuing Animals

- It's great that you want to help every animal you meet. I wish everyone felt the same. But remember that safety has to come first. A frightened, abused animal can strike out at any time. If you find an animal that's in trouble, call your local animal shelter. Then try to find the owner.
- The best way to help a lost pet find its home again is to ask around. You might put a "Found Pet" ad in the paper or make flyers with the animal's picture on it. But be sure to report the find to your local shelter because that's where most owners will go for help in finding a lost pet.
- Report animal cruelty to your local animal shelter or to the humane society.

Author Talk

Dandi Daley Mackall grew up riding horses, taking her first solo bareback ride when she was three. Her best friends were Sugar, a Pinto; Misty, probably a Morgan; and Towaco, an Appaloosa. Dandi and her husband, Joe; daughters, Jen and Katy; and son, Dan, (when forced) enjoy riding Cheyenne, their Paint. Dandi has written books for all ages, including Little Blessings books, *Degrees of Guilt: Kyra's Story*, *Degrees of Betrayal: Sierra's Story*, *Love Rules*, *Maggie's Story*, and the best-selling series Winnie the Horse Gentler. Her books (about 450 titles) have sold more than 4 million copies. She writes and rides from rural Ohio.

Visit Dandi's Web site at
www.dandibooks.com

FOR A NEW NOVEL
essays on fiction

FOR A NEW NOVEL
essays on fiction

ALAIN ROBBE-GRILLET

translated by richard howard

GROVE PRESS, INC. NEW YORK

Originally published by Les Editions de Minuit, Paris, France, as *Pour un nouveau roman*, copyright © 1963 by Les Editions de Minuit.

Earlier versions of "A Future for the Novel" and "Nature, Humanism, Tragedy" were previously published in *Evergreen Review*.

Library of Congress Catalog Card Number: 66-14094

Fourth Printing

Manufactured in the United States of America

DISTRIBUTED BY RANDOM HOUSE, INC., NEW YORK

GROVE PRESS, INC., 53 EAST 11TH STREET,
NEW YORK, NEW YORK 10003

CONTENTS

THE USE OF THEORY

(1955 and 1963)

I am not a theoretician of the novel. I have merely, like all novelists, no doubt, in the past as well as today, been led to make some critical reflections on books I had written, on those I was reading, on those I still plan to write. Most of the time, these reflections were inspired by certain reactions—which seem to me surprising or unwarranted—provoked in the press by my own books.

My novels have not been received, upon publication in France, with unanimous enthusiasm; that is putting it mildly. From the reproachful half-silence that greeted the first (*The Erasers*) to the massive and violent rejection meted out by the newspapers to the second (*The Voyeur*), there was little progress: except for the number of copies printed, which was much larger in the second case. Of course, there was also some praise, here and there, though such appreciations occasionally disconcerted me even more. What most astonished me, in reproaches as in praise, was to encounter in almost every case an implicit—or even explicit—reference to the great novels of the past, which were always held up as the model on which the young writer should keep his eyes fixed.

In the literary magazines, I often found a more serious response. But I was not satisfied to be recognized, enjoyed, studied only by the specialists who had encouraged me from the start; I was eager to write for the "reading public," I resented being considered a "difficult" author. My astonishment, my impatience were probably in proportion to my ignorance of literary circles and their customs. I therefore published, in a politico-literary newspaper with a large circulation (*L'Express*), a series of short articles in which I discussed several ideas that seemed to me no more than obvious: for example, that the novel's forms must evolve in order to remain alive, that Kafka's heroes have only a faint connection with the characters in Balzac, that socialist realism or Sartrean "engagement" are difficult to reconcile with the problematic exercise of literature, as with that of any art.

The result of these articles was not what I expected. They caused some commotion but were declared, by almost everyone, to be both simplistic and silly. Still impelled by the desire to convince, I then reworked the principal points under discussion, developing them in a somewhat longer essay which appeared in the *Nouvelle Revue Française*. The effect, unfortunately, was no better; and this revision—characterized as a "manifesto"—enshrined me as the theoretician of a new "school" of the novel, from which, of course, nothing good was expected, and to which were eagerly relegated, almost at random, any writers who seemed difficult to classify. "*École du regard,*" "Objective Novel," "*École de Minuit*"—the labels varied; as for the intentions attributed to me, they were, indeed, fantastic: to remove man from the world, to impose my own style on other novelists, to destroy every rule of literary composition, etc.

I attempted in new articles to improve matters by emphasizing the elements that had been most neglected, or most distorted, by the critics. This time I was accused of contradicting, of repudiating myself. . . . Thus, impelled alternately by my own explorations and by my detractors, I continued irregularly, from year to year, to publish my reflections on literature. It is this group of texts that appears in the present volume.

These reflections in no way constitute a theory of the novel; they merely attempt to clarify several lines of development which seem to me crucial in contemporary literature. If in many of the pages that follow, I readily employ the term *New Novel*, it is not to designate a school, nor even a specific and constituted group of writers working in the same direction; the expression is merely a convenient label applicable to all those seeking new forms for the novel, forms capable of expressing (or of creating) new relations between man and the world, to all those who have determined to invent the novel, in other words, to invent man. Such writers know that the systematic repetition of the forms of the past is not only absurd and futile, but that it can even become harmful: by blinding us to our real situation in the world today, it keeps us, ultimately, from constructing the world and man of tomorrow.

To praise a young writer in 1965 because he "writes like Stendhal" is doubly disingenuous. On the one hand, there would be nothng admirable about such a feat, as we have just seen; on the other, the thing itself is quite impossible: to write like Stendhal one would first of all have to be writing in 1830. A writer who produces a pastiche skillful enough to contain pages Stendhal might have signed at the time would in no way have the value he would still possess today had he written those same pages under Charles X. It is no paradox that Borges elaborates in *Ficciones*: the twentieth-century novelist who reproduces *Don Quixote* word for word writes a totally different work from that of Cervantes.

Moreover, no one would dream of praising a musician for having composed some Beethoven, a painter for having made a Delacroix, or an architect for having conceived a Gothic cathedral. Many novelists, fortunately, know that the same is true of literature, that literature too is alive, and that the novel, ever since it has existed, has always been new. How could its style have remained motionless, fixed, when everything around it was in evolution—even revolution—during the last hundred and fifty years? Flaubert wrote the new novel of 1860, Proust the new novel of 1910. The writer must proudly consent to bear his own date, knowing that there are no masterpieces in eternity, but only works in history; and that they survive only to the degree that they have left the past behind them and heralded the future.

Nonetheless, if there is one thing in particular which the critics find hard to endure, it is that the artist should explain himself. I certainly realized as much when, after having expressed these and several other notions quite as obvious, I published my third novel (*Jealousy*). Not only was the book attacked, decried as a kind of preposterous outrage against belles-lettres; it was even proved that such an abomination was only to be expected, for *Jealousy* was a self-acknowledged product of premeditation: its author—O the scandal of it!—permitted himself to have opinions concerning his own profession.

Here, too, we see that the myths of the nineteenth century retain all their power; the great novelist, the "genius," is a kind of unconscious monster, irresponsible and fate-ridden, even slightly stupid, who emits "messages" which only the reader may decipher. Anything that risks obscuring the writer's judgment is more or less accepted as favoring the full flowering of his work. Alcoholism, poverty, drugs, mystical passion, madness have so encumbered the more or less romanticized biographies of artists that it henceforth seems quite natural to see them as necessities of the creator's sad condition, to see, in any case, an antinomy between creation and consciousness.

Far from being the result of an honest scrutiny, this attitude betrays a metaphysic. Those pages to which the writer has given birth as though unconsciously, those unpremeditated marvels, those "lost" words reveal the existence of some superior force which has dictated them. The novelist, more than a creator in the strict sense, is thus a simple mediator between ordinary mortals and an obscure power, a force beyond humanity, an eternal spirit, a god. . . .

Actually, it is enough to read Kafka's diaries, for example, or Flaubert's correspondence, to realize straight off the primary role taken, even in the great works of the past, by a creative consciousness, by will, by rigor. Patient labor, methodical construction, the deliberate architecture of each sentence as of the whole of the book—this has always played its part. After *The Counterfeiters*, after Joyce, after *Nausea*, we seem to be tending increasingly toward an age of fiction in which the problems of style and construction will be lucidly considered by the novelist, and in which critical preoccupations, far from sterilizing creation, can on the contrary serve it as a driving force.

There is no question, as we have seen, of establishing a theory, a pre-existing mold into which to pour the books of the future. Each novelist, each novel must invent its own form. No recipe can replace this continual reflection. The book makes its own rules for itself, and for itself alone. Indeed the movement of its style must often lead to jeopardizing them, breaking them, even exploding them. Far from respecting certain immutable forms, each new book tends to constitute the laws of its functioning at the same time that it produces their destruction. Once the work is completed, the writer's critical reflection will serve him further to gain a perspective in regard to it, immediately nourishing new explorations, a new departure.

Hence the attempt to put theoretical views and works of art in contradiction is not very interesting. The only relation that can exist between them is precisely of a dialectical character: an interplay of agreements and oppositions. Nor is it surprising, then, that there should be developments from one essay to another, among those that follow. Not, of course, the crude repudiations mistakenly denounced by readers who have been a little too careless—or ill-disposed—but reconsiderations on a different level, re-examinations, another side of the same idea, or its complement, and in some cases simply a warning against an error of interpretation.

Further, it is obvious that ideas remain of little consequence in relation to works, and that nothing can replace the latter. A novel which is no more than the grammatical example illustrating a rule—even accompanied by its exception—would naturally be useless: the statement of the rule would suffice. While demanding the author's right to the intelligence of his creation, and insisting on the interest afforded by the consciousness of his own exploration, we know that it is chiefly on the level of style that this exploration is made, and that not everything is clear at the moment of decision. Thus, having indisposed the critics by speaking of the literature he dreams of writing, the novelist feels suddenly disarmed when these critics ask him: "Now explain why you wrote this book, what it means, what you were trying to do, what you intended by using this word, by writing that sentence!"

Faced with such questions, the novelist's "intelligence" no longer seems to be of any help to him. What he was trying to do is merely this book itself. Which does not mean that he is always satisfied by it; but the work remains, in every case, the best and the only possible expression of his enterprise. If he had had the capacity to furnish a simpler definition, or to reduce his two or three hundred pages to some message in clear language, to explain its functioning word by word—in short, to give a justification for it, he would not have felt the need to write the book. For the function of art is never to illustrate a truth—or even an interrogation—known in advance, but to bring into the world certain interrogations (and also, perhaps, in time, certain answers) not yet known as such to themselves.

The novelist's critical consciousness can be useful to him only on the level of choices, not on that of their justification. He feels the necessity of using a certain form, of rejecting a certain adjective, of constructing this paragraph in a certain way. He puts all his effort into the search for the right word, and for the right place to put it. But of this necessity he can produce no proof (except, occasionally, after the fact). He implores us to believe him, to trust him. And when we ask him why he has written his book, he has only one answer: "To try and find out why I wanted to write it."

As for saying where the novel is heading, no one, of course, can do so with certainty. Moreover, it is likely that different paths will continue to exist for the novel, in parallel. Yet one such path already seems to be marked more clearly than the rest. From Flaubert to Kafka, a line of descent is drawn, an ancestry that suggests a progeny. That passion to describe, which animates them both, is certainly the same passion we discern in the new novel today. Beyond the naturalism of Flaubert and the metaphysical oneiroticism of Kafka appear the first elements of a realistic style of an unknown genre, which is now coming to light. It is this new realism whose outlines the present collection attempts to describe.

A FUTURE FOR THE NOVEL (1956)

It seems hardly reasonable at first glance to suppose that an entirely *new* literature might one day—now, for instance—be possible. The many attempts made these last thirty years to drag fiction out of its ruts have resulted, at best, in no more than isolated works. And—we are often told—none of these works, whatever its interest, has gained the adherence of a public comparable to that of the bourgeois novel. The only conception of the novel to have currency today is, in fact, that of Balzac.

Or that of Mme. de La Fayette. Already sacrosanct in her day, psychological analysis constituted the basis of all prose: it governed the conception of the book, the description of its characters, the development of its plot. A "good" novel, ever since, has remained the study of a passion—or of a conflict of passions, or of an absence of passion—in a given milieu. Most of our contemporary novelists of the traditional sort—those, that is, who manage to gain the approval of their readers—could insert long passages from *The Princess of Clèves* or *Père Goriot* into their own books without awakening the suspicions of the enormous public which devours whatever they turn out. They would merely need to change a phrase here and there, simplify certain constructions, afford an occasional glimpse of their own "manner" by means of a word, a daring image, the rhythm of a sentence. . . . But all acknowledge, without seeing anything peculiar about it, that their preoccupations as writers date back several centuries.

What is so surprising about this, after all? The raw material—the French language—has undergone only very slight modifications for three hundred years; and if society has been gradually transformed, if industrial techniques have made considerable progress, our intellectual civilization has remained much the same. We live by essentially the same habits and the same prohibitions—moral, alimentary, religious, sexual, hygienic, etc. And of course there is always the human "heart," which as everyone knows is eternal. There's nothing new under the sun, it's all been said before, we've come on the scene too late, etc., etc.

The risk of such rebuffs is merely increased if one dares claim that this new literature is not only possible in the future, but is already being written, and that it will represent—in its fulfillment—a revolution more complete than those which in the past produced such movements as romanticism or naturalism.

There is, of course, something ridiculous about such a promise as "Now things are going to be different!" How will they be different? In what direction will they change? And, especially, why are they going to change now?

The art of the novel, however, has fallen into such a state of stagnation—a lassitude acknowledged and discussed by the whole of critical opinion—that it is hard to imagine such an art can survive for long without some radical change. To many, the solution seems simple enough: such a change being impossible, the art of the novel is dying. This is far from certain. History will reveal, in a few decades, whether the various fits and starts which have been recorded are signs of a death agony or of a rebirth.

In any case, we must make no mistake as to the difficulties such a revolution will encounter. They are considerable. The entire caste system of our literary life (from publisher to the humblest reader, including bookseller and critic) has no choice but to oppose the unknown form which is attempting to establish itself. The minds best disposed to the idea of a necessary transformation, those most willing to countenance and even to welcome the values of experiment, remain, nonetheless, the heirs of a tradition. A new form will always seem more or less an absence of any form at all, since it is unconsciously judged by reference to the consecrated forms. In one of the most celebrated French reference works, we may read in the article on Schoenberg: "Author of audacious works, written without regard for any rules whatever"! This brief judgment is to be found under the heading *Music*, evidently written by a specialist.

The stammering newborn work will always be regarded as a monster, even by those who find experiment fascinating. There will be some curiosity, of course, some gestures of interest, always some provision for the future. And some praise; though what is sincere will always be addressed to the vestiges of the familiar, to all those bonds from which the new work has not yet broken free and which desperately seek to imprison it in the past.

For if the norms of the past serve to measure the present, they also serve to construct it. The writer himself, despite his desire for independence, is situated within an intellectual culture and a literature which can only be those of the past. It is impossible for him to escape altogether from this tradition of which he is the product. Sometimes the very elements he has tried hardest to oppose seem, on the contrary, to flourish more vigorously than ever in the very work by which he hoped to destroy them; and he will be congratulated, of course, with relief for having cultivated them so zealously.

Hence it will be the specialists in the novel (novelists or critics, or overassiduous readers) who have the hardest time dragging themselves out of its rut.

Even the least conditioned observer is unable to see the world around him through entirely unprejudiced eyes. Not, of course, that I have in mind the naive concern for objectivity which the analysts of the (subjective) soul find it so easy to smile at. Objectivity in the ordinary sense of the word—total impersonality of observation—is all too obviously an illusion. But *freedom* of observation should be possible, and yet it is not. At every moment, a continuous fringe of culture (psychology, ethics, metaphysics, etc.) is added to things, giving them a less alien aspect, one that is more comprehensible, more reassuring. Sometimes the camouflage is complete: a gesture vanishes from our mind, supplanted by the emotions which supposedly produced it, and we remember a landscape as *austere* or *calm* without being able to evoke a single outline, a single determining element. Even if we immediately think, "That's literary," we don't try to react against the thought. We accept the fact that what is *literary* (the word has become pejorative) functions like a grid or screen set with bits of different colored glass that fracture our field of vision into tiny assimilable facets.

And if something resists this systematic appropriation of the visual, if an element of the world breaks the glass, without finding any place in the interpretative screen, we can always make use of our convenient category of "the absurd" in order to absorb this awkward residue.

But the world is neither significant nor absurd. It *is*, quite simply. That, in any case, is the most remarkable thing about it. And suddenly the obviousness of this strikes us with irresistible force. All at once the whole splendid construction collapses; opening our eyes unexpectedly, we have experienced, once too often, the shock of this stubborn reality we were pretending to have mastered. Around us, defying the noisy pack of our animistic or protective adjectives, things *are there*. Their surfaces are distinct and smooth, *intact*, neither suspiciously brilliant nor transparent. All our literature has not yet succeeded in eroding their smallest corner, in flattening their slightest curve.

The countless movie versions of novels that encumber our screens provide an occasion for repeating this curious experiment as often as we like. The cinema, another heir of the psychological and naturalistic tradition, generally has as its sole purpose the transposition of a story into images: it aims exclusively at imposing on the spectator, through the intermediary of some well-chosen scenes, the same meaning the written sentences communicated in their own fashion to the reader. But at any given moment the filmed narrative can drag us out of our interior comfort and into this proffered world with a violence not to be found in the corresponding text, whether novel or scenario.

Anyone can perceive the nature of the change that has occurred. In the initial novel, the objects and gestures forming the very fabric of the plot disappeared completely, leaving behind only their *significations:* the empty chair became only absence or expectation, the hand placed on a shoulder became a sign of friendliness, the bars on the window became only the impossibility of leaving. . . . But in the cinema, one *sees* the chair, the movement of the hand, the shape of the bars. What they signify remains obvious, but instead of monopolizing our attention, it becomes something added, even something in excess, because what affects us, what persists in our memory, what appears as essential and irreducible to vague intellectual concepts are the gestures themselves, the objects, the movements, and the outlines, to which the image has suddenly (and unintentionally) restored their *reality*.

It may seem peculiar that such fragments of crude reality, which the filmed narrative cannot help presenting, strike us so vividly, whereas identical scenes in real life do not suffice to free us of our blindness. As a matter of fact, it is as if the very conventions of the photographic medium (the two dimensions, the black-and-white images, the frame of the screen, the difference of scale between scenes) help free us from our own conventions. The slightly "unaccustomed" aspect of this reproduced world reveals, at the same time, the unaccustomed character of the world that surrounds us: it, too, is unaccustomed insofar as it refuses to conform to our habits of apprehension and to our classification.

Instead of this universe of "signification" (psychological, social, functional), we must try, then, to construct a world both more solid and more immediate. Let it be first of all by their *presence* that objects and gestures establish themselves, and let this presence continue to prevail over whatever explanatory theory that may try to enclose them in a system of references, whether emotional, sociological, Freudian or metaphysical.

In this future universe of the novel, gestures and objects will be *there* before being *something;* and they will still be there afterwards, hard, unalterable, eternally present, mocking their own "meaning," that meaning which vainly tries to reduce them to the role of precarious tools, of a temporary and shameful fabric woven exclusively—and deliberately—by the superior human truth expressed in it, only to cast out this awkward auxiliary into immediate oblivion and darkness.

Henceforth, on the contrary, objects will gradually lose their instability and their secrets, will renounce their pseudo-mystery, that suspect interiority which Roland Barthes has called "the romantic heart of things." No longer will objects be merely the vague reflection of the hero's vague soul, the image of his torments, the shadow of his desires. Or rather, if objects still afford a momentary prop to human passions, they will do so only provisionally, and will accept the tyranny of significations only in appearance —derisively, one might say—the better to show how alien they remain to man.

As for the novel's characters, they may themselves suggest many possible interpretations; they may, according to the preoccupations of each reader, accommodate all kinds of comment—psychological, psychiatric, religious, or political—yet their indifference to these "potentialities" will soon be apparent. Whereas the traditional hero is constantly solicited, caught up, destroyed by these interpretations of the author's, ceaselessly projected into an immaterial and unstable *elsewhere*, always more remote and blurred, the future hero will remain, on the contrary, *there*. It is the commentaries that will be left elsewhere; in the face of his irrefutable presence, they will seem useless, superfluous, even improper.

Exhibit X in any detective story gives us, paradoxically, a clear image of this situation. The evidence gathered by the inspectors—an object left at the scene of the crime, a movement captured in a photograph, a sentence overheard by a witness—seem chiefly, at first, to require an explanation, to exist only in relation to their role in a context which overpowers them. And already the theories begin to take shape: the presiding magistrate attempts to establish a logical and necessary link between things; it appears that everything will be resolved in a banal bundle of causes and consequences, intentions and coincidences. . . .

But the story begins to proliferate in a disturbing way: the witnesses contradict one another, the defendant offers several alibis, new evidence appears that had not been taken into account. . . . And we keep going back to the recorded evidence: the exact position of a piece of furniture, the shape and frequency of a fingerprint, the word scribbled in a message. We have the mounting sense that nothing else is *true.* Though they may conceal a mystery, or betray it, these elements which make a mockery of systems have only one serious, obvious quality, which is to *be there.*

The same is true of the world around us. We had thought to control it by assigning it a meaning, and the entire art of the novel, in particular, seemed dedicated to this enterprise. But this was merely an illusory simplification; and far from becoming clearer and closer because of it, the world has only, little by little, lost all its life. Since it is chiefly in its presence that the world's reality resides, our task is now to create a literature which takes that presence into account.

All this might seem very theoretical, very illusory, if something were not actually changing—changing totally, definitively—in our relations with the universe. Which is why we glimpse an answer to the old ironic question, "Why now?" There is today, in fact, a new element that separates us radically this time from Balzac as from Gide or from Mme. de La Fayette: it is the destitution of the old myths of "depth."

We know that the whole literature of the novel was based on these myths, and on them alone. The writer's traditional role consisted in excavating Nature, in burrowing deeper and deeper to reach some ever more intimate strata, in finally unearthing some fragment of a disconcerting secret. Having descended into the abyss of human passions, he would send to the seemingly tranquil world (the world on the surface) triumphant messages describing the mysteries he had actually touched with his own hands. And the sacred vertigo the reader suffered then, far from causing him anguish or nausea, reassured him as to his power of domination over the world. There were chasms, certainly, but thanks to such valiant speleologists, their depths could be sounded.

It is not surprising, given these conditions, that the literary phenomenon par excellence should have resided in the total and unique adjective, which attempted to unite all the inner qualities, the entire hidden soul of things. Thus the word functioned as a trap in which the writer captured the universe in order to hand it over to society.

The revolution which has occurred is in kind: not only do we no longer consider the world as our own, our private property, designed according to our needs and readily domesticated, but we no longer even believe in its "depth." While essentialist conceptions of man met their destruction, the notion of "condition" henceforth replacing that of "nature," the *surface* of things has ceased to be for us the mask of their heart, a sentiment that led to every kind of metaphysical transcendence.

Thus it is the entire literary language that must change, that is changing already. From day to day, we witness the growing repugnance felt by people of greater awareness for words of a visceral, analogical, or incantatory character. On the other hand, the visual or descriptive adjective, the word that contents itself with measuring, locating, limiting, defining, indicates a difficult but most likely direction for a new art of the novel.

ON SEVERAL OBSOLETE NOTIONS (1957)

Traditional criticism has its vocabulary. Though it noisily abstains from offering systematic judgments on literature (claiming, on the contrary, to enjoy this or that work freely, according to such "natural" criteria as good sense, the heart, etc.), one merely needs to read its analyses with a little attention to discover a network of key words, betraying nothing less than a system.

But we are so accustomed to discussions of "character," "atmosphere," "form," and "content," of "message" and "narrative ability" and "true novelists" that it requires an effort to free ourselves from this spider web and realize that it represents an idea about the novel (a ready-made idea, which everyone admits without argument, hence a dead idea), and not at all that so-called "nature" of the novel in which we are supposed to believe.

Even more dangerous, perhaps, are the terms commonly employed to describe the books which escape these accepted rules. The word "avant-garde," for example, despite its note of impartiality, generally serves to dismiss—as though by a shrug of the shoulders—any work that risks giving a bad conscience to the literature of mass consumption. Once a writer renounces the well-worn formulas and attempts to create his own way of writing, he finds himself stuck with the label "avant-garde."

In principle, this means no more than that he is somewhat ahead of his times, and that this way of writing will be used tomorrow by the body of his colleagues. But in fact, the reader, warned by a wink, immediately thinks of some hirsute young men who smirkingly set off their firecrackers under the Academy's armchairs for the sole purpose of making a commotion or shocking the bourgeoisie. "They want to saw off the branch we're sitting on," writes the serious Henri Clouard, quite without malice.

The branch in question is actually dead of natural causes, by the simple action of time; it is not our fault if it is now rotting. And if all those who cling to it so desperately would glance up just once toward the top of the tree, they would discover that new, green, vigorous, hardy branches have grown out long since. *Ulysses* and *The Castle* are already over thirty. *The Sound and the Fury* was translated into French over twenty years ago. Many others have followed. In order not to see them, our good critics have, each time, pronounced one or another of their magic words: "avant-garde," "laboratory," "anti-novel" . . . in other words: "Let's close our eyes and go back to the sane values of the French tradition."

Character

How much we've heard about the "character"! Moreover, I fear we haven't heard the last. Fifty years of disease, the death notice signed many times over by the most serious essayists, yet nothing has yet managed to knock it off the pedestal on which the nineteenth century had placed it. It is a mummy now, but one still enthroned with the same—phony—majesty, among the values revered by traditional criticism. In fact, that is how this criticism recognizes the "true" novelist: "he creates characters". . . .

In order to justify the cogency of this point of view, the customary reasoning is employed: Balzac has given us Père Goriot, Dostoevski has created the Karamazovs, hence writing novels can no longer be anything but that: adding some modern figures to the portrait gallery constituted by our literary history.

A character—everyone knows what the word means. It is not a banal *he*, anonymous and transparent, the simple subject of the action expressed by the verb. A character must have a proper name, two if possible: a surname and a given name. He must have parents, a heredity. He must have a profession. If he has possessions as well, so much the better. Finally, he must possess a "character," a face which reflects it, a past which has molded that face and that character. His character dictates his actions, makes him react to each event in a determined fashion. His character permits the reader to judge him, to love him, to hate him. It is thanks to his character that he will one day bequeath his name to a human type, which was waiting, it would seem, for the consecration of this baptism.

For the character must be unique and at the same time must rise to the level of a category. He must have enough individuality to remain irreplaceable, and enough generality to become universal. One may, for variety's sake, to give oneself some impression of freedom, choose a hero who seems to transgress one of these rules: a foundling, a vagrant, a madman, a man whose uncertain character harbors here and there some small surprise. . . . One must not exaggerate, however, in this direction: that is the road to perdition, which leads straight to the modern novel.

None of the great contemporary works, in fact, corresponds on this point to the norms of criticism. How many readers recall the narrator's name in *Nausea* or in *The Stranger*? Are these human types? Would it not be, on the contrary, the worst absurdity to regard these books as character studies? And does the *Journey to the End of the Night* describe a character? Does anyone suppose, moreover, that it is an accident these three novels are written in the first person? Beckett changes his hero's name and shape in the course of the same narrative. Faulkner purposely gives the same name to two different persons. As for the K of *The Castle*, he is content with an initial, he possesses nothing, has no family, no face; he is probably not even a land surveyor at all.

The examples can be multiplied. As a matter of fact, the creators of characters, in the traditional sense, no longer manage to offer us anything more than puppets in which they themselves have ceased to believe. The novel of characters belongs entirely to the past, it describes a period: that which marked the apogee of the individual.

Perhaps this is not an advance, but it is evident that the present period is rather one of administrative numbers. The world's destiny has ceased, for us, to be identified with the rise or fall of certain men, of certain families. The world itself is no longer our private property, hereditary and convertible into cash, a prey which it is not so much a matter of knowing as of conquering. To have a name was doubtless very important in the days of Balzac's bourgeoisie. A character was important—all the more important for being the weapon in a hand-to-hand struggle, the hope of a success, the exercise of a domination. It was something to have a face in a universe where personality represented both the means and the end of all exploration.

Our world, today, is less sure of itself, more modest perhaps, since it has renounced the omnipotence of the person, but more ambitious too, since it looks beyond. The exclusive cult of the "human" has given way to a larger consciousness, one that is less anthropocentric. The novel seems to stagger, having lost what was once its best prop, the hero. If it does not manage to right itself, it is because its life was linked to that of a society now past. If it does manage, on the contrary, a new course lies open to it, with the promise of new discoveries.

Story

A novel, for most readers—and critics—is primarily a "story." A true novelist is one who knows how to "tell a story." The felicity of "telling," which sustains him from one end of his work to the other, is identified with his vocation as a writer. To invent thrilling, moving, dramatic vicissitudes constitutes both his delight and his justification.

Hence to criticize a novel often comes down to reporting its anecdote, more or less briefly, depending on whether one has six columns or two to fill, with more or less emphasis on the essential passages: the climaxes and denouements of the plot. The judgment made on the book will consist chiefly in an appreciation of this plot, of its gradual development, its equilibrium, the expectations or surprises it affords the panting reader. A loophole in the narrative, a clumsily introduced episode, a lag in interest will be the major defects of the book; vivacity and spontaneity its highest virtues.

The writing itself will never be in question. The novelist will merely be praised for expressing himself in correct language, in an agreeable, striking, evocative manner. . . . Thus the style will be no more than a means, a manner; the basis of the novel, its *raison d'être*, what is inside it, is simply the story it tells.

Yet from serious people (those who admit that literature need not be a mere diversion) to the enthusiasts of the worst sentimental, detective, or exotic junk, everyone is in the habit of demanding a particular quality from the anecdote. It is not enough that it be entertaining, or extraordinary, or enthralling; to have its measure of human truth, it must also succeed in convincing the reader that the adventures he is hearing about have really happened to real characters, and that the novelist is confining himself to reporting, to transmitting events of which he has been the witness. A tacit convention is established between the reader and the author: the latter will pretend to believe in what he is telling, the former will forget that everything is invented and will pretend to be dealing with a document, a biography, a real-life story. To tell a story well is therefore to make what one writes resemble the prefabricated schemas people are used to, in other words, their ready-made idea of reality.

Thus, whatever the unexpected nature of the situations, the accidents, the fortuitous reactions, the narrative must flow without jolts, as though of its own accord, with that irrepressible *élan* which immediately wins our adherence. The least hesitation, the slightest oddity (two contradictory elements, for example, or two that do not exactly match), and unexpectedly the current of the novel ceases to sustain the reader, who suddenly wonders if he is not being "told a story" and who threatens to return to authentic testimonies, about which at least he will not have to ask himself questions as to the verisimilitude of things. Even more than to divert, the issue here is to reassure him.

Lastly, if he wants the illusion to be complete, the novelist is always supposed to know more than he says; the notion of a "slice of life" shows the extent of the knowledge he is supposed to have about what happened before and after. In the very interior of the duration he describes, he must give the impression of offering only the essentials, but of being able, if the reader insisted, to tell much more. The substance of the novel, in the image of reality, must appear inexhaustible.

Lifelike, spontaneous, limitless, the story must, in a word, be natural. Unfortunately, even while admitting that there is still something "natural" in the relations of man and the world, it turns out that writing, like any form of art, is on the contrary an intervention. What constitutes the novelist's strength is precisely that he invents, that he invents quite freely, without a model. The remarkable thing about modern fiction is that it asserts this characteristic quite deliberately, to such a degree that invention and imagination become, at the limit, the very subject of the book.

And no doubt such a development constitutes only one of the aspects of the general change in the relations man sustains with the world in which he lives. The narrative, as our academic critics conceive it—and many readers after them—represents an order. This order, which we may in effect qualify as natural, is linked to an entire rationalistic and organizing system, whose flowering corresponds to the assumption of power by the middle class. In that first half of the nineteenth century which saw the apogee—with *The Human Comedy*—of a narrative form which understandably remains for many a kind of paradise lost of the novel, certain important certainties were in circulation: in particular the confidence in a logic of things that was just and universal.

All the technical elements of the narrative—systematic use of the past tense and the third person, unconditional adoption of chronological development, linear plots, regular trajectory of the passions, impulse of each episode toward a conclusion, etc.—everything tended to impose the image of a stable, coherent, continuous, unequivocal, entirely decipherable universe. Since the intelligibility of the world was not even questioned, to tell a story did not raise a problem. The style of the novel could be innocent.

But then, with Flaubert, everything begins to vacillate. A hundred years later, the whole system is no more than a memory; and it is to that memory, to that dead system, that some seek with all their might to keep the novel fettered. Yet here, too, it is enough to read the great novels of the beginning of our century to realize that, while the disintegration of the plot has become insistently clearer in the course of the last few years, the plot itself had long since ceased to constitute the armature of the narrative. The demands of the anecdote are doubtless less constraining for Proust than for Flaubert, for Faulkner than for Proust, for Beckett than for Faulkner. . . . Henceforth, the issue is elsewhere. To tell a story has become strictly impossible.

Yet it is wrong to claim that nothing happens any longer in modern novels. Just as we must not assume man's absence on the pretext that the traditional character has disappeared, we must not identify the search for new narrative structures with an attempt to suppress any event, any passion, any adventure. The books of Proust and Faulkner are, in fact, crammed with stories; but in the former, they dissolve in order to be recomposed to the advantage of a mental architecture of time; whereas, in the latter, the development of themes and their many associations overwhelms all chronology to the point of seeming to bury again, to drown in the course of the novel what the narrative has just revealed. Even in Beckett, there is no lack of events, but these are constantly in the process of contesting themselves, jeopardizing themselves, destroying themselves, so that the same sentence may contain an observation and its immediate negation. In short, it is not the anecdote that is lacking, it is only its character of certainty, its tranquillity, its innocence.

And if I may cite my own works after these illustrious precursors, I should like to point out that *The Erasers* and *The Voyeur* both contain a plot, an "action" quite readily detectable, rich moreover in elements generally regarded as dramatic. If they at first seem without action to certain readers, is this not simply because the movement of the style is more important to them than that of passions and crimes? But I can readily imagine that in a few decades—sooner, perhaps—when this kind of writing, assimilated, becoming academic, will pass unnoticed in its turn, and when the young novelists, of course, will be doing something else, the criticism of the day, finding once again that nothing happens in their books, will reproach them for their lack of imagination and point to our novels as an example: "Look," they will say, "look how, back in the fifties, people knew how to invent stories!"

Commitment

Since telling a story to divert is "a waste of time," and telling a story to win belief has become suspect, the novelist thinks he sees another course of action: telling a story to teach. Tired of being told with condenscension by "serious" people: "I don't read novels any more, I'm too old for it, it's all right for women (who have nothing to do), I prefer reality . . ." and other inanities, the novelist will fall back on didactic literature. Here at least he hopes to regain the advantage: reality is too disturbing, too ambiguous, for everyone to learn a lesson from it. When it is a question of proving something (whether showing the misery of man without God, explaining the feminine heart, or awakening class consciousness), the invented story may regain its rights: it will be so much more convincing!

Unfortunately, it no longer convinces anyone; the moment the "novelistic" is suspect, it risks, on the contrary, casting discredit on psychology, socialist morality, religion. The man interested in these disciplines will read essays, and risk less. Once again, literature is rejected into the category of the frivolous. The thesis-novel has rapidly become a genre despised more than any other. . . . Yet only a few years ago, we saw it reborn on the Left in new clothes: "commitment," "engagement"; and in the East too, with more naive colors, as "socialist realism."

Of course, the idea of a possible conjunction between an artistic renewal and a politico-economic revolution is one of those which come most naturally to mind. This idea, initially seductive from the emotional viewpoint, also seems to find support in the most obvious logic. Yet the problems raised by such a union are serious and difficult, urgent but perhaps insoluble.

At the start, the relation seems simple enough. On the one hand, the artistic forms which have succeeded one another in the history of nations seem to us to be linked to this or that type of society, to the preponderance of this or that class, to the exercise of an oppression or to the flowering of a liberty. In France, for example, in the realm of literature, it is not gratuitous to see a close relation between Racinian tragedy and the success of a court aristocracy, between the Balzacian novel and the triumph of the bourgeoisie, etc.

Since, further, it is readily admitted, even by our

conservatives, that the great contemporary artists, writers or painters, generally belong (or have belonged in the period of their most important works) to the parties of the Left, we indulge ourselves by constructing this idyllic schema: Art and Revolution advancing hand in hand, struggling for the same cause, passing through the same ordeals, facing the same dangers, gradually achieving the same conquests, acceding finally to the same apotheosis.

Unfortunately, once we turn to the realm of practice, things do not turn out so well. The least we can say, today, is that the *données* of the problem are not so simple. Everyone knows the farces and the dramas which for fifty years have troubled—which trouble still—the various attempts to effect the wonderful marriage that was believed to be one of both love and reason. How could we forget the successive submissions and withdrawals, the echoing quarrels, the excommunications, the imprisonments, the suicides? How could we help seeing what painting has become, to cite only one example, in the nations where the Revolution has triumphed? How keep from smiling before the accusations of "decadence," of "gratuitousness," of "formalism" applied at random by the most zealous of the revolutionaries to everything that counts for us in contemporary art? How avoid fearing to find ourselves caught one day in the same net?

It is too easy—let us say so at once—to accuse bad leaders, bureaucratic routine, Stalin's lack of culture, the stupidity of the French Communist Party. We know from experience that it is just as delicate a matter to plead the cause of art to any politician, within any leftist group. Let us admit quite frankly: the

Socialist Revolution is suspicious of Revolutionary Art and, moreover, there is no reason to believe that it is wrong to be so.

Indeed, from the viewpoint of the Revolution, everything must directly contribute to the final goal: the liberation of the proletariat. . . . Everything, including literature, painting, etc. But for the artist, on the contrary, and despite his firmest political convictions—even despite his good will as a militant revolutionary—art cannot be reduced to the status of a means in the service of a cause which transcends it, even if this cause were the most deserving, the most exalting; the artist puts nothing above his work, and he soon comes to realize that he can create only *for nothing;* the least external directive paralyzes him, the least concern for didacticism, or even for signification, is an insupportable constraint; whatever his attachment to his party or to generous ideas, the moment of creation can only bring him back to the problems of his art, and to them alone.

Yet, even at the moment when art and society, after comparable flowerings, seem to be experiencing parallel crises, it remains obvious that the problems each raises cannot be solved in the same manner. Later on, no doubt, sociologists will discover in the solutions new similarities. But for us, in any case, we must acknowledge honestly, clearly, that the struggle is not the same one, and that, today as always, there is a direct antagonism between the two points of view. Either art is nothing; and in that case, painting, literature, sculpture, music can be enrolled in the service of the revolutionary cause; they will then no longer be anything but instruments, comparable to motorized armies, to mechanized tools, to agricultural tractors;

only their direct and immediate effectiveness will count.

Or else art will continue to exist as art; and in that case, for the artist at least, it will remain *the most important thing in the world*. Vis-à-vis political action, it will then always appear somewhat backward, useless, even frankly reactionary. Yet we know that in the history of peoples, art alone, this supposedly gratuitous art, will find its place, perhaps at the side of the trade unions and the barricades.

Meanwhile, that generous but utopian way of talking about a novel, a painting, or a statue as if they might count for as much in everyday action as a strike, a mutiny, or the cry of a victim denouncing his executioners, is a disservice, ultimately, to both Art and Revolution. Too many such confusions have been perpetrated, in recent years, in the name of socialist realism. The total artistic indigence of the works which insist on its tenets is certainly not the effect of chance: the very notion of a work created *for* the expression of a social, political, economic, or moral content constitutes a lie.

Hence we must now, once and for all, stop taking seriously the accusations of gratuitousness, stop fearing "art for art's sake" as the worst of evils; we must challenge this terrorist apparatus brandished under our noses as soon as we speak of anything besides the class struggle or the anticolonialist war.

Yet not everything was condemnable a priori in that Soviet theory of "socialist realism." In literature, for example, was there not also a reaction against an accumulation of false philosophy which had finally invaded everything, from poetry to the novel? Opposing metaphysical allegories, struggling against abstract "higher worlds" which they imply, as well as against verbal delirium without an object or a vague sentimentalism of the passions, socialist realism could have a healthy influence.

Here the deceptive ideologies and the myths no longer have any currency. Literature simply reveals the situation of man and of the universe with which he is at grips. Along with the earthly "values" of bourgeois society disappear the magical, religious, or philosophical recourses to any spiritual transcendence of our visible world. The themes of despair or absurdity, now fashionable, are denounced as alibis that are too easy. Thus Ilya Ehrenburg did not hesitate to write immediately after the war: "Anxiety is a bourgeois vice. As for us, we are rebuilding."

There was every reason to hope, given such principles, that man and things would be cleansed of their systematic *romanticism*, to adopt the term so dear to Lukacs, and that at last they could be merely *what they are*. Reality would no longer be constantly situated elsewhere, but *here and now*, without ambiguity. The world would no longer find its justification in a hidden meaning, whatever it might be, its existence would no longer reside anywhere but in its concrete, solid, material presence; beyond what we see (what we perceive by our senses) there would henceforth be nothing.

Now let us consider the result. What does socialist realism offer us? Obviously, this time, the good are the good and the wicked the wicked. But precisely, the insistence that this be obvious has nothing to do with what we observe in the world. What progress is made if, in order to escape the doubling of appearances and essences, we fall into a Manicheism of good and evil?

Worse still: when, in less naive narratives, we find ourselves reading about believable men, in a complex world endowed with a sensuous existence, we soon realize in spite of everything that these men have been constructed with a view to an interpretation. Moreover, their authors do not hide it: their primary concern is to illustrate, with the utmost precision, certain historical, economic, social, political behavior.

Yet from the viewpoint of literature, economic truths, Marxist theories of surplus value and usurpation are also abstract "higher worlds." Leftist novels are to have a reality only in relation to these functional explanations of the visible world—explanations prepared in advance, tested, acknowledged—it is difficult to see what their power of discovery or invention can be; and above all, this would be only one more way of denying the world its most certain quality: the simple fact that it is there. An explanation, whatever it may be, can only be *in excess*, confronted with the presence of things. A theory of their social function, if it has governed their description, can only confuse their outline, falsify them in exactly the same way as the old psychological and moral theories, or the symbolism of metaphysical allegories.

Which explains, ultimately, why socialist realism has no need of any experiment in novelistic form, why it so mistrusts any innovation in the technique of the arts, why what suits it best, as we see every day, is the most "bourgeois" expression.

But for some time, an uneasiness has been growing in Russia and in the Peoples' Republics. The leaders are coming to understand that they have taken the wrong path, and that despite appearances, the so-called "laboratory" experiments with the structure and language of the novel, even if they interest only specialists at first, are perhaps not so futile as the party of the Revolution affects to believe.

Then what remains of commitment? Sartre, who had seen the danger of this moralizing literature, advocated a *moral* literature, which claimed only to awaken political awareness by stating the problems of our society, but which would escape the spirit of propaganda by returning the reader to his liberty. Experience has shown that this too was a utopia: once there appears the concern to signify something (something external to art), literature begins to retreat, to disappear.

Let us, then, restore to the notion of commitment the only meaning it can have for us. Instead of being of a political nature, commitment is, for the writer, the full awareness of the present problems of his own language, the conviction of their extreme importance, the desire to solve them *from within.* Here, for him, is the only chance of remaining an artist and, doubtless too, by means of an obscure and remote consequence, of some day serving something—perhaps even the Revolution.

Form and Content

One thing must trouble the partisans of socialist realism, and that is the precise resemblance of their arguments, their vocabulary, their values to those of the most hardened bourgeois critics. For example, in the matter of separating the "form" of a novel from its "contents," that is, of contrasting the *style* (choice of words and their arrangement, use of grammatical tenses and persons, structure of the narrative, etc.) with the anecdote it serves to report (events, actions of the characters, their motivations, morality implied or revealed).

Only the doctrine differs, between the academic literature of the West and that of the nations of the East. Moreover, it does not differ as much as either side claims. The story told remains in any case (according to their common optic) the important thing; a good novelist remains the one who invents splendid stories or who tells them best; thus the "great" novel, in either case, is merely one whose signification transcends its anecdote, transcends it in the direction of a profound human truth, a morality, or a metaphysic.

Hence it is natural that the accusation of "formalism" should be one of the most serious in the mouths of our critics on both sides. Here again, in spite of all they say, the word reveals a systematic decision about the novel; and here again, for all its "natural" look, the system conceals the worst abstractions—if not the worst absurdities. Further, we can discern in it a certain contempt for literature, implicit but flagrant, which is as surprising coming from its official champions—the defenders of art and tradition—as from those who have made of mass culture their favorite warhorse.

What, precisely, do they mean by formalism? Clearly enough, what is meant is an excessively marked concern for form—and, in the specific instance, for the technique of the novel—at the expense of the story and of its meaning, its signification. That leaky old boat—the academic opposition of form and content—has not yet been entirely scuttled.

In fact, quite the contrary, it seems that this stock notion has broken out more virulently than ever. If we encounter the reproach of formalism under the pens of the worst enemies reconciled on this point (enthusiasts of belles-lettres and the minions of Zhdanov), it is obviously not the result of a fortuitous encounter; they are in agreement on at least one essential point: to deny art its principal condition of existence, freedom. On one hand they choose to see literature only as one more instrument in the service of the Socialist Revolution, on the other, they require it to express that vague humanism which has survived the heyday of a society now on the wane, of which they are the last defenders.

In both cases, the point is to reduce the novel to a signification external to it, to make the novel a means of achieving some value which transcends it, some spiritual or terrestrial "beyond," future Happiness or eternal Truth. Whereas if art is something, it is *everything*, which means that it must be self-sufficient, and that there is nothing *beyond*.

There is a famous Russian cartoon in which a hippopotamus, in the bush, points out a zebra to another hippopotamus: "You see," he says, "now that's formalism." The existence of a work of art, its weight, are not at the mercy of interpretative grids which may or may not coincide with its contours. The work of art, like the world, is a living form: it *is*, it has no need of justification. The zebra is real, to deny it would not be reasonable, though its stripes are doubtless meaningless. The same is true of a symphony, a painting, a novel: it is in their form that their reality resides.

But—and this is where our socialist realists must beware—it is also in their form that their meaning resides, their "profound signification," that is, their content. There are not, for a writer, two possible ways to write the same book. When he thinks of a future novel, it is always a *way of writing* which first of all occupies his mind, and demands his hand. He has in mind certain rhythms of sentences, certain architectures, a vocabulary, certain grammatical constructions, exactly as a painter has in mind certain lines and colors. What will happen in the book comes afterward, as though secreted by the style itself. And, once the work is concluded, what will strike the reader is again this form so many affect to despise, a form whose meaning he often cannot define in any exact way, but which for him will constitute the writer's individual world.

We can make the experiment with any important work of our literature. Take *The Stranger*, for instance. It suffices to change the tense of its verbs, to replace that first person in the perfect tense (whose quite uncustomary use extends throughout the narrative) by the usual third person in the past tense, for Camus' universe to disappear at once, and all the interest of his book with it; as it suffices to change the arrangement of the words, in *Madame Bovary*, for there to be nothing left of Flaubert.

Whence the embarrassment we feel in the "committed" novels which claim to be revolutionary because they treat the condition of the workers and the problems of socialism. Their literary form, which generally dates from before 1848, makes them the most backward of bourgeois novels: their real signification, which is quite evident upon reading, the values they enjoin, are identical to those of our capitalist nineteenth century, with its humanitarian ideals, its morality, its mixture of rationalism and spirituality.

Thus it is the style, the *écriture*, and it alone which

is "responsible," to adopt a word so often abused by those who accuse us of betraying our mission as writers. To speak of the content of a novel as something independent of its form comes down to striking the genre as a whole from the realm of art. For the work of art contains nothing, in the strict sense of the term (that is, as a box can hold—or be empty of—some object of an alien nature). Art is not a more or less brilliantly colored envelope intended to embellish the author's "message," a gilt paper around a package of cookies, a whitewash on a wall, a sauce that makes the fish go down easier. Art endures no servitude of this kind, nor any other pre-established function. It is based on no truth that exists before it; and one may say that it expresses nothing but itself. It creates its own equilibrium and its own meaning. It stands all by itself, like the zebra; or else it falls.

We thus see the absurdity of that favorite expression of our traditional criticism: "X has something to say and says it well." Might we not advance on the contrary that the genuine writer has nothing to say? He has only a way of speaking. He must create a world, but starting from nothing, from the dust. . . .

It is then the reproach of "gratuitousness" which is lodged against us, on the pretext that we assert our nondependence. Art for art's sake does not have a good press: it suggests a game, imposture, dilettantism. But the *necessity* a work of art acknowledges has nothing to do with utility. It is an internal necessity, which obviously appears as gratuitousness when the system of references is fixed *from without:* from the viewpoint of the Revolution, for example, as we have said, the highest art may seem a secondary, even absurd enterprise.

Here is where the difficulty—one is tempted to say the impossibility—of creation resides: the work must seem necessary, but necessary *for nothing;* its architecture is without use; its strength is untried. If such obvious points appear today as paradoxes in connection with the novel, whereas everyone readily admits them in the case of music, this is only because of what we must call the *alienation* of literature in the modern world. This alienation, which the writers themselves generally suffer without even realizing it, is maintained by the quasi-totality of our critics, beginning with those of the extreme Left who claim, in all other realms, to be combating the alienated condition of man. And we see that the situation is still worse in the socialist countries, where the liberation of the workers is, it is said, a *fait accompli.*

Like every alienation, this one effects, of course, a general inversion of values as well as of vocabulary, so that it becomes quite difficult to react against it, and so that one hesitates to use words in their normal acceptation. Such is the case for the term "formalism." Taken in its pejorative sense, it should actually apply—as Nathalie Sarraute has pointed out—only to the novelists overly concerned with their "content" who, to make themselves more clearly understood, abjure any exploration of style likely to displease or surprise: those who, precisely, adopt a form—a mold—which has given its proofs, but which has lost all force, all life. They are formalists because they have accepted a ready-made, sclerotic form which is no more than a formula, and because they cling to this fleshless carcass.

The public in its turn readily associates a concern for form with coldness. But this is no longer true from the moment form is invention and not formula. And coldness, like formalism, is entirely on the side of respect for dead rules. As for all the great novelists of the last hundred years or so, we know from their journals, their correspondence, that the constant focus of their work, the thing that constituted their passion, their most spontaneous requirement, their life, in fact, was precisely this form, by which their work has survived.

NATURE, HUMANISM, TRAGEDY (1958)

Tragedy is merely a means of "recovering" human misery, of subsuming and thereby justifying it in the form of a necessity, a wisdom, or a purification: to refuse this recuperation and to investigate the techniques of not treacherously succumbing to it (nothing is more insidious than tragedy) is today a necessary enterprise. —Roland Barthes

As recently as two years ago, trying to define the direction of a still tentative development in the art of the novel, I described as a constant factor "the destitution of the old myths of depth." The violent and almost unanimous reactions of the critics, the objections of many readers of apparent good faith, the reservations formulated by several sincere friends have persuaded me that I went too far too fast. Apart from several men themselves engaged in comparable investigations—artistic, literary, or philosophical—no one would grant that such an assertion did not necessarily involve the negation of Man himself. Loyalty to the old myths showed itself to be, as matter of fact, quite tenacious.

That writers as different as François Mauriac and André Rousseaux, for example, should concur in denouncing the exclusive description of "surfaces" as a gratuitous mutilation, the blind folly of a young rebel, a kind of sterile despair leading to the destruction of art nonetheless seemed quite in order. More unexpected, more disturbing, was the position—identical, from many points of view—of certain materialists who, in order to judge my enterprise, referred to "values" remarkably similar to the traditional values of Christianity. Yet for them there was no question of a confessional *parti pris*. But on either side, what was offered as a principle was the indefectible solidarity between our mind and the world, while art was reduced to its "natural," reassuring role as mediator; and I was condemned in the name of the "human."

Finally I was quite naive, it was said, to attempt to deny this depth: my own books were interesting, were readable, only to the degree—and the degree was disputed—to which they were, unknown to me, its expression.

That there is no more than a rather loose parallelism between the three novels I have published up to now and my theoretical views on a possible novel of the future is certainly obvious enough. Moreover, it will be regarded as only natural that a book of two or three hundred pages should be more complex than an article of ten; and also, that it is easier to indicate a new direction than to follow it, without failure—partial or even complete—being a decisive, definitive proof of the error committed at the outset.

Finally, it must be added that the characteristic of humanism, whether Christian or not, is precisely to recover *everything*, including whatever attempts to trace its limits, even to impugn it as a whole. This is, in fact, one of the surest resources of its functioning.

There is no question of seeking to justify myself at any price; I am merely trying to see the matter more clearly. The critical positions cited above help me do so in a notable way. What I am undertaking today is less to refute their arguments than to define their scope, and to define at the same time what separates me from such points of view. It is always futile to engage in polemics; but if a true dialogue is possible, one must on the contrary seize the opportunity to engage in it. And if dialogue is not possible, it is important to know why. In any case, we are doubtless all, on one side as on the other, interested enough in these problems to make it worth while discussing them again, however bluntly.

Is there not, first of all, a certain fraudulence in this word *human* which is always being thrown in our faces? If it is not a word quite devoid of meaning, what meaning does it really have?

It seems that those who use it all the time, those who make it the sole criterion of all praise as of all reproach, identify—deliberately, perhaps—a precise (and limited) reflection on man, his situation in the world, the phenomena of his existence, with a certain anthropocentric atmosphere, vague but imbuing all things, giving the world its so-called *signification*, that is, investing it from within by a more or less disingenuous network of sentiments and thoughts. Simplifying, we can summarize the position of our new inquisitors in two sentences; if I say, "The world is man," I shall always gain absolution; while if I say, "Things are things, and man is only man," I am immediately charged with a crime against humanity.

The crime is the assertion that there exists something in the world which is not man, which makes no sign to him, which has nothing in common with him. The crime, above all, according to this view, is to remark this separation, this distance, without attempting to effect the slightest sublimation of it.

What could be, in other words, an "inhuman" work? How, in particular, could a novel which deals with a man, and follows his steps from page to page, describing only what he does, what he sees, or what he imagines, how could such a novel be accused of turning away from man? And it is not the character himself, let us make that clear at once, who is involved in this judgment. As a "character," as an individual animated by torments and passions, no one will ever reproach him with being inhuman, even if he is a sadistic madman and a criminal—the contrary, it would seem.

But now suppose the eyes of this man rest on things without indulgence, insistently: he sees them, but he refuses to appropriate them, he refuses to maintain any suspect understanding with them, any complicity; he asks nothing of them; toward them he feels neither agreement nor dissent of any kind. He can, perhaps, make them the prop of his passions, as of his sense of sight. But his sense of sight is content to take their measurements; and his passion, similarly, rests on their surface, without attempting to penetrate them since there is nothing inside, without feigning the least appeal since they would not answer.

To condemn, in the name of the human, the novel which deals with such a man is therefore to adopt the *humanist* point of view, according to which it is not enough to show man where he is: it must further be proclaimed that man is everywhere. On the pretext that man can achieve only a subjective knowledge of the world, humanism decides to elect man the justification of everything. A true bridge of souls thrown between man and things, the humanist outlook is pre-eminently a pledge of solidarity.

In the literary realm, the expression of this solidarity appears chiefly as the investigation, worked up into a system, of analogical relations.

Metaphor, as a matter of fact, is never an innocent figure of speech. To say that the weather is "capricious" or the mountain "majestic," to speak of the "heart" of the forest, of a "pitiless" sun, of a village "huddled" in the valley, is, to a certain degree, to furnish clues as to the things themselves: shape, size, situation, etc. But the choice of an analogical vocabulary, however simple, already does something more than account for purely physical data, and what this *more* is can scarcely be ascribed only to the credit of belles-lettres. The height of the mountain assumes, willy-nilly, a moral value; the heat of the sun becomes the result of an intention. . . . In almost the whole of our contemporary literature, these anthropomorphic analogies are repeated too insistently, too coherently not to reveal an entire metaphysical system.

More or less consciously, the goal for the writers who employ such a terminology can only be to establish a constant relation between the universe and the being who inhabits it. Thus man's sentiments will seem alternately to derive from his contacts with the world and to find in that world their natural correspondence if not their fulfillment.

Metaphor, which is supposed to express only a comparison, without any particular motive, actually introduces a subterranean communication, a movement of sympathy (or of antipathy) which is its true *raison d'être*. For, as comparison, metaphor is almost always a useless comparison which contributes nothing new to the description. What would the village lose by being merely "situated" in the valley? The word "huddled" gives us no complementary information. On the other hand it transports the reader (in the author's wake) into the imagined soul of the village; if I accept the word "huddled," I am no longer entirely a spectator; I myself become the village, for the duration of a sentence, and the valley functions as a cavity into which I aspire to disappear.

Taking this possible adherence as their basis, the defenders of metaphor reply that it thereby possesses an advantage: that of making apparent an element which was not so. Having himself become the village, they say, the reader participates in the latter's situation, hence understands it better. Similarly in the case of the mountain: I shall make it easier to see the mountain by saying it is majestic than by measuring the apparent angle from which my gaze registers its height. . . . And this is true sometimes, but it always involves a more serious reversal: it is precisely this participation which is problematical, since it leads to the notion of a hidden unity.

It must even be added that the gain in descriptive

value is here no more than an alibi: the true lovers of metaphor seek only to impose the idea of a communication. If they did not possess the verb "huddle," they would not even mention the position of the village. The height of the mountain would be nothing to them, if it did not offer the moral spectacle of "majesty."

Such a spectacle, for them, never remains entirely *external.* It always implies, more or less, a gift received by man: the things around him are like the fairies in the tale, each of whom brought as a gift to the newborn child one of the traits of his future character. The mountain might thus have first communicated to me the feeling of the majestic—that is what is insinuated. This feeling would then be developed in me and, by a natural growth, engender others: magnificence, prestige, heroism, nobility, pride. In my turn I would refer these to other objects, even those of a lesser size (I would speak of a proud oak, of a vase of noble lines), and the world would become the depository of all my aspirations to greatness, would be both their image and their justification, for all eternity.

The same would be true of every feeling, and in these incessant exchanges, multiplied to infinity, I could no longer discern the origin of anything. Was majesty to be located first within, or around me? The question itself would lose its meaning. Only a sublime communion would remain between the world and me.

Then, with habit, I would easily go much farther. Once the principle of this communion was admitted, I would speak of the melancholy of a landscape, of the indifference of a stone, of the fatuousness of a coal scuttle. These new metaphors no longer furnish appreciable information about the objects subject to my scrutiny, but the world of things has been so thoroughly contaminated by my mind that it is henceforth susceptible of any emotion, of any character trait. I will forget that it is I, I alone, who feels melancholy or suffers solitude; these affective elements will soon be considered as the *profound reality* of the material universe, the sole reality—to all intents and purposes—worthy of engaging my interest in it.

Hence there is much more involved than describing our consciousness by using things as raw material, as one might build a cabin out of logs. To identify in this way my own melancholy with that which I attribute to a landscape, to admit this link as more than superficial, is thereby to acknowledge a certain predestination for my present life: this landscape existed *before* me; if it is really the landscape which is sad, it was *already* sad before me, and this correspondence I experience today between its form and my mood were here waiting for me long before I was born; this melancholy has been fated for me forever. . . .

We see to what point the idea of a human *nature* can be linked to the analogical vocabulary. This nature, common to all men, eternal and inalienable, no longer requires a God to establish it. It is enough to know that Mont Blanc has been waiting for me in the heart of the Alps since the tertiary era, and with it all my notions of greatness and purity!

This nature, moreover, does not merely belong to man, since it constitutes the link between his mind and things: it is, in fact, an essence common to all "creation" that we are asked to believe in. The universe and I now have only one soul, only one secret.

Belief in a *nature* thus reveals itself as the source of all humanism, in the habitual sense of the word. And it is no accident if Nature precisely—mineral, animal, vegetable Nature—is first of all clogged with an anthropomorphic vocabulary. This Nature—mountain, sea, forest, desert, valley—is simultaneously our model and our heart. It is, at the same time, within us and around us. It is neither provisional nor contingent. It encrusts us, judges us, and ensures our salvation.

To reject our so-called "nature" and the vocabulary which perpetuates its myth, to propose objects as purely external and superficial, is not—as has been claimed—to deny man; but it is to reject the "pananthropic" notion contained in traditional humanism, and probably in all humanism. It is no more in the last analysis than to lay claim, quite logically, to my freedom.

Therefore nothing must be neglected in this mopping-up operation. Taking a closer look, we realize that the anthropocentric analogies (mental or visceral) are not the only ones to be arraigned. *All* analogies are just as dangerous. And perhaps the most dangerous ones of all are the most secret, those in which man is not named.

Let us give some examples, at random. To discover the shape of a horse in the heavens may, of course, derive from a simple process of description and not be of any consequence. But to speak of the "gallop" of the clouds, or of their "flying mane," is no longer entirely innocent. For if a cloud (or a wave or a hill) possesses a mane, if later on the mane of a stallion "flings arrows," if the arrow . . . etc., the reader of such images will emerge from the universe of forms to find himself plunged into a universe of significations. Between the wave and the horse, he will be tempted to conceive an undifferentiated profundity: passion, pride, power, wildness. . . . The idea of a nature leads infallibly to that of a nature common to all things, that is, a *superior* or *higher* nature. The idea of an interiority always leads to the idea of a transcendence.

And the task extends step by step: from the bow to the horse, from the horse to the wave—and from the sea to love. A common nature, once again, must be the eternal answer to the *single question* of our Greco-Christian civilization; the Sphinx is before me, questions me, I need not even try to understand the terms of the riddle being asked, there is only one answer possible, only one answer to everything: man.

This will not do.

There are *questions*, and *answers*. Man is merely, from his own point of view, the only witness.

Man looks at the world, and the world does not look back at him. Man sees things and discovers, now, that he can escape the metaphysical pact others had once concluded for him, and thereby escape servitude and terror. That he can . . . that he *may*, at least, some day.

He does not thereby refuse all contact with the world; he consents on the contrary to utilize it for material ends: a utensil, *as* a utensil, never possesses "depth"; a utensil is entirely form and matter—and purpose.

Man grasps his hammer (or a stone he has selected) and pounds on a stake he wants to drive into the ground. While he uses it in this way, the hammer (or the stone) is merely form and substance: its weight, the striking surface, the other extremity which allows him to hold it. Afterward, man sets the tool down in front of him; if he no longer needs it, the hammer is no more than a thing among things: outside of his use, it has no signification.

And man today (or tomorrow) no longer experiences this absence of signification as a lack, or as a laceration. Confronting such a void, he henceforth feels no dizziness. His heart no longer needs an abyss in which to lodge.

For if he rejects communion, he also rejects tragedy.

Tragedy may be defined, here, as an attempt to "recover" the distance which exists between man and things as a new value; it would be then a test, an ordeal in which victory would consist in being vanquished. Tragedy therefore appears as the last invention of humanism to permit nothing to escape: since the correspondence between man and things has finally been denounced, the humanist saves his empire by immediately instituting a new form of solidarity, the divorce itself becoming a major path to redemption.

There is still almost a communion, but a *painful* one, perpetually in doubt and always deferred, its effectiveness in proportion to its inaccessible character. Divorce-as-a-form-of-marriage is a trap—and it is a falsification.

We see in effect to what degree such a union is perverted: instead of being the quest for a good, it is now the benediction of an evil. Unhappiness, failure, solitude, guilt, madness–such are the accidents of our existence which we are asked to entertain as the best pledges of our salvation. To entertain, not to accept: it is a matter of feeding them at our expense while continuing to struggle against them. For tragedy involves neither a true acceptance nor a true rejection. It is the sublimation of a difference.

Let us retrace, as an example, the functioning of "solitude." I call out. No one answers me. Instead of concluding that there is no one there–which could be a pure and simple observation, dated and localized in space and time–I decide to act as if there *were* someone there, but someone who, for one reason or another, will not answer. The silence which follows my outcry is henceforth no longer a *true* silence; it is charged with a content, a meaning, a depth, a soul–which immediately sends me back to my own. The distance between my cry, to my own ears, and the mute (perhaps deaf) interlocutor to whom it is addressed becomes an anguish, my hope and my despair, a meaning in my life. Henceforth nothing will matter except this false void and the problems it raises for me. Should I call any longer? Should I shout louder? Should I utter different words? I try once again. . . . Very quickly I realize that no one will answer; but the invisible presence I continue to create by my call obliges me to hurl my wretched cries into the silence forever. Soon the sound they make begins to stupefy me. As though bewitched, I call again . . . and again. My solitude, aggravated, is ultimately transmuted into a superior necessity for my alienated consciousness, a promise of my redemption. And I am obliged, if this redemption is to be fulfilled, to persist until my death, crying out for nothing.

According to the habitual process, my solitude is then no longer an accidental, momentary datum of my existence. It becomes part of me, of the entire world, of all men: it is our nature, once again. It is a solitude forever.

Wherever there is distance, separation, doubling, cleavage, there is the possibility of experiencing them as suffering, then of raising this suffering to the height of a sublime necessity. A path toward a metaphysical Beyond, this pseudo-necessity is at the same time the closed door to a realistic future. Tragedy, if it consoles us today, forbids any solider conquest tomorrow. Under the appearance of a perpetual motion, it actually petrifies the universe in a sonorous malediction. There can no longer be any question of seeking some remedy for our misfortune, once tragedy convinces us to love it.

We are in the presence of an oblique maneuver of contemporary humanism, which may deceive us. Since the effort of recuperation no longer bears on things themselves, we might suppose, at first sight, that the divorce between them and man is in any case consummated. But we soon realize that nothing of the kind is the case: whether the pact is concluded with things or with their distance from us comes down to the same thing; the "bridge of souls" subsists between them and us; in fact it is actually reinforced from the operation.

This is why the tragic sense of life never seeks to suppress the distances: it multiplies them, on the contrary, at will. Distance between man and other men, distance between man and himself, between man and the world, between the world and itself—nothing remains intact: everything is lacerated, fissured, divided, displaced. Within the most homogeneous objects as in the least ambiguous situations appears a kind of secret distance. But this is precisely an *interior distance*, a false distance, which is in reality a well-marked path, that is, already a reconciliation.

Everything is contaminated. It seems, though, that the favorite domain of tragedy is the narrative complication, the romanesque. From all mistresses-turned-nuns to all detective-gangsters, by way of all tormented criminals, all pure-souled prostitutes, all the just men constrained by conscience to injustice, all the sadists driven by love, all the madmen pursued by logic, a good "character" in a novel must above all be *double*. The plot will be "human" in proportion to its *ambiguity*. Finally the whole book will be true in proportion to its contradictions.

It is easy to ridicule. It is less so to free oneself from the tragic conditioning our mental civilization imposes upon us. One might even say that the rejection of the ideas of "nature" and of predestination lead *first* to tragedy. There is no important work in contemporary literature that does not contain at the same time the assertion of our freedom and the "tragic" germ of its abandonment.

Two great works at least, in recent decades, have offered us two new forms of the fatal complicity: absurdity and nausea.

Albert Camus, as we know, has named *absurdity* the impassable gulf which exists betwen man and the world, between the aspirations of the human mind and the world's incapacity to satisfy them. Absurdity is in neither man nor things, but in the impossibility of establishing between them any relation other than *strangeness.*

Every reader has noticed, nonetheless, that the hero of *The Stranger* maintains an obscure complicity with the world, composed of rancor and fascination. The relations of this man with the objects surrounding him are not at all innocent: absurdity constantly involves disappointment, withdrawal, rebellion. It is no exaggeration to claim that it is things, quite specifically, which ultimately lead this man to crime: the sun, the sea, the briliant sand, the gleaming knife, the spring among the rocks, the revolver. . . . As, of course, among these things, the leading role is taken by Nature.

Thus the book is not written in a language as *filtered* as the first pages may lead one to believe. Only, in fact, the objects already charged with a flagrant human content are carefully neutralized, and *for moral reasons* (such as the old mother's coffin, whose screws are described in terms of their shape and the depth they penetrate into the wood). Alongside this we discover, increasingly numerous as the moment of the murder approaches, the most revealing classical metaphors, naming man or infected by his omnipresence: the countryside is "swollen with sunlight," the evening is "like a melancholy truce," the rutted road reveals the "shiny flesh" of the tar, the soil is "the color of blood," the sun is a "blinding rain," its reflection on a shell is "a sword of light," the day has "cast anchor in an ocean of molten metal"–not to mention the "breathing" of the "lazy" waves, the "somnolent" headland, the sea that "pants" and the "cymbals" of the sun. . . .

The crucial scene of the novel affords the perfect

image of a painful solidarity: the implacable sun is always "the same," its reflection on the blade of the knife the Arab is holding "strikes" the hero full in the face and "searches" his eyes, his hand tightens on the revolver, he tries to "shake off" the sun, he fires again, four times. "And it was—he says—as though I had knocked four times on the door of unhappiness."

Absurdity, then, is really a form of tragic humanism. It is not an observation of the separation between man and things. It is a lover's quarrel, which leads to a crime of passion. The world is accused of complicity in a murder.

When Sartre writes (in *Situations I*) that *The Stranger* "rejects anthropomorphism," he is giving us, as the quotations above show, an incomplete view of the work. Sartre has doubtless noticed these passages, but he supposes that Camus, "unfaithful to his principle, is being poetic." Can we not say, rather, that these metaphors are precisely the explanation of the book? Camus does not reject anthropomorphism, he utilizes it with economy and subtlety in order to give it more weight.

Everything is in order, since the point is ultimately, as Sartre points out, to show us, according to Pascal's phrase "the natural unhappiness of our condition."

And what does *Nausea* offer us? It is evidently concerned with strictly visceral relations with the world, dismissing any effort of description (called futile) in favor of a suspect intimacy, presented moreover as illusory, but which the narrator does not imagine he can avoid yielding to. The important thing, in his eyes, is in fact to yield to it as much as possible, in order to arrive at self-awareness.

It is significant that the three first perceptions recorded at the beginning of the book are all gained by the sense of touch, not that of sight. The three objects which provoke revelation are, in effect, respectively, the pebble on the beach, the bolt of a door, the hand of the Self-Taught Man. Each time, it is the physical contact with the narrator's hand which provokes the shock. We know that the sense of touch constitutes, in everyday life, a much more *intimate* sensation than that of sight: no one is afraid of contracting a contagious disease merely by looking at a sick man. The sense of smell is even more suspect: it implies a penetration of the body by the alien thing. The domain of sight itself, moreover, involves different qualities of apprehension: a shape, for example, will generally be more certain than a color, which changes with the light, with the background accompanying it, with the subject considering it.

Hence we are not surprised to note that the eyes of Roquentin, the hero of *Nausea*, are more attracted by colors—particularly by the less determined shades—than by outlines; when it is not his sense of touch, it is almost always the sight of an ill-defined color which provokes the nausea. We recall the importance assumed, at the beginning of the book, by Cousin Adolphe's suspenders, which are scarcely visible against the blue of his shirt: they are "mauve . . . buried in the blue, but with false humility . . . as if, having started out to become violet, they had stopped on the way without abandoning their pretensions. One feels like telling them: 'Go on, *become* violet and get it over with.' But no, they remain in suspension, checked by their incompleted effort. Sometimes the blue that surrounds them slides over them and covers them completely: I remain without seeing them for a moment. But this is only a transition, soon the blue pales in places, and I see patches of the hesitant mauve reappearing, which spread, connect, and reconstitute the suspenders." And the reader will continue to be ignorant of the suspenders' shape. Later, in the park, the famous root of the chestnut tree finally concentrates all its absurdity and its hypocrisy in its black color: "Black? I felt the word draining, emptying out its meaning with an extraordinary rapidity. Black? The root *was not* black, *that* wasn't black there on that piece of wood . . . but rather the vague effort to *imagine black* on the part of someone who had never seen it and who could not have decided on it, who would have imagined an ambiguous being, beyond colors." And Roquentin comments on himself: "Colors, tastes, smells were never real, never truly themselves and nothing but themselves."

As a matter of fact, colors afford him sensations analogous to those of the sense of touch: they are for him an appeal, immediately followed by a withdrawal, then another appeal, etc.; this is a "suspect" contact accompanied by unnamable impressions, demanding an adherence and rejecting it at the same time. Color has the same effect on his eyes as a physical presence on the palm of his hand: it manifests above all an indiscreet (and, of course, double) "personality" of the object, a kind of shameful insistence which is simultaneously complaint, challenge, and denial. "Objects . . . they touch me, it's unbearable. I'm afraid of entering into contact with them, just as if they were living creatures." Color changes, hence it is *alive;* that is what Roquentin has discovered: things are alive, *like himself*.

Sounds seem to him similarly corrupted (aside from musical tunes, which do not *exist*). There remains the visual perception of outlines; we feel that Roquentin avoids attacking these. Yet he rejects in turn this last refuge of coincidence with himself: the only lines which coincide exactly are geometric lines, the circles for example, "but the circle too does not exist."

We are, once again, in an entirely *tragedified* universe: fascination with doubling, solidarity with things *because* they bear their own negation within themselves, redemption (here: accession to consciousness) by the very impossibility of achieving a true correspondence; in other words, the final recuperation of all distances, of all failures, of all solitudes, of all contradictions.

Hence analogy is the only mode of description seriously envisaged by Roquentin. Facing the cardboard box containing his bottle of ink, he discovers the futility of geometry in this realm: to say that it is a parallelepiped is to say nothing at all "about it." On the contrary, he tells us about the *real* sea which "crawls" under a thin green film made to "fool" people, he compares the "cold" brightness of the sun to a "judgment without indulgence," he notices the "happy gurgle" of a fountain, a streetcar seat is for him "a dead donkey" drifting, its red plush "thousands of tiny feet," the Self-Taught Man's hand is a "big white worm," etc. Each object would have to be cited, for all are deliberately presented in this fashion. The one most charged with transformations is, of course, the chestnut root, which becomes, successively, "black nail," "boiled leather," "mildew," "dead snake," "vulture's talon," "sealskin," etc., until nausea.

Without trying to limit the book to this particular

point of view (though it is an important one), one can say that *existence* in it is characterized by the presence of interior distances, and that *nausea* is man's unhappy visceral penchant for these distances. The "smile in complicity with things" ends in a grimace: "All the objects that surrounded me were made of the same substance as myself, of a kind of shoddy suffering."

But are we not incited, under these conditions, to accord Roquentin's melancholy celibacy, his lost love, his "wasted life," the lugubrious and laughable fate of the Self-Taught Man—all the malediction weighing on the terrestrial world—the status of a superior necessity? Where, then, is freedom? Those who are unwilling to accept this malediction are all the same threatened with the supreme moral condemnation: they will be "filthy swine," *salauds*. Everything happens, then, as if Sartre—who can nonetheless hardly be accused of "essentialism"—had, in this book at least, brought the ideas of *nature* and of *tragedy* to their highest point. Once again, to struggle against these ideas is initially to do no more than to confer new powers upon them.

Drowned in the *depth* of things, man ultimately no longer even perceives them: his role is soon limited to experiencing, in their name, totally *humanized* impressions and desires. "In short, it is less a matter of observing the pebble than of installing oneself in its heart and of seeing the world with its eyes . . ."; it is apropos of Francis Ponge that Sartre writes these words. He makes the Roquentin of *Nausea* say: "I *was* the chestnut root." The two positions are not unrelated: it is a matter, in both cases, of thinking "with things" and not *about* them.

Ponge too, as a matter of fact, is not at all concerned to describe. He knows perfectly well, no doubt, that his texts would be of no help to a future archaeologist seeking to discover what a cigarette or a candle might have been in our lost civilization. Without our daily frequentation of these objects, Ponge's phrases concerning them are no more than lovely hermetic poems.

On the other hand, we read that the hamper is "annoyed to be in a clumsy position," that the trees in spring "enjoy being fooled" and "release a green vomit," that the butterfly "takes revenge for its long amorphous humiliation as a caterpillar."

Is this really to take the "side" of things, to represent them from "their own point of view"? Ponge obviously cannot be deceiving himself to this degree. The openly psychological and moral anthropomorphism which he continues to practice can have as its goal, on the contrary, only the establishment of a human, general, and absolute order. To assert that he speaks *for* things, *with* them, in their *heart*, comes down, under these conditions, to denying their reality, their opaque presence: in this universe populated by things, they are no longer anything but mirrors for a man that endlesly reflect his own image back to him. Calm, tamed, they stare at man with his own gaze.

Such a *reflection*, in Ponge, is not of course gratuitous. This oscillating movement between man and his natural doubles is that of an active consciousness, concerned to understand itself, to reform itself. Throughout his subtle pages, the smallest pebble, the least stick of wood gives him endless lessons, expresses and judges him at the same time, instructs him in a progress to be made. Thus man's contemplation of the world is a permanent apprenticeship to life, to happiness, to wisdom and to death.

So that ultimately it is a definitive and smiling reconciliation that we are being offered here. Again we have come back to the humanist affirmation: the world is man. But at what cost! For if we abandon the moral perspective of self-improvement, Ponge's *le Parti pris des choses* is no longer of any help to us. And if, in particular, we prefer freedom to wisdom, we are obliged to break all these mirrors so artfully arranged by Francis Ponge in order to get back to the hard, dry objects which are behind them, unbroached, as alien as ever.

François Mauriac, who—he said—had once read Ponge's *Hamper* on Jean Paulhan's recommendation, must have remembered very little of this text when he baptized *Hamper Technique* the description of objects advocated in my own writings. Or else I had expressed myself very badly.

To describe things, as a matter of fact, is deliberately to place oneself outside them, confronting them. It is no longer a matter of appropriating them to oneself, of projecting anything onto them. Posited, from the start, as *not being man*, they remain constantly out of reach and are, ultimately, neither comprehended in a natural alliance nor recovered by suffering. To limit oneself to description is obviously to reject all the other modes of approaching the object: sympathy as unrealistic, tragedy as alienating, comprehension as answerable to the realm of science exclusively.

Of course, this last point of view is not negligible. Science is the only honest means man possesses for turning the world around him to account, but it is a material means; however disinterested science may be, it is justified only by the establishment, sooner or later, of utilitarian techniques. Literature has other goals. Only science, on the other hand, can claim to know the *inside* of things. The interiority of the pebble, of the tree, or of the snail which Francis Ponge gives us ridicules science, of course (and even more than Sartre seems to think); hence it in no way represents what is *in* these things, but what man can put into them of his own mind. Having observed certain behavior, with more or less rigor, Ponge is inspired by these appearances to human analogies, and he begins talking about man, always about man, supporting himself on things with a careless hand. It matters little to Ponge that the snail does not "eat" earth, or that the chlorophyllic function is an absorption and not an "exhalation" of carbon gas; his eye is as casual as his recollections of natural history. The only criterion is the truth of the sentiment expressed in terms of these images—of the human sentiment, obviously, and of the human nature which is the nature of all things!

Mineralogy, botany, or zoology, on the contrary, pursue the *knowledge* of textures (internal and external alike), of their organization, of their functioning, and of their genesis. But, outside their domain, these disciplines too are no longer of any use, except for the abstract enrichment of our intelligence. The world around us turns back into a smooth surface, without signification, without soul, without values, on which we no longer have any purchase. Like the workman who has set down the tool he no longer needs, we find ourselves once again *facing* things.

To describe this surface then is merely to constitute this externality and this independence. Probably I have no more to say "about" the box my ink bottle came in than "with" it; if I write that it is a parallelipiped, I make no claim to defining any special essence of it; I have still less intention of handing it over to the reader so that his imagination can seize upon and embellish it with polychrome designs: I should prefer to keep him from doing so, in fact.

The most common criticisms made of such geometric information—"it says nothing to the mind," "a photograph or a diagram would show the shape better," etc.—are strange indeed: wouldn't I have thought of them first of all? As a matter of fact, there is something else involved. The photograph or the diagram aims only at reproducing the object; they are successful to the degree that they suggest as many interpretations (and the same errors) as the model. Formal description, on the other hand, is above all a limitation: when it says "parallelipiped," it knows it achieves no Beyond, but at the same time it cuts short any possibility of seeking one.

To record the distance between the object and myself, and the distances of the object itself (its *exterior* distances, i.e., its measurements), and the distances of objects among themselves, and to insist further on the fact that these are *only distances* (and not divisions), this comes down to establishing that things are here and that they are nothing but things, each limited to itself. The problem is no longer to choose between a happy correspondence and a painful solidarity. There is henceforth a rejection of all complicity.

There is, then, first a rejection of the analogical vocabulary and of traditional humanism, a rejection at the same time of the idea of tragedy, and of any other notion leading to the belief in a profound, and higher, nature of man or of things (and of the two together), a rejection, finally, of every pre-established order.

The sense of sight immediately appears, in this perspective, as the privileged sense, particularly when applied to outlines and contours (rather than to colors, intensities, or transparencies). Optical description is, in effect, the kind which most readily establishes distances: the sense of sight, if it seeks to remain simply that, leaves things in their respective place.

But it also involves risks. Coming to rest, without preparation, on a detail, the sense of sight isolates it, extracts it, seeks to develop it, fails, insists, no longer manages either to develop the detail or return it to its place . . .; "absurdity" is not far away. Or else contemplation is intensified to the point where everything begins to vacillate, to move, to dissolve . . .; then "fascination" begins, and "nausea."

Yes these risks remain among the least, and Sartre himself has acknowledged the cleansing power of the sense of sight. Troubled by a contact, by a suspect tactile impression, Roquentin lowers his eyes to his hand: "The pebble was flat, dry on one side, wet and muddy on the other. I was holding it by the edges, my fingers far apart to keep from getting dirty." He no longer understands what has moved him; similarly, a little later on, at the moment of entering his room: "I stopped short, because I felt in my hand a cold object which attracted my attention by a kind of personality. I opened my hand, I looked: I was simply holding the doorknob." Then Roquentin attacks colors, and his eye no longer manages to exercise its displacing action: "The black root did not *get through*, it remained there in my eyes, as a piece that is too big remains stuck in the throat. I could neither accept nor reject it." There has already been the "mauve" of the suspenders and the "suspect transparency" of the glass of beer.

We must work with the means at hand. The sense of sight remains, in spite of everything, our best weapon, especially if it keeps exclusively to outlines. As for its "subjectivity"—principal argument of the opposition—how is its value diminished thereby? Obviously I am concerned, in any case, only with the world as *my point of view* orients it; I shall never know any other. The relative subjectivity of my sense of sight serves me precisely to define *my situation in the world*. I simply keep myself from helping to make this situation a servitude.

Thus, though Roquentin thinks "the sense of sight is an abstract invention, a scoured, simplified idea, a human idea," it nonetheless remains, between the world and myself, the most effective operation.

For effectiveness is the point. To measure the distances—without futile regret, without hatred, without despair—between what is separated will permit us to identify what is *not* separated, what *is one*, since it is false that everything is double—false, or at least provisional. Provisional with regard to man, that is our hope. False already with regard to things: once scoured clean, they no longer refer to anything except to themselves, without a flaw for us to slip into, without a tremor.

One question persists: Is it possible to escape tragedy? Today its rule extends to all my feelings and all my thoughts, it conditions me utterly. My body can be satisfied, my heart content, my consciousness remains unhappy. I assert that this unhappiness is *situated* in space and time, like every unhappiness, like everything in this world. I assert that man, some day, will free himself from it. But of this future I possess no proof. For me, too, it is a wager. "Man is a sick animal," Unamuno wrote in *The Tragic Sense of Life*; the wager consists in believing he can be cured, and that it would therefore be a mistake to imprison him in his disease. I have nothing to lose. This wager, in any event, is the only reasonable one.

I have said that I possessed no proof. It is easy to perceive, nonetheless, that the systematic *tragedification* of the universe I live in is often the result of a deliberate intention. This suffices to cast a doubt on any proposition tending to posit tragedy as natural and definitive. Now, from the moment doubt has appeared, I cannot do otherwise than seek still farther.

This struggle, I shall be told, is precisely the tragic illusion par excellence: if I seek to combat the idea of tragedy, I have already succumbed to it; and it is so natural to take objects as a refuge . . . perhaps. But perhaps not. And, in that case. . . .

ELEMENTS OF A MODERN ANTHOLOGY

The several works that will be rapidly analyzed or discussed in the following pages are far from being the only ones whose investigations have marked the literature of the first half of the twentieth century. Nor in all cases are these even the works which have most impressed me personally. The absence of Kafka, among others, will be noticed at once, and the presence, on the contrary, of writers of much less importance. It will surely be pointed out that Joë Bousquet is quite dated from some points of view, that Godot *is too fashionable, and that often it is not the most accomplished works which have been chosen to represent the authors under consideration.*

All of which is true. The fact is that the five brief essays reprinted here will serve principally as examples, which will permit me to focus on certain themes and characteristic forms of this literature still in progress.

The earliest of these examples already date back some fifty years, the latest belong to our own postwar period. All of them offer, from my point of view, something profoundly immediate; it is that something *which I am trying to isolate here, and which it would not be difficult to recognize in most contemporary explorations.*

ENIGMAS AND TRANSPARENCY IN RAYMOND ROUSSEL (1963)

Raymond Roussel describes; and beyond what he describes there is nothing, nothing of what can traditionally be called a *message*. To adopt one of the favorite expressions of academic literary criticism, Roussel almost seems to have "nothing to say." No transcendence, no humanist metamorphosis can be applied to the series of objects, gestures, and events which constitute, at first glance, his universe.

On occasion, in order to satisfy the requirements of a very strict descriptive line, he must relate some psychological anecdote, or some imaginary religious custom, an account of primitive mores, a metaphysical allegory. . . . But these elements never have any "content," any depth; they cannot make in any case the most modest contribution to the study of human character or of the passions, the least contribution to sociology, inspire the slightest philosophical meditation. As a matter of fact, it is always frankly conventional sentiments that are involved (filial love, dedication, self-sacrifice, betrayal—always treated in a copybook manner), or else "gratuitous" rituals, or recognized symbolisms and well-worn philosophies. Between absolute non-sense and an exhausted sense, there remain once again only things themselves, objects, gestures, etc.

On the linguistic level, Roussel answers the requirements of criticism no better. Many have already pointed this out, and of course negatively: Raymond Roussel writes badly. His style is lusterless, neutral. When he abandons the order of observation—that is, of avowed platitude: the realm of "there is" and "is located at a certain distance"—he always employs a banal image, a hackneyed metaphor, itself the stand-by of some arsenal of literary conventions. Lastly the auditory organization of the sentences, the rhythm of the words, their music does not seem to raise any problem for the author's ear. The result is almost continuously without attraction from the point of view of belles-lettres: a prose alternating between simple-minded monotony and laborious cacophonous jumbles, alexandrines that must be counted out on the fingers to reveal their complement of the proper twelve feet.

Thus we are dealing with the exact opposite of what is conventionally called a good writer: Raymond Roussel has nothing to say, and says it badly. . . . And yet his *oeuvre* is beginning to be acknowledged as one of the most important in French literature in the early part of this century, one which has exercised its spell over several generations of writers and artists, one which we must count among the direct ancestors of the modern novel; whence the continually growing interest that attaches today to his opaque and disappointing works.

Let us consider first the opacity. It is, quite as much, an excessive transparency. Since there is never anything beyond the thing described, that is, since no supernature is hidden in it, no symbolism (or else a symbolism immediately proclaimed, explained, destroyed), the eye is forced to rest on the very surface of things: a machine of ingenious and useless functioning, a post card from a seaside resort, a celebration whose progress is quite mechanical, a demonstration of childish witchcraft, etc. A total transparency, which allows neither shadow nor reflection to subsist, this amounts, as a matter of fact, to a *trompe-l'oeil* painting. The more that scruples, specifications, details of shape and size accumulate, the more the object loses its depth. What we get, then, is an opacity without mystery: as behind a painted back cloth, there is nothing behind these surfaces, no inside, no secret, no hidden motive.

Yet by an impulse of contradiction frequent in modern writing, mystery is one of the formal themes most readily used by Roussel: search for a hidden treasure, problematic origin of some character or object, enigmas of all kinds proposed to the reader as to the heroes in the form of riddles, puns, codes, allusions, apparently absurd series of articles, etc. Concealed exits, underground passageways connecting two apparently unrelated sites, sudden revelations as to the mysteries of a contested consanguinity keep turning up in this rationalistic world in the best tradition of Gothic novels, momentarily transforming the geometric space of the situations and dimensions into a new *Castle of*

Otranto. . . . Actually not, however: the mysteries here are too well controlled. Not only are these enigmas set forth too clearly, analyzed too objectively, and too evidently asserted as enigmas, but even, at the end of a more or less extended discourse, they are actually solved and explained, and this time too with the greatest simplicity considering the extreme complication of the various clues. After having read the description of the disconcerting machinery, we are entitled to the rigorous description of its functioning. After the rebus comes the explanation, and everything is back where it belongs.

It is for this reason that the explanation becomes futile in its turn. It answers the questions asked so well, it so totally exhausts the subject that it seems, ultimately, to be a useless duplication of the machinery itself. And even when we see it functioning and we know to what end, the machinery remains mystifying: for example, the famous pile driver that serves to compose decorative mosaics with human teeth by using the energy of the sun and the wind! The decomposition of the whole into its tiniest parts, the perfect identity of the latter with their function, merely leads to the pure spectacle of a gesture deprived of meaning. Once again, a signification that is too transparent coincides with a total opacity.

Elsewhere, we are initially offered an assemblage of words, as heterogeneous as possible—placed, for example, under a statue, itself possessing many disconcerting features (and described as such)—and we are then at great length told the meaning (always *immediate*, on the verbal level) of the riddle-sentence, and how it is directly related to the statue, whose strange details are then revealed to be entirely necessary, etc. Now these chain elucidations, extraordinarily complex, ingenious, and farfetched as they are, seem so preposterous, so disappointing that it is as if the mystery remained intact. But it is henceforth a mystery that has been filtered, drained, a mystery that has become unnamable. Opacity no longer hides anything. We have the impression of having found a locked drawer, then a key; and this key opens the drawer quite impeccably . . . and the drawer is empty.

Roussel himself seems to have been somewhat mistaken about this aspect of his work, imagining he could lure crowds to the Châtelet theater to attend a cascade of these—as he believed—thrilling enigmas and their successive solution by a patient and subtle hero. Experience, alas, quickly disabused him, as could easily be foreseen. For what he offers is actually riddles *in the void*, concrete but theoretical investigations without event and therefore unable to "catch" anything. Though there are traps on every page, they are merely made to function before our eyes, exhibiting all their secret workings and revealing, in fact, how to avoid becoming their victim. Moreover, even if he has not already been initiated into the Rousselian operations and the necessary disappointment which accompanies their execution, any reader will immediately be struck by the total absence of anecdotal interest—the utter gratuitousness—of the mysteries proposed to his attention. Here again, we have either a complete dramatic blank or else the drama of panoply, with all its conventional accessories. And in this case, whether or not the stories told exceed the limits of the stupefying, the mere way in which they are presented, the naïveté with which the questions are asked (in the genre of "All those present were highly intrigued by . . ." etc.), the style, finally—as remote as possible from the elementary rules of suspense—would be enough to detach the best-disposed reader from these amateur inventors of science fiction and from these folkloric pages controlled like a parade of marionettes.

Then what are these forms which so concern us? And how do they act upon us? What is their meaning? The last two questions it is still, no doubt, too early to answer. The Rousselian forms have not yet become academic; they have not yet been digested by the culture; they have not yet reached the status of values. We can already attempt, however, to name some of them at least. And to begin with, precisely that *investigation* which destroys, in the writing itself, its own object.

This investigation, as we have said, is purely formal. It is above all an itinerary, a logical path which leads from a given condition to another condition—one very similar to the first, though it is achieved by a long detour. We find a new example of this—one which has the additional advantage of being located entirely in the realm of language—in the brief posthumous texts whose architecture has been explained by Roussel himself: two sentences which when spoken sound identical almost to the letter, but whose meanings are totally without connection, on account of the different acceptations in which the similar words are taken. The trajectory here is the story, the anecdote permitting us to unite the two sentences, which will constitute respectively the first and last sentences of the text. The most absurd episodes will thus be justified by their function as utensils, as vehicles, as intermediaries; the anecdote no longer has any explicit content, but a movement, an order, a composition; it too is no longer anything but a mechanism: simultaneously a reproduction-machine and a modification-machine.

For we must emphasize the importance Roussel attaches to that very slight *modification* in sound separating the two key sentences, not to mention the general modification of the meaning. The narrative has effected, before our eyes, on the one hand a profound change in what the world—and language—means, and on the other a tiny superficial displacement (the altered letter); the text "devours its own tail," but with a slight irregularity, a little wrench—which changes everything.

Frequently, too, we find a simple plastic *reproduction*, like that mosaic produced by the above-mentioned pile driver. Examples abound, whether in the novels, the plays, or the poems, of these images of all kinds: statues, engravings, paintings, or even crude drawings without any artistic character. The best known of these objects is the miniature view set in the shaft of a penholder. Of course, precision of detail is here as great as if the author were showing us a real scene, life-size or even enlarged by some optical device, binoculars, or microscope. An image a few millimeters square thus causes us to see a beach including various persons on the sand, or on the water in boats; there is never anything vague about their gestures, or in the lines of the setting. On the other side of the bay passes a road; and on this road is a car, and in the car is seated a man; this man is holding a cane, whose engraved handle represents . . . , etc.

Sight, the privileged sense in Roussel, rapidly achieves an obsessive acuity, tending to infinity. This characteristic is made doubtless still more provocative by the fact that what is involved is a reproduction. Roussel almost prefers to describe, as we have pointed out, a universe which is not given as real but as already represented. He likes to place an intermediary artist between himself and the world of men. The text we are offered is a relation concerning a double. The excessive enlargement of certain remote or miniature elements here assumes, therefore, a particular value; for the observer has not been able to approach in order to consider at close hand the detail that catches his attention. From all appearances, he too invents, after the fashion of these numerous creators—of machines or methods—who people the entire work. Sight here is an *imaginary* sense.

Another striking characteristic of these images is what we might call their *instantaneity*. The wave about to break, the child rolling a hoop on the beach, elsewhere the statue of a person making an eloquent gesture (even if its meaning is initially missing, a riddle), or an object represented halfway between the ground and the hand which has just dropped it—everything is given as in movement, but frozen in the middle of that movement, immobilized by the representation which leaves in suspense all gestures, falls, conclusions, etc., eternalizing them in the imminence of their end and severing them from their meaning.

Empty enigmas, arrested time, signs which refuse to signify, giant enlargement of the tiny detail, narratives which come full circle: We are in a *flat* and *discontinuous* universe where each thing refers only to itself. A universe of fixity, of repetition, of absolute obviousness, which enchants and discourages the explorer. . . .

And thus the trap reappears, but it is of another nature. Obviousness, transparency preclude the existence of *higher worlds*, of any transcendence; yet, from this world before us we discover we can no longer escape. Everything is at a standstill, everything endlessly reproduces itself, the child forever holds his stick above the leaning hoop, and the foam of the motionless wave is about to fall back. . . .

ZENO'S SICK CONSCIENCE (1954)

Zeno Cosini, a rich Triestine businessman (pre-World War I Trieste), writes his psychoanalyst an account of the principal events of his past existence. Indeterminate university studies, father's death, unrequited passion for a young girl, marriage to her sister, happy and comfortable family life, mistresses, more or less risky business deals, generally unsuccessful—nothing of all this in appearance has serious consequences for him: his wife lovingly runs their home, an investment councilor carefully manages the bulk of his fortune. The aging Zeno, moreover, does not take an excessive interest in these rather ordinary facts, he resuscitates and discusses them with only one purpose: to prove he is sick and to describe his sickness. Despite his aspect, which we guess to be flourishing, the label *imaginary invalid* does not quite suit him; he knows that medicine has little power over his diseases, he always ends up quarreling with the doctors, whose diagnoses merely produce new symptoms; if he collects medications—or even takes them sometimes—it is hardly with therapeutic intent, strictly speaking; of course, he is as skeptical of psychoanalysis as of electrotherapy or gymnastics. At the very beginning of the book we read his profession of faith: "Sickness is a conviction, and I was born with that conviction." Something, all in all, like Grace.

The precise nature and the exclusive importance of this conviction—that is what his narrative seeks to illuminate in some four hundred pages. The universe into which he plunges us, a universe simultaneously grotesque, fantastic, and utterly banal, immediately attains—and retains to the end—an exceptional degree of *presence*. Zeno is indeed *in the world;* he is the prey of no symbolism; he escapes quite as completely the claustration of withdrawal. His condition can inspire neither incredulity nor irritation; it is obvious, necessary, incurable. The opposite of that morbid complacency in which the sufferer snuggles into his pains as into a kind of warm bed, Zeno engages in a continual struggle to conquer "good health," regarded as the supreme good, which is simultaneously accompanied by an utter inner repose—harmony of spirit, goodness, purity, *innocence*—and by external manifestations of a more practical nature: elegance, coolness, cunning, success in business, the capacity to seduce women and to play the violin well—instead of drawing from the latter instrument only horrible squeals, as from the rest of existence. The healthy man, moreover, does not benefit from these gifts in order to lead a scattered life: he confines himself, for instance, to a strict monogamy. This is not a contradiction, because, if for some people everything is good health, for others everything is disease.

This is particularly true of relations with time. Zeno's time is a diseased time. It is for this reason that, among other calamities, he can play no musical instrument properly: "The basest creature, once he knows what thirds, fourths, sixths are, also knows how to shift from one to another. . . . But when I have produced one of these figures, I can no longer free myself from it; it sticks to me, it contaminates the next figure and distorts it." When in conversation he speaks a sentence, however simple, at the same moment he tries to remember another sentence which he has uttered shortly before. If he has only five minutes in which to perform an important action, he wastes them calculating whether or not he would have needed more in order to complete it satisfactorily. He decides to stop smoking because tobacco is the cause of all his suffering; immediately his time is divided and devoured by the successive and always postponed dates of his "last cigarette," which he writes in advance on the walls of his bedroom—so that, once the walls are covered, he must soon move out. But amid the paralysis, death strikes friends and relatives around him, and each time he is caught unprepared, suddenly realizing that now he can never persuade them of his good will and his innocence.

Zeno does not "enjoy" poor health. He tries not to talk about it, behaves like everyone else insofar as he can. He has even "permanently assumed the aspect of a happy man." From the family dinner table, at which he arrives on time for meals as a good husband should, to the office where he zealously functions (without pay) as a bookkeeper, from Lloyds to the

Exchange, from his mistress' bed to the house of his affectionate parents-in-law, we eagerly follow the saunterings of this huntsman mercilessly tracking himself down. And we unhesitatingly place him beside his brothers: here indeed is the passion of a Michael Kohlhaas seeking his unjustly confiscated horses, the periodic dejection of a Dimitri Karamazov running after the money he must borrow at any price, the jolting progress of a Josef K. pursuing both his lawyer and his judges. The infirmities by which Zeno is abruptly stricken (stiffness of the knee because a lame friend has told him about the fifty-four muscles used in walking, or pain in the side because another has drawn him in a caricature with an umbrella sticking into him), and from which he subsequently suffers for the rest of his days, are closely related to those of Captain Ahab who has lost his leg in the struggle against the White Whale, or of Molloy who is gradually immobilized by a paralysis starting in one foot. Zeno knows his death in advance: it will begin by the gangrene of the lower limbs. Even his "unredeemed" city of Trieste, where not Italian but a dialect mixture of German and Croatian is spoken, reminds us of Kafka's Germano-Czech Prague, and of Joyce's Anglo-Irish Dublin—fatherlands of all those who are not at home in their own language. "A written confession is always a lie, and we [Triestines] lie with each Tuscan word we speak!"

Further, the narrator is of bad faith. Prefacing his account, the psychoanalyst warns us that it contains a good many lies. Zeno himself points out some in passing. But how can anything here be called a lie, since each event is accompanied by a long analysis which discredits and denies it? One day when he has not managed by this method to confuse the situation sufficiently, Zeno declares: "It was so clear that I no longer understood anything about it." After having accumulated the evidence of a classical Oedipus complex with many transferences, he turns on the physician who has not been able to avoid remarking on it; then he deliberately goes on to add, in support of this thesis, several false elements. He proceeds analogously in his relations with his family or friends: "If I had not distorted everything, I would have felt it was useless to open my mouth." At the end, he discovers that his analysis is capable of converting health into disease; that need be no obstacle: he then decides that he must treat his health.

This health that he wants to attend to—this bad health—this *conscience*, as the Italian title of the book indicates, Zeno ends by calling simply "life," which "unlike other diseases, is always mortal."

War breaks out between Italy and Austria. Paradoxically, the hero claims to discover his equilibrium in the frenzied commercial transactions to which the extension of the conflict gives rise. And the book ends on an astonishing note of hope: one day, a man "made like all other men of flesh and blood, but a little more ill than the others," will set off an explosive, of a power still unknown, in the center of the earth. "And there will be a tremendous explosion, but no one will hear it, and the earth will return to its nebulous state and continue on its way through the sky, freed from men—without parasites, without diseases."

Sick time, sick language, sick libido, sick body, sick life, sick conscience . . . we must not, of course, see in these some vague allegory of original sin, or any other metaphysical lamentation. It is a question of everyday life and of direct experience of the world. What Italo Svevo tells us in his way is that in our modern society nothing is any longer *natural*. Nor is there even any reason to be upset about it. We can be quite happy, talk, make love, do business, wage war, write novels; but nothing of all this will any longer be done without thinking about it, the way one breathes. Under our gaze, the simple gesture of holding out our hand becomes bizarre, clumsy; the words we hear ourselves speaking suddenly sound false; the time of our minds is no longer that of the clocks; and the style of a novel, in its turn, can no longer be innocent.

JOË BOUSQUET THE DREAMER (1953)

> *A man knew himself as the product of this world. He sought to become its consciousness: a way of dreaming that he would embody its salvation.* —J. B.

Joë Bousquet is in his room, captive, weak, *immobile*, he writes:

> I am here, but not the way you are here: if you could only see my eyes working! . . .
>
> My shadow turns around me, you turn around your shadow.
>
> It is difficult to make others understand that I do not live the way they do. They are in space like fish in water. Not me. I am a hole in the river bed.

When, at the age of twenty, Bousquet is suddenly "cut off from life" by the war wound which paralyzes him for the rest of his days, he thinks first of suicide "out of love for life." But he soon realizes his error:

if he has lost the use of his legs, life, on the other hand, cannot escape him. Better still, his physical diminution gives him a new strength to construct the universe around himself—a strength which his body's agitation had hitherto doubtless diverted or disguised. And, if this *life* he elaborates seems to have looked to him, at first, as a kind of replacement product—marvelous for him, but of secondary interest, in spite of everything, for the man who has a choice—he soon recognizes it as the most precious, the most profound, probably the only life to be *real*. . . .

> If all men lived motionless, like me, they would have a name rich with doubt to designate the facts which turn in circles in order to surround them. . . .

If men lived motionless, if they consented to be that "hole in the river bed," they would see the water flow toward them from all sides, the currents organized in a new, more comprehensible way, and the whole river take its true direction.

Bousquet has not sought to make this dramatic experiment for himself alone, and more perhaps than by his strictly poetic or fictional works, it is by these everyday reflections, in which he strives to make us understand his situation, that he reveals himself to be irreplaceable. For his situation is merely a cruel image of the creator's own.

The sensuous world that surrounds him is no longer, like dreams, like memory, anything but the substance to which he must lend his imagination in order to redeem it from nothingness. He is a prisoner in his room, he is condemned to inaction by the bullet he stopped, but it is he, after all, who gives an organized existence to his prison, it is he who redeems from chance and from chaos that stray bullet which has paralyzed him. The point here is no longer to awaken a consciousness, after the fact, to phenomena that already have a life of their own: without this creation, substance could have no form; Bousquet discovers finally that he has inflicted his mutilation upon himself.

In *Le Meneur de Lune* we follow the progression from page to page:

> The accident which mutilates a man does not affect the sources of his existence; it is mortal only to his habits. Physical misfortune corrupts only what there was to be corrupted.
>
> "Then after having been thrown on your invalid's bed, you have found your life coming toward you?"
>
> "Alas! What else have I embodied than the accident of which I was the victim?"

And later on:

> Create your life in the image of the best that is within yourself. If it imposes upon you a law you have not conceived, do not cut yourself off from it on this pretext. You are, your life and you, the product of the same will.

But then: "What comes to you, you had desired. . . ."

What comes to you: These are first the memories of youth which recompose themselves in settings and events stripped of their halo, molded henceforth in a less friable clay. The operation has nothing impoverishing about it, on the contrary; it is not a schematic model which is substituted for a too complex reality; it is actually *the stone and the water* which this labor "constructs and clears."

> It's not possible, [a girl he has known since childhood tells him] it's as if the country where we lived is a hundred feet underground and you go down there, when we think we see you.

But Bousquet is not mistaken; he knows that he "shelters among his memories a secret and profound experience": the point is not to *go down* to the buried village, but to reconstruct it, or rather to bring it to light for the first time; for the garden, the cottage at the water's edge, the railroad at his feet—none of all this has yet existed. Only the inattentive witnesses can confuse them with the scattered fragments, corrupted by the years and by distance, to which these constructions are supposed to relate. Bousquet knows that their luster, their quality "of immutable coherence and density" belong only to a *new world*, this time recovered forever. This *snow of another age* will not melt in the first sunbeam.

> In my evocations of Marceillens, or of the village where I grew up, the reference to memory becomes a kind of concession less and less readily granted. . . . It seems increasingly to me that nothing in this operation is, indeed, as fictive and conventional as the determination to attribute it to my memory. . . .
>
> My experience as a prisoner has enlightened me; as a free man, I engendered the space in which I believed I moved as an object. Immobilized, I realize that the beating of my heart relentlessly created the space in which I so often thought I recognized the stereotyped setting of my childhood. Had I kept the use of my legs, I should have long ago mobilized the wooded hillside of a stroll, and dissolved in the effort of climbing the sensation whose qualities the throbbing of my blood distributed upon the docile slope of my field of vision.

Now I grasp better the operation which remains incomplete. Imagining I am reviving memories, I create on a past model a landscape into which I no longer have the means to penetrate, but where I make the weather rain, occasionally advancing a white page across the hallowed wires of the magic operation.

The discovery is crucial, it marks the accession of art by freeing literature from the task of transcribing or testifying. Reportage demands of its conscientious author a physical displacement, in which the essential is always more or less "dissolved in the effort of climbing"; as it is here defined, *creation* is on the contrary inseparable from confinement—with which, moreover, the popular image prefers to embellish it: the poet in his ivory tower, Sade in his cell, Marcel Proust in his cork-lined room. The attempt has often been made to limit this prison to a certain quality of solitude, almost always understood as a solitude in relation to men. We must see it as something more, and even something quite different in its scope: not only a more serious isolation which cuts off, just as radically, both objects and surroundings, but also a new dimension created by the impossibility of approaching them. This is what is stated so precisely by the last sentence of the paragraph—"a landscape into which *I no longer have the means to penetrate*, but where *I make the weather rain* . . ."—the two phenomena (*paralysis* of the creator and *life* of the creation) here being not juxtaposed but linked by a very strict causal relation. As if this faculty of giving life could not function, paradoxically, without a certain incapacity to live; an incapacity against which those stricken by it rebel—though they continue, at the same time, to desire an ultimate extension of their own misfortune ("if we could only take root!"), of which death is at once the end, the most perfect image—and the mockery.

> If only my existence, like that of a tree, were the fixity of a site. . . . Or else, like that of my mind, the obliteration of all sites. But I am like that passer-by over there; watch him walk, he seems to be running after a car. He is himself, as the feather that flies is a bird.

There is also the false sleep of dreams, which gives us a less alarming approximation of the *ideal state*—temporary and reversible, in any case—and at the same time more effective. Like many of his surrealist friends, Bousquet duly records his dreams; he likes "the sovereign solitude of the dream"; he dreads "the anguish which imprisons him at the moment of waking," "a typical anguish which makes us sickeningly aware of all the space we are losing." He therefore soon reaches the point of instigating his dreams himself; he seeks "to enter, head high, that world which is called imaginary." Eyelids half closed over "petrified" eyes, he senses the transformation of the space around him:

> . . . The whole house is changed, and seems to grow and fall silent, to construct around me a solitude in which the mounting silence of space introduces the majesty and the seething of a sea. A word that comes to my lips completes my fascination with the vision of this structure suddenly open to the invisible and to the void. This word is: absence.

But Bousquet reveals to us the secret of this universe of dreams, which has given rise, under other pens or brushes, to so many hallucinations and to so much poetic charlatanism. The secret is one of extreme simplicity, which at the same time illuminates the *enigmatic* relations which link everyday life to what art should be. Here again, rather than giving a more or less inexact paraphrase of what he has to say, let us quote the paragraph *in extenso:*

> The dream is more real than waking life because in it the object is never negligible: the revolver, the needle, and the clock here *summarize events which without them would not exist. Event and object are here rigorously interchangeable*, as in those adventures in which a hotel room tells the whole of a crime the detective imagination is incapable of reinventing on the spot. And, reading detective stories or certain pages of Raymond Roussel, we experience the thrill of a man who has entered by the oblique means of fictive relations into *the most necessary and the most exact of his functions.*

This is then first of all, it appears, a significant universe; the absurd and the gratuitous are restored to their place, that of signs not yet elucidated, which for the detective inspecting the "hotel room" will gradually become clues. Further, everything is revealed, objectified, whether in the form of palpable matter (the tools of the "crime") or of traces theoretically more fugitive. Words and phrases, for example, also become *objects*, whose shape may give rise later on to the same analyses. Everyone has experienced—often even without attaching importance to it— the abnormal clarity affecting, in the most ordinary dreams, a chair, a pebble, a hand, the fall of some debris (which produces the strange impression that it is going to *recur*, as often as one likes, as if the detached fragment were *eternalized in the falling state*), or, in exactly the same way, two or three words (spoken by whom? one no longer recalls) whose image has remained in the mind as precisely as if they had been carved on a signpost at a crossroads.

And we quickly realize that the utilitarian meaning of these words, like the anecdotal signification of these criminal objects, is of no real interest. These are only possible by-products of the things themselves, which alone remain necessary, irreplaceable. They impose themselves upon our senses with a rigor which owes nothing to the explanations subsequently discovered for them. Their presence is such that it suffices to convince us and to satisfy us totally.

It is not surprising, under these conditions, that a world so perfect (that is, completed, not simplified and necessarily single in meaning, but in which ambiguity itself is unobscured), a world which is no longer the promise of a *beyond* but one which on the contrary frees us from all nostalgia—it is not surprising that this world attracts us so forcefully. The popular expression says: *to take refuge* in dreams. Actually something quite different is involved; it is the key to *this world* we are holding in our hand, and suddenly we understand that the dreams Bousquet is telling us about are not quite the dreams of our uneasy nights. It would be too easy if it were enough to close our eyes in order to discover the real contours of our life. The necessary disjunction is less easy to provoke, and doubtless we can do so more effectively by not falling asleep. As we suspected, this *waking dream* could simply be *art*, of which sleep, it is true, affords fragments on occasion but which only a conscious activity permits us to assemble and unite.

Thus, just as memory was only an alibi, oneirotic events and landscapes are only a means of penetrating the opacity of the more urgent phenomena which concern us on every hand, and whose urgency, precisely, confuses us; once again, it is the "effort of climbing" which it is essential to avoid.

For those who possess a healthy body, who let themselves be ruled by it and who every day dissolve a little more in the play of joints and muscles, the point is to react against nocturnal visions. "*To dream* is a good word for what happens in the imagination of a man immobilized by sleep." This word, charged with all kinds of vaguely pejorative hints, commonly serves men of action to maintain the integrity of their moral health. Yet Joë Bousquet perceives that he has brothers, nonetheless, among his "ex-fellow men."

"I agree," he writes, "that on his way to his office a man may tell himself he had dreamed the steps which he is actually taking. But I, who move no more awake than asleep—how should I adopt your ways, my friends, of distinguishing these two states?"

Perhaps dreams will therefore be of still greater help to these "friends" who stand, who walk, if they can benefit by the *immobile* view which is thus lent to them; and ultimately it is for the same enterprise—the interpretation of the same universe, or rather its creation, that dreams will serve them as well as Bousquet himself. "It would be," he admits, "no more than an absurd game to consider my dreams if I did not relate the impression they had given me to the objects of the day."

Further, "nothing distinguishes dreams from life awake: the objects in them are identical to those of waking life." Only we see them better, because the light by which we see them "falls from higher up."

Thus we are incontestably back on earth: it is indeed the "objects of life awake" that we must deal with, and the admirable clarity we had momentarily glimpsed is, in reality, their own. . . . At least it *should* be. It is in order to acquire it that they demand our cooperation.

> Do not imitate reality, collaborate with it. Put your thoughts and your expressive gifts in the service of the days and the facts which distinguish them, subject yourself to the existence of things, if you are not what they lack, you are nothing, you will enrich what exists by what, in yourself, was its presentiment.

That is what dreams are: the "presentiment" of what the real world will be when our minds have given matter its definitive form. Unfortunately, these glimpsed fragments do not suffice to convince man of his necessity to be what things lack, so that, out of frivolity or lack of imagination, he generally prefers to ignore the partial revelations of which he has been the witness. His situation *in* the world increases his blindness still further.

> The world's mediocrity derives from the imperfection of our vision, from our incapacity to pay attention. Our vision of things remains vague and cloudy, like the prospect carved out of the night by the headlights of a car, and so imperfect that the driver's imagination must continually interpret and paraphrase the signs glimpsed. At night, one sees a road well only by tearing oneself away from what one sees of it.

More serious than our "incapacity to interpret signs" is the reluctance the demand to do so meets in us. If we cannot, it is chiefly because we will not. We are conscious of the imperfection of the phenomena which constitute our universe, but we convince ourselves that it does not concern us. Along with the responsibility for chaos, we gladly abandon to some higher power the task of completing the job as if our condition as *mortals* were a sufficient excuse for us to desist.

> Adapted to the life whose phenomena it reflects, thought forbids itself to form a part of its totality. We see only the fact in a fact, we forbid ourselves to discover in it an episode of a life doomed to death.
>
> Our thought does not choose to be the thought of our life. We watch things pass by in order to forget that they are watching us die.

Opposing this unacceptable abdication, Bousquet develops a kind of stubborn sermon, whose essential themes appear in all his work. *Real matter*, he says, is still invisible: "What you called by that name is not even its image. True matter is masked. Your soul must mingle with it in order for it to be revealed to you." Similarly, time and space are the work of man, or rather *will be* his work. What is to be saved is not oneself, "it is the earth, the pebble, the ash. *Your duty is to enact the salvation of space and time.*" There is, in the determination to become this savior, both much pride and the greatest humility, for the human person totally disappears into it, to the benefit of a problematic creation which alone is granted an *ideal* status. But, out of clumsy vanity, man wants first "to exist," which is precisely what constitutes his nothingness. "You do not exist. . . . You are not even accursed. Malediction is merely the site of your absurd and monstrous freedom."

The highest quality of our mind is merely the faculty (and in terms of morality, the duty) of conceiving a form which can give unity to the world and "raise it to our image." This will be, by an appropriate turnabout, the true accession of man, of that man who is "to come."

"Man-the-nebula must be made real. . . ."

Facts are difficult to penetrate. Yet we discover in them, gradually, the design of our life. Speaking of his own, Bousquet—whose existence seemed to have been wrecked by a tragic fate—writes: "There is no event, no phenomenon which is not a feature of my soul." And further: "I am both the subject and the product of my will. . . . Man exists by his adherence to events, by his way of achieving, through them, the event he will be." Who better than this wounded veteran, bedridden for twenty years, could make such a lesson so moving, and so explicit?

It is not enough to "recuperate" chance. Even better camouflaged than events that are absurd a priori are those which already seem integrated in an order, superficial but reassuring, which takes the place of a signification for them. Such events pass quite unnoticed, we forget to mistrust them, and they smother us only all the more certainly.

> The most innocent facts, those most surely linked to their causes, seem to submit to subterranean relations for which our soul has supplied the channels. Intervening in a cooled-off world, they adhere however for a very brief period to wishes which we formed in their regard. It is as if they had encountered each other while seeking us and, even while yielding to physical laws, have already accommodated themselves, far from us, in the manner of a dream. Indeed, they have been our memory before being our adventure.

No doubt the most serious achievement of surrealism has been to restore, by systematic investigation, to the "apparent miracles which cast so lively a doubt on the common vision of reality" all their value and all their weight: those of "evident pledges of an unknown order"; it is by relentlessly tracking them down that we shall enter "into the castle of each moment." It is futile, on the other hand, to waste one's strength in "arbitrarily bringing together an iron and a celluloid collar"; "the impossibility of ever finding the gratuitous in the most daring juxtapositions" dispenses us from such amusements; the everyday world offers riches enough so that we can avoid such extravagances. The most ordinary phenomena will be, ultimately, the most marvelous.

We must, finally, guard against allegorical constructions and against symbolism. (Here again we find an idea dear to the friends of André Breton.) Each object, each event, each form is in effect its own symbol: "*Do not say that there are wooden crosses and the sign of the cross.* There would be an unreal sign and a thing signified, which would be real. One and the other are, simultaneously, realities and signs."

Bousquet's universe—ours—is a universe of signs. Everything in it is a sign; and not the sign of something else, something more perfect situated out of our reach, but a sign of itself, of that reality which asks only to be revealed.

For this we possess a singular weapon, which is the body of speech and writing, *language*. Even the word "weapon" is only half appropriate to designate what seems to us both a means and an end: being the sign par excellence (the representation of all signs), language cannot also have a signification entirely outside itself. Nothing, then, can be exterior to it.

> Language is not contained in consciousness, but contains it. . . . The experience of language encloses all others. . . . After having written to a woman "I shall take you in my arms," I have no more than her phantom to embrace. . . .

Hence beyond language there is probably nothing else. The world "creates itself in us" and "ends in speech," for speech is truth: "Truth when by the act of naming an object it produces the accession of man." To write is "to give our reality to truth, from which we derived it, in order to become once again, within it, light as dreams."

> Let us have the courage to admit this. Man exists only outside himself, he is only the negative of existence and it would be a marked progress for him to suppress himself altogether. The paradox seems of a piece. Is our existence still to be won? Frankly, I believe so. Man is the being in the falling state, in exile, as far removed from life as the mortal cold which nonetheless is privileged to purify the atmosphere and give coherence and solidity to a mass of water. I have understood. I seek to collect my nothingness in the shadow of a reality worthy of the light, and to forge with my own hands an object which obliterates my tracks.

A text both "dense and irreducible," so perfect that it does not seem "to have been touched," an object so perfect that it would obliterate our tracks. . . . Do we not recognize here the highest ambition of every writer?

Doubtless it is by this constant reflection on literary (or in a more general sense, on artistic) creation that Joë Bousquet's *oeuvre* remains so precious for us. And on this account, we must overlook what may be annoying in these pages: a man who talks of "falling" and of "exile" seems quite close to talking of original sin. Even without holding his frequent use of the word "soul" against him when the word *imagination* would certainly suit his purpose more clearly, we cannot help being irritated by the kind of mysticism (heretical, moreover) which imbues all of Bousquet's thinking. More serious than a suspect vocabulary ("soul," "salvation," etc.), there is in Bousquet that attempt at a *total recuperation* of the universe by the human mind. The notion of *totality* always leads more or less directly to that of absolute truth, that is, to a higher truth and thence to the notion of God.

Here, however, it is man himself who must "give unity to the world and raise it to his own image." We regret, especially, that Bousquet has not specified that the operation will remain on the human scale and will have importance for man only, that it will not thereby attain to any essence of things, and that the creation, finally, to which we are invited will always have to be begun again, by ourselves and by those who come after us.

It is then, as a matter of fact, that the *invention* of the world can assume its entire meaning—a permanent invention which, as we are told, belongs to artists but also to all men. In dreams, in memory, as in the sense of sight, our imagination is the organizing force of our life, of *our* world. Each man, in his turn, must reinvent the things around him. These are real things, clear, hard, and brilliant, of the real world. They refer to no other world. They are the sign of nothing but themselves. And the only contact man can make with them is to imagine them.

SAMUEL BECKETT, OR PRESENCE ON THE STAGE (1953 and 1957)

The human condition, Heidegger says, is *to be there*. Probably it is the theater, more than any other mode of representing reality, which reproduces this situation most naturally. The dramatic character *is on stage*, that is his primary quality: he is *there*.

Samuel Beckett's encounter with this requirement afforded a priori, an exceptional interest: at last we would see Beckett's man, we would see *Man*. For the novelist, by carrying his explorations ever farther, managed only to reduce more on every page our possibilities of apprehending him.

Murphy, Molloy, Malone, Mahood, Worm—the hero of Beckett's narratives deteriorates from book to book, and faster and faster. Feeble, but still capable of traveling on a bicycle, he rapidly loses the use of his limbs, one after the other; no longer able even to drag himself along, he then finds himself imprisoned in a room, in which his senses gradually abandon him. The room, shrinking, is soon reduced to a simple jar in which a rotting and obviously mute trunk ultimately falls apart altogether. At the end there remains no more than this: "the shape of an egg and the consistency of glue." But this shape and this consistency are themselves immediately denied by one absurd sartorial detail: the character wears garters, which is especially impossible for an egg. We are therefore once again put on our guard: man—man is not yet *that*.

Thus all these creatures which have paraded past us served only to deceive us; they occupied the sentences of the novel in place of the ineffable being who still refuses to appear there, the man incapable of recuperating his own existence, the one who never manages to be present.

But now we are in the theater. And the curtain goes up. . . .

The set represents nothing, or just about. A road? Let's say, in a more general way: *outdoors*. The only notable detail consists of a tree, sickly, scarcely more than a bush, and without a single leaf; let's say, a skeleton of a bush.

Two men are on stage, of no particular age, without profession, without family situation. And also without domicile; hence: two *vagabonds*. Physically, they seem to be intact. One takes off his shoes, the other speaks of the Gospels. They eat a carrot. They have nothing to say to each other. They address each other by two diminutives which seem to refer to no identifiable names: Gogo and Didi.

They look to the right, to the left, they prepare to leave, to leave each other, and always come back, side by side, to the middle of the stage. They cannot go anywhere else: they are waiting for someone named Godot, about whom nothing is known except that he will not come; from the start, that, at least, is obvious to everyone.

And no one is surprised when a young boy arrives (Didi, moreover, thinks he has already seen him the day before) bringing this message: "Mr. Godot won't come this evening but surely tomorrow." Then the light rapidly wanes; night falls. The two tramps decide to leave and come back the next day. But they do not move. The curtain falls.

Previously, two other characters have appeared, creating a diversion: Pozzo, of flourishing aspect, who keeps his servant Lucky on a leash; Lucky is a total wreck. Pozzo sits himself down on a folding stool, eats a chicken leg, smokes a pipe; then he undertakes an inflated description of the twilight. Lucky, on his orders, executes a few hops by way of a "dance" and mouths at top speed an incomprehensible tirade, stammering his way through fragments of gibberish.

So much for the first act.

Act two: the next day. But is it really the next day? Or after? Or before? In any case, the setting is the same, except for one detail: the tree now has three leaves.

Didi is singing a song, on this theme: a dog stole a crust of bread, was beaten to death, and on his tombstone was written: a dog stole a crust of bread . . . (*ad libitum*). Gogo puts his shoes back on, eats a radish, etc. He does not remember having already come to this place.

Pozzo and Lucky return: Lucky is mute, Pozzo is blind and remembers nothing. The same little boy returns, bearing the same message: "Mr. Godot won't come this evening but he'll come tomorrow." No, the child does not know the two tramps, he has never seen them before.

Again, it is night. Gogo and Didi would like to try hanging themselves—the tree's branches may be strong enough—but unfortunately they have no rope. . . . They decide to leave and come back the next day. But they do not move. The curtain falls.

This is called *Waiting for Godot*. The performance lasts nearly three hours.

From this point of view alone, there is something surprising: during these three hours, the play *holds together*, without a hollow, though it consists of nothing but emptiness, without a break, though it would seem to have no reason to continue or to conclude. From beginning to end, the audience follows; it may lose countenance sometimes, but remains somehow compelled by these two beings, who do nothing, who say virtually nothing, who have no other quality than to be present.

From the very first performance, the virtually unanimous critics have emphasized the *public* character of the spectacle. As a matter of fact, the words "experimental theater" no longer apply here: what we have is simply theater, which everyone can see, from which everyone immediately derives his enjoyment.

Is this to say that no one misjudges it? Of course not. *Godot* is misjudged in every way, just as everyone misjudges his own misery. There is no lack of explanations, which are offered from every side, left and right, each more futile than the next:

Godot is God. Don't you see that the word is the

diminutive of the root-word *God* which the author has borrowed from his mother tongue? After all, why not? Godot—why not, just as well?—is the earthly ideal of a better social order. Do we not aspire to a better life, better food, better clothes, as well as to the possibility of no longer being beaten? And this Pozzo, who is precisely *not* Godot—is he not the man who keeps thought enslaved? Or else Godot is death: tomorrow we will hang ourselves, if it does not come all by itself. Godot is silence; we must speak *while waiting for it:* in order to have the right, ultimately, to keep still. Godot is that inaccessible *self* Beckett pursues through his entire *oeuvre*, with this constant hope: "This time, perhaps, it will be me, at last."

But these images, even the most ridiculous ones, which thus try as best they can to limit the damages, do not obliterate from anyone's mind the reality of the drama itself, that part which is both the most profound and quite superficial, about which there is nothing else to say: Godot is that character for whom two tramps are waiting at the edge of a road, and who does not come.

As for Gogo and Didi, they refuse even more stubbornly any other signification than the most banal, the most immediate one: they are men. And their situation is summed up in this simple observation, beyond which it does not seem possible to advance: they are *there*, they are on the stage.

Attempts doubtless already existed, for some time, which rejected the stage movement of the bourgeois theater. *Godot*, however, marks in this realm a kind of finality. Nowhere had the risk been so great, for what is involved this time, without ambiguity, is what is essential; nowhere, moreover, have the means employed been so *poor;* yet never, ultimately, has the margin of misunderstanding been so negligible. To such a degree that we must turn back in order to measure this risk and this poverty.

It seemed reasonable to suppose, until recent years, that although the novel for example could free itself of many of its rules and traditional accessories, the theater at least had to show more discretion. The dramatic work, as a matter of fact, accedes to its true life only on condition of an understanding with a public of some kind or other; hence the latter must be surrounded with attentions: it must be offered unusual characters, it must be interested by piquant situations, it must be caught up in the complications of a plot, or else it must be violently taken out of itself by a continuous verbal invention, deriving more or less from delirium or from poetic lyricism.

What does *Waiting for Godot* offer us? It is hardly enough to say that nothing happens in it. That there should be neither complications nor plot of any kind has already been the case on other stages. Here, it is *less than nothing*, we should say: as if we were watching a kind of regression *beyond* nothing. As always in Samuel Beckett, what little had been given to us at the start—and which seemed to be nothing—is soon corrupted before our eyes, degraded further, like Pozzo who returns deprived of sight, dragged on by Lucky deprived of speech—and like, too, that carrot which in the second act is no longer anything but a radish. . . .

"This is becoming really insignificant," one of the vagabonds says at this point. "Not enough," says the other. And a long silence punctuates his answer.

It will be evident, from these two lines, what distance we have come from the verbal delirium mentioned above. From start to finish, the dialogue of *Godot* is *moribund*, extenuated, constantly located at those frontiers of agony where all of Beckett's "heroes" move, concerning whom we often cannot even be certain that they are still on this side of their death. In the middle of these silences, these repetitions, these ready-made phrases (typical: "One is what one is. The inside doesn't change."), one tramp or the other proposes, now and then, in order to pass the time, that they make conversation, "repent," hang themselves, tell stories, insult each other, play "Pozzo and Lucky," but each time the attempt breaks down and peters out, after a few uncertain exchanges, into suspension points, renunciations, failures.

As for the argument, it is summarized in four words: "We're waiting for Godot"—which continually recur, like a refrain. But like a stupid and tiresome refrain, for such waiting interests no one; it does not possess, as waiting, the slightest stage value. It is neither a hope, nor an anguish, nor even a despair. It is barely an alibi.

In this general dilapidation, there is a kind of culminating point—that is to say, under the circumstances, the reverse of a culminating point: a nadir, an oubliette. Lucky and Pozzo, feeble now, have collapsed on top of each other in the middle of the road; they cannot get back up. After a long argument, Didi comes to their aid, but he stumbles and falls on top of *them;* he must call for help in his turn. Gogo holds out his hand, loses his balance, and falls. There is no longer a single character standing up. There is nothing left on stage but this wriggling, whining heap, in which we then observe Didi's face light up as he says, in a voice almost calm again, "We are men!"

We all know what the "theater of ideas" was: a healthy exercise of the intelligence, which had its public (though it sometimes treated situations and dramatic development in a rather cavalier way). We were somewhat bored in this theater, but we "thought" hard there, out front as well as on stage. Thought, even subversive thought, always has something reassuring about it. Speech—beautiful language—is reassuring too. How many misunderstandings a noble and harmonious discourse has created, serving as a mask either for ideas or for their absence!

Here, no misunderstanding: in *Godot* there is no more thought than there is beautiful language; neither one nor the other figures in the text except in the form of parody, of *inside out* once again, or of corpse.

Language is that "twilight" described by Pozzo; announced as a set-piece by a great deal of throat-clearing and whip-cracking, crammed with sounding phrases and dramatic gestures, but sabotaged at the same time by sudden interruptions, familiar exclamations, grotesque lapses in inspiration:

> (*Lyrical.*) An hour ago (*he looks at his watch, prosaic*) roughly (*lyrical*) after having poured forth ever since (*he hesitates, prosaic*) say ten o'clock in the morning (*lyrical*) tirelessly torrents of red and white light it begins to lose its effulgence, to grow pale (*gesture of the two hands lapsing by stages*) pale, ever a little paler, a little paler until (*dramatic pause, ample gesture of the two hands flung wide apart*) pppfff! finished! it comes to rest. But—(*hand raised in admonition*)—but behind this veil of gentleness and peace night is charging (*vibrantly*) and will burst upon us (*snaps his fingers*)

pop! like that! (*his inspiration leaves him*) just when we least expect it. (*Silence. Gloomily.*) That's how it is on this bitch of an earth. (*Long silence.*)

And then comes the thought. The two tramps have asked Pozzo a question, but no one can recall what it was. All three simultaneously take off their hats, raise their hands to their foreheads, concentrate intensely. Long silence. Suddenly Gogo makes an exclamation, he has remembered: "Why doesn't he put down his bags?"

He is referring to Lucky. This is, as a matter of fact, the question which had been asked some moments before, but in the interval the servant has put down the bags; hence Didi convinces everyone by concluding: "Since he has put down his bags it is impossible we should have asked why he does not do so." Which is logic itself. In this universe where time does not pass, the words *before* and *after* have no meaning; only the present situation counts: the bags *are* down, as if forever.

Such reasoning was already to be found in Lewis Carroll or in Jarry. Beckett does better: he gives us a specialized thinker, Lucky; on the command of his master ("Think, pig!"), he begins:

> Given the existence as uttered forth in the public works of Puncher and Wattmann of a personal God quaquaquaqua with white beard quaquaquaqua outside time without extension who from the heights of divine apathia divine athambia divine aphasia loves us dearly with some exceptions for reasons unknown but time will tell and suffers . . . [etc.]

In order to shut him up, the others are forced to knock him over, beat him up, trample on him, and—the only really effective method—to take off his hat. As one of the two vagabonds says: "Thinking isn't the worst."

We cannot overemphasize the seriousness of such reflections. Over seventy centuries of analysis and metaphysics have a tendency, instead of making us modest, to conceal from us the weakness of our resources when it comes to essentials. As a matter of fact, everything happens as if the real importance of a question was measured, precisely, by our incapacity to apply honest thinking to it, unless to make it retrogress.

It is this movement—this dangerously contagious retrogression—which all of Beckett's work suggests. The two confederates, Pozzo and Lucky, have thus declined from one act to the other, in the fashion of Murphy, Molloy, Malone, etc. The carrots have been reduced to radishes. As for the cyclical song of the thieving dog, Didi has even ended by losing the thread of it. And this is in keeping with all the other accessories of the play.

But the two tramps remain intact, unchanged. Hence we are certain, this time, that they are not mere marionettes whose role is confined to concealing the absence of the protagonist. It is not this Godot they are supposed to be waiting for *who has "to be,"* but they, Didi and Gogo.

We grasp at once, as we watch them, this major function of theatrical representation: to show of what the fact of *being there* consists. For it is this, precisely, which we had not yet seen on a stage, or in any case which we had not seen so clearly, with so few concessions. The dramatic character, in most cases, merely *plays a role*, like the people around us who evade their own existence. In Beckett's play, on the contrary, everything happens as if the two tramps were on stage *without having a role.*

They *are there*; they must explain themselves. But they do not seem to have a text prepared beforehand and scrupulously learned by heart, to support them. They must invent. They are free.

Of course, this freedom is without any use: just as they have nothing to recite, they have nothing to *invent* either; and their conversation, which no plot sustains, is reduced to ridiculous fragments: stock responses, puns, more or less abortive phony arguments. They try a little bit of everything, at random. The only thing they are not free to do is to leave, to cease *being there:* they must remain because they are waiting for Godot. They are there in the first act, from the beginning to the end, and when the curtain falls it does so, despite the announcement of their departure, on two men who continue waiting. They are still there in the second act, which brings nothing new; and again, despite the announcement of their departure, they remain on stage when the curtain falls. They will still be there the next day, the day after that, and so on . . . *tomorrow and tomorrow and tomorrow . . . from day to day . . .* alone on stage, standing there, futile, without past or future, irremediably present.

But then man himself, who is there before our eyes, ends by disintegrating in his turn. The curtain rises on a new play: *Endgame*, an "old endgame lost of old," specifies Hamm, the protagonist.

No more than his predecessors, Didi and Gogo, has Hamm the possibility of leaving to go elsewhere. But the reason for this has become tragically physical:

he is paralyzed, sitting in an armchair in the middle of the stage, and he is blind. Around him nothing but high bare walls, without accessible windows. Clov, a kind of attendant, half-impotent himself, tends as well as he can to the moribund Hamm: he manages to take him for a "turn," dragging the latter's chair on its casters around the edge of the stage, along the walls.

In relation to the two tramps, Hamm has therefore lost that ridiculous freedom they still possessed: it is no longer he who chooses *not to leave*. When he asks Clov to build a raft and to put him on it, in order to abandon his body to the ocean currents, it can this time only be a joke; as if Hamm, by immediately abandoning this project, were trying to give himself the illusion of a choice. As a matter of fact, he appears to us somehow imprisoned in his retreat; if he has no desire to emerge from it, he now does not have the means to do so either. This is a notable difference: the question for man is no longer one of affirming a position, but of suffering a fate.

And yet, within his prison, he still performs a parody of choice: he interrupts his "turn" at once, he insists on being pushed to the center, the exact center of the stage; although seeing nothing, he claims to be sensitive to the slightest irregularity in one direction or another.

To be in the middle, to be motionless, is not enough: he must also be rid of all useless accessories; Hamm soon casts out of reach all that he still possesses: a whistle, a stick that he could use, if necessary, to move his chair, a rag dog he could caress. Finally, there must be solitude: "It's the end, Clov, we've come to the end. I don't need you any more."

As a matter of fact, the companion's role does come

to an end: there is no more biscuit, no more pain-killer, there is no more *anything* to give to the invalid. There is nothing left for Clov to do but leave. He does so . . . or at least he decides to do so, but, hat on his head and bag in his hand, while Hamm calls him in vain and perhaps believes he is already far away, Clov remains there, near the open door, his eyes fixed on Hamm, who veils his face with a bloody handkerchief, as the curtain falls.

Thus, even in this final image, we come back to the essential theme of *presence*: everything that is *is here*, off-stage there is only nothingness, nonbeing. It is not enough that Clov, up on a ladder to get to the tiny windows that open onto the outside pseudo-world, informs us with a phrase as to the landscape: an empty gray sea on one side and a desert on the other. In reality this sea, this desert–invisible, moreover, to the spectator–are uninhabitable in the strictest sense of the word: as much as a back cloth would be, on which might be painted the water or the sand. Whence this dialogue: "Why do you stay with me?" "Why do you keep me?" "There's no one else." "There's nowhere else." Hamm, moreover, constantly emphasizes: "Outside of here it's death!" "Gone from me you'd be dead," "Far from me is death," etc.

Similarly, everything is present in time as it is in space. To this ineluctable *here* corresponds an eternal *now*: "Yesterday! What does that mean? Yesterday!" Hamm exclaims several times. And the conjunction of space and time merely affords, with regard to a possible third character, this certitude: "If he exists he'll die there or he'll come here."

Without past, without place elsewhere, without any future but death, the universe thus defined is necessarily deprived of sense in the two acceptations of the term in French: it excludes any idea of *direction* as well as any *signification.*

Hamm is suddenly struck by a doubt: "We're not beginning to . . . to . . . mean something?" he asks with feeling. Clov immediately reassures him: "Mean something! You and I, mean something! *(Brief laugh.)* Ah that's a good one!"

But this waiting for death, this physical misery which grows worse, these threats Hamm brandishes at Clov ("One day you'll be blind, like me. You'll be sitting there, a speck in the void, in the dark, for ever, like me. One day you'll say . . . I'm hungry, I'll get up and get something to eat. But you won't get up . . ."), all this gradual rot of the present constitutes, in spite of everything, a future.

Whence the fear of "meaning something" is perfectly justified: by this accepted consciousness of a tragic development, the world has thereby recovered its whole signification.

And in parallel, before such a threat (this future simultaneously terrible and fatal), one can say that the present is no longer anything, that it disappears, conjured away in its turn, lost in the general collapse. "No more pain-killer . . ." "No more biscuit . . ." "No more bicycle . . ." "No more nature. . . ." *There is no more present*, Clov could finally announce, in the same gloomy and triumphant voice.

"Moments for nothing, now as always . . ." Hamm says in his final monologue, logical conclusion to the phrase repeated many times: "What's happening?" "Something is taking its course." And, finally, Hamm is driven to the acknowledgment of his failure: "I was never there. Clov! . . . I was never there . . . Absent, always. It all happened without me. . . ."

Once again the fatal trajectory has ben made. Hamm and Clov, successors to Gogo and Didi, have again met with the common fate of all Beckett's characters: Pozzo, Lucky, Murphy, Molloy, Malone, Mahood, Worm, etc.

The stage, privileged site of *presence*, has not resisted the contagion for long. The progress of the disease has occurred at the same sure rate as in the narratives. After having believed for a moment that we had grasped the real man, we are then obliged to confess our mistake. Didi was only an illusion, that is doubtless what gave him that dancing gait, swaying from one leg to the other, that slightly clownlike costume. . . . He, too, was only the creature of a dream, temporary in any case, quickly falling back into the realm of dreams and fiction.

"I was never there," Hamm says, and in the face of this admission nothing else counts, for it is impossible to understand it other than in its most general form: *No one was ever there.*

And if, after *Godot* and *Endgame*, there now comes a third play, it will probably be *The Unnamable* again, third panel of the trilogy of novels. Hamm already enables us to imagine its tone, by the novel he makes up as he goes along, creating sham situations and manipulating phantoms of characters into action. Since he is not there himself, there is nothing left for him now but to tell himself stories, to operate marionettes, in his place, to help pass the time. . . . Unless Samuel Beckett is reserving new surprises for us. . . .

A NOVEL THAT INVENTS ITSELF (1954)

"I can't get it out of my mind: a book—what a presumption in one sense, but what an extraordinary wonder if it is spoiled in its broad outlines." Thus Robert Pinget informs us of his ambitions, and this honest writer (the type is not so frequent), who has focused all his attention for several years now on *spoiling* his books in their broad outlines, is going virtually unnoticed—even by the specialists, professionally drowned in the daily flood of linear narratives, successful ones—whereas these books (Pinget's), apparently *without head or tail*, may already be precisely the "extraordinary wonders" prophesied.

We must try to retrace, if not their anecdotes—which are described and dissolved on every page in contradictions, variants, and dangerous leaps resulting, more often than not, in fantastic reversals—at least the *movement* which, if it is sometimes difficult to grasp amid this permanent sabotage, is never, ultimately, either foolhardy or conventional.

Mahu ou le Materiau [Mahu or the Raw Material]: this title is already a program. The characters of this *novel* belong neither to the realm of psychology nor to that of sociology, nor even to symbolism, still less to history or ethics; they are *pure creations* which derive only from the spirit of creation. Their existence, beyond a confused past of dreams and ineffable impressions, is merely a process without purpose, subject from sentence to sentence to the most extravagant mutations, at the mercy of the least thought passing through the mind, of the least word in the air, of the most fugitive suspicion. Yet they *make themselves*, but instead of each of them creating his own reality, it is an *ensemble* that is produced, a kind of living tissue each cell of which sprouts and shapes its neighbors; these characters continuously create each other, the world around them is merely a secretion—one could almost say the *waste product*—of their suppositions, of their lies, of their delirium. Of course, this mode of growth is not very healthy, it suggests some pathological proliferation more than the development of the grain of wheat directly oriented toward the productive sheaf. The story, in this regard, can only turn in circles, unless it stops short, unashamedly turning back on itself; still elsewhere it branches off, divides into two or more parallel series which immediately react on each other, destroy each other, or unite in an unexpected synthesis.

Here are the novelist Lattirail, Mademoiselle Lorpailleur, also a novelist, the postal clerk Sinture who delays and falsifies the mail, Petite-Fiente, a perverse little girl who *makes up stories*, Juan Simon, Mahu's boss, the Pinson boy, Julia, etc. We are already not sure whether some of them may not have been invented by the others. What can we say, then, of the host of more or less episodic walk-ons, materializations of the thoughts of one or another protagonist, who appear and vanish, transform themselves, multiply, drop out and create in their turn new fictions which mingle with the story and soon turn against the reality from which they had emerged.

Mahu himself—is he really a witness of this phantasmagoria? Or is he its god? Or quite simply, is he, like the others, one of the fictions with a humorously tragic fate which haunt this country between Fantoine and Agapa, absurd suburb of reality? Mahu first emerges with difficulty from his sleep and from a series of fourteen brothers of the same age; he thinks he must find an office *to go to,* like the others. He takes only the photograph which decorated the wall of his room: some figs which "make a hole" in him when he looks at them. He finds an employer, Juan Simon, who tries to correspond with his clientele without the intervention of the postal clerk Sinture. Petite-Fiente, Juan Simon's daughter, claims to have been slapped by Mahu . . . or not to have been slapped, we don't know . . . or rather to have slapped him herself. . . . The account develops in a few pages an extraordinarily uncomfortable complexity, which it is unfortunately not possible to analyze here; also, later when the two novelists and the postal clerk, all of whom openly claim to be *writing the story,* intervene, the story then cheerfully exceeds the limits of the incomprehensible. At a loss, Mahu goes back home, rid at last, he believes, of all this jumble of "soft characters." The last hundred pages of the book are no more than raw material, brief fragments of decomposed reality which turn out to be at least as curious as all that preceded, as rich, as fascinating: words which fall from the sky without leaving traces, children who speak "backwards," a little piece of ear that moves near a column in a public meeting. . . . It is henceforth impossible to say whether Robert Pinget is a scrupulous experimenter in his laboratory or a visionary abusing his drugs. The narrative closes on this *enigmatic* conclusion: "There. I have nothing more to say, nonetheless everything is left in me, I have won."

But inescapably, for "the honor of continuing," everything begins all over again. This time it is called *Le Renard et la Boussole* [The Fox and the Compass]. The new novel begins in a sort of gray shadow with an awakening, as usual; *possibilities* lurk in the corners —possible lives, possible literatures. . . . A novel, we are told, a real novel should begin with an "I was born . . ." but something else is trying to slip under the pen here, turns, returns insistently: "I was pricked with a long needle. . . ." This must be made clear: "The birth of an object, I have noticed, does not take place today, there is movement all around which keeps it from showing its head and tomorrow you realize that it exists. Consequently the best explanation of origins would be to begin by mouth noises and to shift gradually in the direction of articulated words until the moment when the listener without asking himself a single question is participating in your story." This is precisely what happens here; gradually, among digressions and collapses, a spot of reddish color establishes itself in the picture (the heroes are painters in *Le Renard*, as they were novelists in *Mahu*). This initially indistinct mass soon assumes the shape of a fox, which decomposes into several characters, one of whom is none other than David, the Wandering Jew. This fox invents a journey, a trip to Israel. There follows a kind of report on life in the *kibbutzim*, occasionally interrupted by Biblical evocations and other digressions, apparitions of pharaohs and sultans, still more unexpected encounters—those for example of Don Quixote and of his Castilian desert. The documentary peters out, in the heat of the Palestinian summer. The narrator is anxious about the lassitude he detects in the reader and in himself, as in his travelers: "This isn't going well," he says, "could they have come back already?" Yet Renard and David then make the acquaintance of Marie-Madeleine, known as "Mama," who will help them to re-embark, then the more important acquaintance of the crouching Scribe: "Be careful. . . . Don't talk to him, he writes everything down." As a matter of fact, he immediately transcribes his own encounter. . . . "A fact, one among billions, they are denied all value in practice, they are transcribed, they are transcribed, that's all."

And as if it were the most natural thing in the world, Renard, who has for a long time been identified with the narrator (named John Tintouin Porridge), finds himself back in Fantoine. Mahu and the others reproach him for having left them for a while. Doesn't he like them any more? "But of course I like you, we're bound together for life . . . here I am." Amid the apéritifs and the muddy strolls of the return appears Mademoiselle Lorpailleur, the novelist; she asks John what he was planning to do. He vaguely recalls that he was planning a study of Mary Stuart, he has mentioned *origins*, "afterwards it branched out." Then she gives him this advice: a book—a book always begins with "I was born. . . ." And this one ends paradoxically with a whole collection of possible beginnings, all opening with these three words, but degenerating at the end into a cacophony of unfinished sentences, cries, stammerings, and other "mouth noises."

Once again, everything is to be done all over again. Yet, in a sense (the only one that matters to us), Robert Pinget has still "won."

NEW NOVEL, NEW MAN

(1961)

A great deal has been written about the "New Novel" in the last few years. Unfortunately, among the criticism that has been lavished upon it, and also, frequently, among the praise, there have been so many extreme simplifications, so many errors, so many misunderstandings, that a kind of monstrous myth has been promulgated in the mind of the public at large, for whom, apparently, the New Novel is henceforth precisely the opposite of what it is for us.

And so it will suffice for me to pass in review the most obvious of these absurd notions that circulate from pen to mouth with regard to the New Novel, in order to give a good idea of the general program of our movement's actual enterprise: each time that general supposition, or the specialized criticism which both reflects and sustains it, attributes an intention to us, it can be asserted without much risk of error that our intention is exactly the contrary.

So much for intentions. Of course, there are the works, and they are what count. But of the works, the writers themselves are obviously not the judges. Further, it is always for what are supposedly our intentions that we are condemned: the detractors of our novels claim that they are the result of our pernicious theories, while those who find our novels good insist they have been written *against* our theories!

Here then is the charter of the New Novel as general supposition circulates it: 1) The New Novel has codified the laws of the future novel. 2) The New Novel has made a *tabula rasa* of the past. 3) The New Novel seeks to eliminate man from the world. 4) The New Novel aims at a perfect objectivity. 5) The New Novel, difficult to read, is addressed only to specialists.

And now, taking the exact opposite of each of these notions, here is what it would be more reasonable to say:

The New Novel is not a theory, it is an exploration.

It has therefore codified no law. Which means that there is no question of a literary school in the narrow sense of the phrase. We are the first to realize that there are among our respective works—between those of Claude Simon and my own, for example—considerable differences, and we believe that this is a good thing. What interest would there be in the two of us writing, if we were writing the same thing?

But have such differences not always existed within all "schools"? What is found in common between individuals, in each of the literary movements of our history, is chiefly the desire to escape a sclerosis, the need for *something else*. Around what have artists always grouped themselves, if not the rejection of the outworn forms still being imposed on them? Forms live and die, in all the realms of art, and in all periods they have had to be continually renewed: the composition of the novel of the nineteenth-century type, which was life itself a hundred years ago, is no longer anything but an empty formula, serving only as the basis for tiresome parodies.

Hence, far from dictating rules, theories, laws, either for others or for ourselves, we have, on the contrary, come together in a struggle against laws that are too rigid. There was, there still is, particularly in France, a theory of the novel implicitly recognized by everyone or nearly everyone, a theory that is thrown up like a wall against all the books we have published. We are told: "You do not create characters, hence you are not writing true novels," "you are not telling stories, hence you are not writing true novels," "you are not studying psychology or milieu, you are not analyzing passions, hence you are not writing true novels," etc.

But we, on the contrary, who are accused of being theoreticians, we do not know what a novel, a true novel, should be; we know only that the novel today will be what we make it, today, and that it is not our job to cultivate a resemblance to what it was yesterday, but to advance beyond.

The New Novel is merely pursuing a constant evolution of the genre.

The error is to suppose that the "true novel" was set once and for all in the Balzacian period, with strict and definitive rules. Not only has the development been considerable since the middle of the nineteenth century, but it began immediately, in Balzac's own period. Did not Balzac already note the "confusion" in the descriptions of *The Charterhouse of Parma*? It is obvious that the Battle of Waterloo, as described by Stendhal, no longer belongs to the Balzacian order.

And, since then, the evolution has become increasingly evident: Flaubert, Dostoevski, Proust, Kafka, Joyce, Faulkner, Beckett. . . . Far from making a *tabula rasa* of the past, we have most readily reached an agreement on the names of our predecessors; and our ambition is merely to continue them. Not to *do better*, which has no meaning, but to situate ourselves in their wake, now, in our own time.

The construction of our books is, moreover, disconcerting only if one insists on looking in them for the trace of elements which have actually disappeared in the last twenty, thirty, or forty years from all living novels, or have at least singularly disintegrated: characters, chronology, sociological studies, etc. The New Novel will in any case have had the merit of bringing to the awareness of a rather large (and continually growing) public a general evolution of the genre, whereas there has been a persistent attempt to deny it, relegating in principle Kafka, Faulkner, and all the others to vague marginal zones, when they are, quite simply, the great novelists of the first half of the century.

And in the last twenty years, no doubt, matters have accelerated, but not only in the realm of art, as everyone will agree. If the reader sometimes has difficulty getting his bearings in the modern novel, it is in the same way that he sometimes loses them in the very world where he lives, when everything in the old structures and the old norms around him is giving way.

The New Novel is interested only in man and in his situation in the world.

Since there were not, in our books, "characters" in the traditional sense of the word, it was concluded, somewhat hastily, that men were not to be found there at all. This was to read them very badly indeed. Man is present on every page, in every line, in every word. Even if many objects are presented and are described with great care, there is always, and especially, the eye which sees them, the thought which reexamines them, the passion which distorts them. The objects in our novels never have a presence outside human perception, real or imaginary; they are objects comparable to those in our daily lives, as they occupy our minds at every moment.

And, if the object is taken in its general sense (object, according to the dictionary: whatever affects the senses), it is natural that there should be only objects in my books: there is also, in my life, the furniture in my room, the words I hear, or the woman I love, that woman's gestures, etc. And, in a broader sense (object, according to the dictionary once again: whatever preoccupies the mind), objects will be, further, memory (by which I turn back to past objects), intention (which projects me toward future objects: if I decide to go swimming, I already see the beach and the sea in my mind), and every form of imagination.

As for what is called more precisely *things*, there

have always been many of them in the novel. Recall Balzac: houses, furnishings, clothes, jewels, tools, machines, everything described with a care which has nothing to envy in modern works. If such objects are, as it is said, more "human" than ours, it is only—and we shall come back to this—that man's situation in the world he inhabits is no longer the same today as it was a hundred years ago. And not at all because our description is too neutral, too objective, since in fact it is not "neutral" at all.

The New Novel aims only at a total subjectivity.

Since there were many objects in our books, and since there was something unaccustomed about them, a special meaning was quickly attached to the word "objectivity," uttered in their regard by certain critics, though in a very special sense: oriented toward the object. Taken in its habitual sense—neutral, cold, impartial—the word became an absurdity. Not only is it *a man* who, in my novels for instance, describes everything, but it is the least neutral, the least impartial of men: *always* engaged, on the contrary, in an emotional adventure of the most obsessive kind, to the point of often distorting his vision and of producing imaginings close to delirium.

Hence it is easy to show that my novels—like those of all my friends—are more subjective in fact than Balzac's, for example. Who is describing the world in Balzac's novels? Who is that omniscient, omnipresent narrator appearing everywhere at once, simultaneously seeing the outside and the inside of things, following both the movements of a face and the impulses of conscience, knowing the present, the past, and the future of every enterprise? It can only be a God.

It is God alone who can claim to be objective. While in our books, on the contrary, it is *a man* who sees, who feels, who imagines, a man located in space and time, conditioned by his passions, a man like you and me. And the book reports nothing but his experience, limited and uncertain as it is. It is a man here, now, who is his own narrator, finally.

It is doubtless sufficient to cease blinding oneself to this evident truth to realize that our books are within the grasp of any reader, once he agrees to free himself from ready-made ideas, in literature as in life.

The New Novel is addressed to all men of good faith.

For what is at issue here is an experience of life, not reassuring—and at the same time despairing—schemas which try to limit the damages and to assign a conventional order to our existence, to our passions. Why seek to reconstruct the time of clocks in a narrative which is concerned only with human time? Is it not wiser to think of our own memory, which is *never* chronological? Why persist in discovering what an individual's name is in a novel which does not supply it? Every day we meet people whose names we do not know, and we can talk to a stranger for a whole evening, when we have not even paid any attention to the introductions made by the hostess.

Our books are written with the words, the phrases of everyone, of every day. They afford no special difficulty to those who are not trying to paste on them a grid of dated interpretations which have already ceased to be valid for nearly fifty years. We may even inquire if a certain literary culture, in fact, does not make it more difficult to understand them: a culture which came to an end around 1900. While quite simple people, who do not know Kafka perhaps, but who are also not beclouded by the Balzacian forms, find themselves able to deal with books in which they recognize the world they live in and their own thoughts, and which, instead of deceiving them as to the signification of their existence, will help them to consider it more lucidly.

The New Novel does not propose a ready-made signification.

Which brings us to the major question: does our life have a meaning? What is it? What is man's place on earth? We see at once why the Balzacian objects were so reassuring: they belonged to a world of which man was the master; such objects were chattels, properties, which it was merely a question of possessing, or retaining, or acquiring. There was a constant identity between these objects and their owner: a simple waistcoat was already a character and a social position at the same time. Man was the reason for all things, the key to the universe, and its natural master, by divine right. . . .

Not much of all this is left today. While the bourgeois class was gradually losing its justifications and its prerogatives, thought was abandoning its essentialist bases, phenomenology was increasingly occupying the whole field of philosophical investigations, the physical sciences were discovering the realm of the discontinuous, psychology itself was undergoing, in a parallel fashion, a transformation just as total.

The significations of the world around us are no more than partial, provisional, even contradictory, and always contested. How could the work of art claim to illustrate a signification known in advance, whatever it might be? The modern novel, as we said at the start, is an exploration, but an exploration which itself creates it own significations, as it proceeds. Does reality have a meaning? The contemporary artist cannot answer this question: he knows nothing about it. All he can say is that this reality will perhaps have a meaning after he has existed, that is, once the work is brought to its conclusion.

Why regard this as a pessimism? In any case, it is the contrary of a renunciation. We no longer believe in the fixed significations, the ready-made meanings which afforded man the old divine order and subsequently the rationalist order of the nineteenth century, but we project onto man all our hopes: it is the forms man creates which can attach significations to the world.

The only possible commitment for the writer is literature.

It is not reasonable, henceforth, to claim in our novels to serve a political cause, even a cause which seems just to us, even if in our political life we advocate its victory. Political life ceaselessly obliges us to assume certain known significations: social, historical, moral. Art is more modest—or more ambitious: in art, nothing is ever known in advance.

Before the work of art, there is nothing—no certainty, no thesis, no message. To believe that the novelist has "something to say" and that he then looks for a way to say it represents the gravest of misconceptions. For it is precisely this "way," this manner of speaking, which constitutes his enterprise as a writer, an enterprise more obscure than any other, and which will later be the uncertain content of his book. Ultimately it is perhaps this uncertain content of an obscure enterprise of form which will best serve the cause of freedom. But who knows how long that will take?

TIME AND DESCRIPTION IN FICTION TODAY (1963)

Criticism is a difficult thing, much more so than art, in a sense. Whereas the novelist, for example, can rely on his sensibility alone, without always trying to understand its options, and while the mere reader is satisfied to know whether or not he is affected by the book, whether or not the book interests him, whether or not he likes it, whether or not it offers him something, the critic, on the other hand, is supposed to give the reasons for all this: he must account for what the book gives, say why he likes it, offer absolute value judgments.

Now there are values only for the past. These values, which alone can serve as criteria, have been instituted upon the great works of our fathers, of our grandfathers, often even upon works still older. It is these works which, once rejected because they did not correspond to the values of the period, have brought new significations into the world, new values, new criteria on which we are living today.

But today, as yesterday, new works have no reason to exist unless they bring into the world in their turn new significations, still unknown to the authors themselves, significations which will exist only later, thanks to these works, and on which society will institute new values . . . which again will be of no use, or even be harmful, when it comes to judging the literature in progress.

The critic is thus put in this paradoxical position: he is obliged to judge contemporary works by employing criteria which, at best, do not concern them. Which means that the artist is right to be dissatisfied with criticism, but that he is wrong to believe in a deliberate nastiness or stupidity on the part of the critic. Since he is in the process of inventing a new world, and new measurements, he must admit that it is difficult, if not impossible, to measure it himself and to establish a just accounting of its merits and its faults.

The best possible method is still to extrapolate, and this is precisely what vital criticism attempts to do. Taking as its foundation the historical evolution of forms and of their significations, in the Western novel, for example, criticism can attempt to imagine what tomorrow's significations will be, and then to offer a provisional judgment as to the forms the artist affords it today.

It is evident that such a method may be dangerous, for it supposes an evolution that follows predictable rules. And things are further complicated when we are dealing with too recent an art—the cinema, for example, in which the lack of perspective makes any extrapolation impracticable. Hence it is not always useless for authors, though they possess by nature no more insight than critics, to offer their "theoretical" contribution to this investigation.

Notice has often been taken, and with reason, of the considerable space occupied by descriptions in what is conventionally called the New Novel, in particular in my own books. Although these descriptions—motionless objects or fragments of scenes—have in general acted on the readers in a satisfactory fashion, the judgment many specialists make of them remains pejorative. They are found to be useless and confused: useless, because without real relation to the action; confused, because not playing what should be, apparently, their fundamental role: to make the reader see.

It has even been said, with reference to the supposed intentions of the authors, that these contemporary novels were merely abortive films, and that the camera should be performing the function of the inadequate pen. First, the cinematographic image would show at once in a few seconds' projection what literature vainly tries to represent in some dozens of pages; further, the superfluous details would of necessity be restored to their proper place, the apple pip on the floor no longer threatening to invade the entire setting in which the scene takes place.

All of which would be true if this were not to misunderstand precisely what constitutes the meaning of these descriptions offered in the novel today. Once again, it seems that it is indeed by reference to the past that the present explorations are judged (and condemned).

Let us admit, first of all, that description is not a modern invention. The great French novels of the nineteenth century in particular, Balzac's first of all, are crammed with houses, furnishings, costumes, exhaustively and scrupulously described, not to mention faces, bodies, etc. And it is certain that such descriptions have as their goal to make the reader see, and that they succeed in doing so. It was then generally a question of establishing a setting, of defining the context of the action, of presenting the physical appearance of the protagonists. The weight of things thus posited in a precise fashion constituted a stable and certain universe, to which one could then refer, and which guaranteed by its resemblance to the "real" world the authenticity of the events, the words, the gestures which the novelist would cause to occur there. The calm assurance with which the arrangement of sites, the decoration of interiors, the style of costumes were established, as also the social or characterological signs contained in each element and by which the latter justified its presence, finally the proliferation of these precise details on which it seemed that one could draw indefinitely, all this could only convince the reader of the objective existence—outside literature—of a world which the novelist seemed merely to reproduce, to copy, to transmit, as if one were dealing with a chronicle, a biography, a document of some kind.

This world of the novel lived, indeed, the same life as its model: in it one followed in the wake of the years. Not only from one chapter to the next, but often at the first encounter, it was easy to recognize in the most modest domestic object, in the least feature of a countenance, the patina created by use, the erosion caused by time.

Thus this setting was already the image of man: each of the walls or the furnishings of the house represented a double of the person who inhabited it—rich or poor, severe or vainglorious—and was in addition subject to the same destiny, to the same fatality. The reader overly concerned to know the story could even consider himself justified in skipping the descriptions: they involved only a frame, which moreover happened to have a meaning identical to that of the picture it was to contain.

Obviously, when this same reader skips the descriptions in our books, he is in danger of finding himself, having turned all the pages one after the other with a rapid forefinger, at the end of the volume whose contents will have escaped him altogether; imagining he has been dealing hitherto with nothing but the frame, he will still be looking for the picture.

This is because the place and the role of description have changed completely. While the preoccupations of a descriptive order were invading the entire novel, they were at the same time losing their traditional meaning. Preliminary definitions are no longer in question. Description once served to situate the chief contours of a setting, then to cast light on some of its particularly revealing elements; it no longer mentions anything except insignificant objects, or objects which it is concerned to make so. It once claimed to reproduce a pre-existing reality; it now asserts its creative function. Finally, it once made us see things, now it seems to destroy them, as if its intention to discuss them aimed only at blurring their contours, at making them incomprehensible, at causing them to disappear altogether.

It is not rare, as a matter of fact, in these modern novels, to encounter a description that starts from nothing; it does not afford, first of all, a general view, it seems to derive from a tiny fragment without importance—what most resembles a *point*—starting from which it invents lines, planes, an architecture; and such description particularly seems to be inventing its object when it suddenly contradicts, repeats, corrects itself, bifurcates, etc. Yet we begin to glimpse something, and we suppose that this something will now become clearer. But the lines of the drawing accumulate, grow heavier, cancel one another out, shift, so that the image is jeopardized as it is created. A few paragraphs more and, when the description comes to an end, we realize that it has left nothing behind it: it has instituted a double movement of creation and destruction which, moreover, we also find in the book on all levels and in particular in its total structure—whence the *disappointment* inherent in many works of today.

The concern for precision which sometimes borders on the delirious (those notions so nonvisual as "right" and "left," those calculations, those measurements, those geometric points of reference) does not manage to keep the world from moving even in its most material aspects, and even at the heart of its apparent immobility. It is no longer a question here of time passing, since gestures paradoxically are on the contrary shown only frozen in the moment. It is matter itself which is both solid and unstable, both present and imagined, alien to man and constantly being invented in man's mind. The entire interest of the descriptive pages—that is, man's place in these pages—is therefore no longer in the thing described, but in the very movement of the description.

We thus see how false it is to say that such writing tends toward photography or toward the cinematographic image. That image, taken in isolation can only make us see, in the fashion of Balzacian description, and would therefore seem made on the contrary to replace the latter, which the naturalistic cinema, in fact, does not fail to do.

The definite attraction which cinematographic creation exercises upon many new novelists must be sought elsewhere. It is not the camera's objectivity which interests them, but its possibilities in the realm of the subjective, of the imaginary. They do not conceive the cinema as a means of expression, but of exploration, and what most captures their attention is, quite naturally, what has most escaped the powers of literature: which is not so much the image as the sound track—the sound of voices, noises, atmospheres, music—and above all the possibility of acting on two senses at once, the eye and the ear; finally, in the image as in the sound, the possibility of presenting with all the appearance of incontestable objectivity what is, also, only dream or memory—in a word, what is only imagination.

There is in the sound the spectator hears, in the image he sees, a primary quality: it is *there*, it is present. The breaks of cutting, the repetitions of scene, the contradictions, the characters suddenly paralyzed as in amateur photographs afford this perpetual present all its force, all its violence. It is, then, no longer a question of the nature of the images but of their composition, and it is only here that the novelist can recognize, though transformed, certain of his literary preoccupations.

These new cinematic structures, this movement of images and sounds, turn out to be directly apparent to the unprejudiced spectator; it even seems that for many, their power is infinitely stronger than that of literature. But they also set up, within traditional criticism, even more powerful defense reactions.

I discovered this from personal experience during the release of my second film (*L'Immortelle*). Of course, there is no occasion to be surprised at the unfavorable judgments offered by the majority of newspaper reviewers; but it may be interesting to note certain of their censures, often more revealing than praise. Here, then, are the points on which the most frequent and the most violent attacks were centered: first of all, the lack of "naturalness" in the performance of the actors; then the impossibility of distinguishing clearly what is "real" from what is mental (memory or hallucination); lastly, the tendency of the elements with a strong emotional charge to be transformed into "post cards" (sightseeing for the city of Istanbul, erotic for the heroine, etc.).

We see that these three censures constitute, basically, one and the same reproach: the film's structure does not afford enough confidence in the objective truth of things. Two remarks on this subject come to mind. First, Istanbul is a *real* city, and it is indeed Istanbul that we see from one end of the film to the other; similarly, the heroine is embodied on the screen by a *real* woman. Further, with regard to the story, it is obvious that it is untrue: neither the actor nor the actress died during the making of the film, nor did even the dog. What disturbs the spectators fond of "realism" is that there is no longer any effort to make them believe in anything—I would almost say: on the contrary. . . . The *real*, the *false*, and *illusion* become more or less the subject of all modern works; this one, instead of claiming to be a piece of reality, is developed as a reflection on reality (or on the *dearth of reality*, as Breton calls it). It no longer seeks to conceal its necessarily deceptive character by offering itself as a "real-life story." So that we rediscover here, in the cinematographic style, a function related to that assumed by description in literature: the image thus treated (with regard to the actors, the set, the cutting, in its relations with the sound, etc.) keeps us from believing at the same time what it affirms, just as description kept us from seeing what it was showing. . . .

It is this same paradoxical movement (to construct while destroying) that we also find in the treatment of time. The film and the novel present themselves initially in the form of temporal sequences—contrary, for example, to plastic works, paintings or sculptures. The film, like the musical work, is even timed in a definitive fashion (whereas the duration of a reading can vary infinitely, from one page to the next, and from one individual to the next). On the other hand, as we have said, the cinema knows only one grammatical mode: the present tense of the indicative. In any case, film and novel today meet in the construction of moments, of intervals, and of sequences which no longer have anything to do with those of clocks or calendars. Let us try to specify their role a little.

It has very often been repeated in recent years that time was the chief "character" of the contemporary novel. Since Proust, since Faulkner, the flashback, the break in chronology seem in effect at the basis of the very organization of the narrative, of its architecture. The same is obviously true of the cinema: every modern cinematographic work is a reflection on human memory, its uncertainties, its persistence, its dramas, etc.

All of which is said a little too quickly. Or rather,

if passing time is indeed the essential character of many works of the early part of this century, and of those which follow them, as it had been, moreover, of works of the last century, present investigations seem on the contrary to be concerned, most often, with private mental structures of "time." And this is precisely what makes them on first exposure so disconcerting. I shall take several examples, again from my own books or films, whose meaning, on this point, has almost always been falsified by the critics.

Last Year at Marienbad, because of its title and because, too, of the works previously directed by Alain Resnais, has from the start been interpreted as one of those psychological variations on lost love, on forgetting, on memory. The questions most often asked were: Have this man and this woman really met before? Did they love each other last year at Marienbad? Does the young woman remember and is she only pretending not to recognize the handsome stranger? Or has she really forgotten everything that has happened between them? etc. Matters must be put clearly: such questions have no meaning. The universe in which the entire film occurs is, characteristically, that of a perpetual present which makes all recourse to memory impossible. This is a world without a past, a world which is self-sufficient at every moment and which obliterates itself as it proceeds. This man, this woman begin existing only when they appear on the screen the first time; before that they are nothing; and, once the projection is over, they are again nothing. Their existence lasts only as long as the film lasts. There can be no reality outside the images we see, the words we hear.

Thus the duration of the modern work is in no way

a summary, a condensed version, of a more extended and more "real" duration which would be that of the anecdote, of the narrated story. There is, on the contrary, an absolute identity between the two durations. The entire story of *Marienbad* happens neither in two years nor in three days, but exactly in one hour and a half. And when at the end of the film the hero and heroine meet in order to leave together, it is as if the young woman were admitting that there had indeed been something between them last year at Marienbad, but we understand that it was precisely last year during the entire projection, and that we were at Marienbad. This love story we were being told as a thing of the past was in fact actually happening before our eyes, here and now. For of course an *elsewhere* is no more possible than a *formerly*.

But, it will be asked, what do the scenes we have watched represent, under these conditions? What, in particular, is signified by these successions of daylight and nighttime shots or these excessive costume changes, incompatible with such a brief duration? It is at this point, of course, that matters become complicated. It can here be a question only of a subjective, mental, personal occurrence. These things must be happening in someone's mind. But whose? The narrator-hero's? Or the hypnotized heroine's? Or else, by a constant exchange of images between them, in the minds of both, together? It would be better to admit a solution of another order: just as the only time which matters is that of the film itself, the only important "character" is the spectator; *in his mind* unfolds the whole story, which is precisely *imagined* by him.

Once again, the work is not a testimony offered in

evidence concerning an external reality, but is its own reality for itself. Hence it is impossible for the author to reassure a spectator concerned about the fate of the hero after the words "The End." After the words "The End" nothing at all happens, by definition. The only future which the work can accept is a new, identical performance: by putting the reels back in the projection camera.

Similarly, it was absurd to suppose that in the novel *Jealousy*, published two years earlier, there existed a clear and unambiguous order of events, one which was not that of the sentences of the book, as if I had diverted myself by mixing up a pre-established calendar the way one shuffles a deck of cards. The narrative was on the contrary made in such a way that any attempt to reconstruct an external chronology would lead, sooner or later, to a series of contradictions, hence to an impasse. And this not with the stupid intention of disconcerting the Academy, but precisely because there existed for me no possible order outside of that of the book. The latter was not a narrative mingled with a simple anecdote external to itself, but again the very unfolding of a story which had no other reality than that of the narrative, an occurrence which functioned nowhere else except in the mind of the invisible narrator, in other words of the writer, and of the reader.

How could this present conception of the work permit time to be the chief character of the book, or of the film? Is it not rather to the traditional novel, to the Balzacian novel, for example, that this definition would apply? There time played a role, and the chief one: it completed man, it was the agent and measurement of his fate. Whether involved in an ascent or a collapse, it realized a process, at once a pledge of the triumph of a society conquering the world, and a fatality of nature: man's mortal condition. Passions, like events, could be envisaged only in a temporal development: birth, growth, paroxysm, decline and fall.

But in the modern narrative, time seems to be cut off from its temporality. It no longer passes. It no longer completes anything. And this is doubtless what explains the disappointment which follows the reading of today's books, or the projection of today's films. As much as there was something satisfying in a "destiny," even a tragic one, by so much do the finest works of our contemporaries leave us empty, out of countenance. Not only do they claim no other reality than that of the reading, or of the performance, but further they always seem to be in the process of contesting, of jeopardizing themselves in proportion as they create themselves. Here space destroys time, and time sabotages space. Description makes no headway, contradicts itself, turns in circles. Moment denies continuity.

Now, if temporality gratifies expectation, instantaneity disappoints it; just as spatial discontinuity *dissolves* the trap of the anecdote. These descriptions whose movement destroys all confidence in the things described, these heroes without naturalness as without identity, this present which constantly invents itself, as though in the course of the very writing, which repeats, doubles, modifies, denies itself, without ever accumulating in order to constitute a past—hence a "story," a "history" in the traditional sense of the word—all this can only invite the reader (or the spectator) to another mode of participation than the one to which he was accustomed. If he is sometimes led to condemn the works of his time, that is, those which most directly address him, if he even complains of being deliberately abandoned, held off, disdained by the authors, this is solely because he persists in seeking a kind of communication which has long since ceased to be the one which is proposed to him.

For, far from neglecting him, the author today proclaims his absolute need of the reader's cooperation, an active, conscious, *creative* assistance. What he asks of him is no longer to receive ready-made a world completed, full, closed upon itself, but on the contrary to participate in a creation, to invent in his turn the work—and the world—and thus to learn to invent his own life.

FROM REALISM TO REALITY
(1955 and 1963)

All writers believe they are realists. None ever calls himself abstract, illusionistic, chimerical, fantastic, falsitical. . . . Realism is not a theory, defined without ambiguity, which would permit us to counter certain writers by certain others; it is, on the contrary, a flag under which the enormous majority—if not all—of today's novelists enlist. And no doubt we must believe them all, on this point. It is the real world which interests them; each one attempts as best as can to create "the real."

But if they are mustered under this flag, it is not to wage common combat there; it is in order to tear one another to pieces. Realism is the ideology which each brandishes against his neighbor, the quality which each believes he possesses for himself alone. And it has always been the same: out of a concern for realism each new literary school has sought to destroy the one which preceded it; this was the watchword of the romantics against the classicists, then of the naturalists against the romantics; the surrealists themselves declared in their turn that they were concerned only with the real world. Realism, among writers, seems as widely distributed as "common sense" according to Descartes.

And, here too, we must conclude that all of them are right. If they do not understand each other, it is because each one has different ideas about reality. The classicists believed that it is classical, the romantics that it is romantic, the surrealists that it is surreal, Claudel that it is of a divine nature, Camus that it is absurd, the "committed" writers that it is chiefly economic and tends toward socialism. Each speaks of the world as he sees it, but no one sees it in the same way.

It is easy, moreover, to understand why literary revolutions have always been made in the name of realism. When a form of writing has lost its initial vitality, its force, its violence, when it has become a vulgar recipe, an academic mannerism which its followers respect only out of routine or laziness, without even questioning its necessity, then it is indeed a return to the real which constitutes the arraignment of the dead formulas and the search for new forms capable of continuing the effort. The discovery of reality will continue only if we abandon outworn forms. Unless we suppose that the world is henceforth entirely discovered (and, in that case, the wisest thing would be to stop writing altogether), we can only attempt to go farther. It is not a question of "doing better," but of advancing in ways as yet unknown, in which a new kind of writing becomes necessary.

What is the use, it will be asked, if it only concludes,

after a more or less long interval, in a new formalism, soon as sclerotic as the old one was? Which comes down to asking why we should go on living, since we must die and make way for others. Art is life. Nothing, in art, is ever won *for good*. Art cannot exist without this permanent condition of being *put in question*. But the movement of these evolutions and revolutions constitutes its perpetual renaissance.

And then the world, too, changes. On the one hand, it is no longer objectively the same, on many points, as a hundred years ago, for example; material life, intellectual life, political life have been considerably modified, as has the physical aspect of our cities, our houses, our villages, our roads, etc. On the other hand, our knowledge of what is within us and of what surrounds us (scientific knowledge, whether involving the sciences of matter or the sciences of man) has undergone, in parallel fashion, extraordinary upheavals. On account of the one and the other, the subjective relations we entertain with the world have utterly changed.

The objective modifications of reality, combined with the "progress" of our physical knowledge, have reverberated profoundly–and continue to reverberate–in our philosophical conceptions, our metaphysics, our ethics. Hence, even if the novel were only to reproduce reality, it would scarcely be natural for the foundations of its realism not to have evolved in parallel with these transformations. To account for what is real today, the nineteenth-century novel would not be at all the "good tool" which Soviet criticism–with even more tranquil assurance than bourgeois criticism–constantly reproaches the New Novel for casting away, when it could still serve (we are told) to reveal to the masses the evils of today's world and the remedies in fashion, with (if need be) some improvements in detail, as if it were a matter of perfecting a hammer or a sickle. To keep to this image of the tool, no one regards a diesel thresher as a perfected version of the sickle, a fortiori in the case of a machine which serves in a harvest without any relation to that of wheat.

But there is something more serious involved. As we have already had occasion to specify in the course of this work, the novel is not a tool at all. It is not conceived with a view to a task defined in advance. It does not serve to set forth, to translate things existing before it, outside it. It does not express, it explores, and what it explores is itself.

Academic criticism in the West, as in the Communist countries, employs the word "realism" as if reality were already entirely constituted (whether for good and all, or not) when the writer comes on the scene. Thus it supposes that the latter's role is limited to "explaining" and to "expressing" the reality of his period.

Realism, according to this point of view, merely requires from the novel that it respect the truth. The author's qualities would be, chiefly, perspicacity in observation and the constant concern for plain speaking (often allied to plain speech). Apart from socialist realism's absolute repugnance for adultery and sexual deviations, it would then be a matter of the unveiled representation of harsh or painful scenes (without fear, O Irony, of shocking the reader!), with, of course, particular attention to the problems of material life and chiefly to the domestic difficulties of the poorer classes. The factory and the shantytown would thus, by nature, be more "realistic" than idleness and luxury, adversity more realistic than happiness. It would be a matter, in short, of merely giving the world certain colors and a signification stripped of prettiness, following a more or less bastardized formula of Emile Zola.

Now all this has scarcely any meaning the moment we realize that not only does each of us see in the world his own reality, but that the novel is precisely what creates it. The style of the novel does not seek to inform, as does the chronicle, the testimony offered in evidence, or the scientific report, it *constitutes* reality. It never knows what it is seeking, it is ignorant of what it has to say; it is invention, invention of the world and of man, constant invention and perpetual interrogation. All those–politicians and others–who ask of a book only stereotypes, and who fear above all the spirit of contestation, can only mistrust literature.

Like everyone else, I have been the victim, on occasion, of the *realistic illusion.* At the period when I was writing *The Voyeur*, for example, while I was trying to describe exactly the flight of sea gulls or the movement of waves, I had occasion to make a brief trip in winter to the coast of Brittany. On the way, I told myself: here is a good opportunity to observe things "from life" and to "refresh my memory." But from the first gull I saw, I understood my error: on the one hand, the gulls I now saw had only very confused relations with those I was describing in my book, and on the other it couldn't have mattered less to me whether they did or not. The only gulls that mattered to me at that moment were those which were inside my head. Probably they came there, one way or another, from the external world, and perhaps from Brittany; but they had been transformed, becoming at the same time somehow more real *because* they were now imaginary.

Sometimes, too, exasperated by objections such as: "Things don't happen that way in life"; "There is no hotel like the one in *Marienbad*"; "A jealous husband doesn't behave like the one in *Jealousy*"; "The Turkish adventures of your Frenchman, in *L'Immortelle*, are unconvincing"; "Your soldier lost *In the Labyrinth* isn't wearing his military insignia in the right place"; etc., I myself try to situate my arguments on the realistic level, and I speak of the subjective existence of that hotel, or of the direct psychological truth (hence, not susceptible to analysis) of this agonized husband fascinated by his wife's suspect (or too natural) behavior. And no doubt I hope that my novels and films are defensible from this point of view as well. But I know perfectly well that my intention is elsewhere. I do not transcribe, I construct. This had been even the old ambition of Flaubert: to make something out of nothing, something that would stand alone, without having to lean on anything external to the work; today this is the ambition of the novel as a whole.

We measure how far the "lifelike" and the "typical" are from being able to serve as criteria still. It would seem, in fact, as if the *false*—that is at once the possible, the impossible, lies, hypotheses, etc.—had become one of the privileged themes of modern fiction; a new kind of narrator is born: no longer a man who describes the things he sees, but at the same time a man who invents the things around him and who sees the things he invents. Once these hero-narrators begin ever so little to resemble "characters," they are immediately liars, schizophrenics, or victims of hallucinations (or even writers, who are creating their own story). We must emphasize the importance here, in this perspective, of the novels of Raymond Queneau (*Le Chiendent* and *The Skin of Dreams* in particular) whose texture often, and whose movement always, are rigorously those of the imagination.

In this new realism, it is therefore no longer *verisimilitude* that is at issue. The little detail which "rings true" no longer holds the attention of the novelist, in the spectacle of the world or in literature; what strikes him—and what we recognize after many avatars in his writings—is more likely, on the contrary, the little detail that rings *false*.

Thus, even in Kafka's diaries, when the writer notes down what he has noticed during the day in the course of a walk, he retains merely fragments which are not only without importance, but further, which seem to him cut off from their signification, hence from their *verisimilitude:* the stone abandoned for no good reason in the middle of a street, the bizarre gesture of a passer-by, incomplete, clumsy, not seeming to correspond to any function or precise intention. Partial objects, detached from their use, moments immobilized, words separated from their context, or cross-conversations, whatever rings a little false, that lacks "naturalness"—it is precisely this which rings truest to the novelist's ear.

Is it a question of what is called the *absurd*? Certainly not. For, elsewhere, an entirely rational and common element suddenly establishes itself with the same character of obviousness, of unmotivated presence, of inessential necessity. It *is*, that's all. But there is a risk for the writer: with the suspicion of absurdity the metaphysical danger returns. Non-sense, a-causality, and the void irresistibly attract higher worlds and supernatures.

Kafka's misfortune in this realm is exemplary. This *realistic* author (in the new sense which we are trying to define: creator of a material world, of a visionary presence) is also the one who has been most charged with meanings—"profound" meanings—by his admirers and exegetes. He has quickly become, above all in the eyes of the public, the man who pretended to be speaking about things of this world, but with the sole purpose of revealing the problematic existence of a beyond. Thus he describes the tribulations of his persistent (false) surveyor among the villagers; but his novel has no other concern than to make us dream about the near and remote life of a mysterious castle. When he describes the offices, the staircases, and the corridors where Josef K. pursues justice, it is solely to involve us in the theological notion of "Grace." And the rest in keeping.

Kafka's narratives would thus be no more than allegories. Not only would they require an explanation (which would summarize them perfectly, to the point where their entire content would be exhausted), but further, this signification would destroy in a radical way the tangible universe which constituted their texture. Thus literature would always consist, and in a systematic way, in speaking of *something else*. There would be a present world and a real world; the first would be the only visible one, the second the only important one. The novelist's role would be that of an intercessor: by a fake description of visible things—themselves entirely futile—he would evoke the "reality" hidden behind.

Now, on the contrary, if there is one thing of which an unprejudiced reading convinces us it is the absolute reality of the things Kafka describes. The visible world of his novels is certainly for him the real world, and what is behind (if there *is* something) seems without value, faced with the manifest nature of objects, gestures, words, etc. The hallucinatory effect derives from their extraordinary clarity and not from mystery or mist. Nothing is more fantastic, ultimately, than precision. Perhaps Kafka's staircases lead *elsewhere*, but they are *there*, and we look at them, step by step, following the detail of the banisters and the risers. Perhaps his gray walls hide something, but it is on them that the memory lingers, on their cracked whitewash, their crevices. Even what the hero is searching for vanishes before the obstinacy of his pursuit, his trajectories, his movements; they alone are made apparent, they alone are made real. In the whole of Kafka's work, man's relations with the world, far from having a symbolic character, are constantly direct and immediate.

The same is true of profound metaphysical significations as of political, psychological, or moral significations. To take those which are already known, in order to express them, goes counter to the major requirement of literature. As for those which the novel will have ultimately contributed to the world of the future, the best thing (both the most honest and the most astute) is not to be concerned about it today. In twenty years we have had occasion to judge how little subsisted of the Kafkaesque universe in the work of his so-called descendants, when the latter were merely reproducing the metaphysical content and forgetting the master's realism.

There remains, then, that immediate signification of things (descriptive, partial, always contested)—in other words, the signification which takes its place within the story, the anecdote of the book, as the profound (transcendent) signification takes its place outside it. It is on this immediate signification that the effort of exploration and creation will henceforth be brought to bear. From it, as a matter of fact, there can be no question of freeing oneself, or else we risk seeing the anecdote take over, and soon even transcendence (metaphysics loves a vacuum, and rushes into it like smoke up a chimney); for, within immediate signification, we find the absurd, which is theoretically nonsignification, but which as a matter of fact leads immediately, by a well-known metaphysical recuperation, to a new transcendence; and the infinite fragmentation of immediate meaning thus establishes a new totality, quite as dangerous, quite as futile. Even within signification, there is nothing left but the sound of words.

But the various levels of signification of language which we have just remarked have among them many interferences. And it is likely that the new realism will destroy certain of these theoretical oppositions. Today's life, today's science are dissolving many of the categorical antinomies established by the rationalism of past centuries. It is natural that the novel, which, like every art, claims to precede systems of thought and not to follow them, should already be in the process of melting down the terms of other pairs of contraries: matter-form, objectivity-subjectivity, signification-absurdity, construction-destruction, memory-presence, imagination-reality, etc.

It is repeated, by the extreme Right as by the extreme Left, that this new art is unhealthy, decadent, inhuman, and black. But the good health to which this judgment alludes is that of blinkers and formaldehyde, that of death. One is always decadent in comparison to things of the past: reinforced concrete in comparison to stone, socialism in comparison to paternalist monarchy, Proust in comparison to Balzac. And it is scarcely being inhuman to want to build a new life for man; such a life looks black only if—still mourning the old colors—we do not try to see the new beauties which illuminate it. What today's art proposes to the reader, to the spectator, is in any case a way of living in the present world, and of participating in the permanent creation of tomorrow's world. In order to succeed in this, the New Novel merely asks the public to have some confidence, still, in the power of literature, and it asks the novelist to be ashamed no longer of producing it.

A very widespread idea concerning the New Novel—one that has existed ever since articles were first written about it—is that it is a "passing fashion." This opinion, when one thinks about it a little, appears doubly preposterous. Even by identifying a certain kind of writing with a fashion (and there are always, certainly, followers who sniff the wind and imitate the modern forms without feeling their necessity, without even understanding their functioning, and of course without seeing that their handling requires at least some rigor), the New Novel would be, at worst, the movement of fashions, which destroy themselves as they develop in order to engender, continually, new ones. And that the forms of the novel change and pass is precisely what the New Novel is saying!

We find in this kind of remark—on the passing fashion, the pacification of the rebellious, the return to the healthy tradition, and other nonsense—only the good old attempt to prove, imperturbably, desperately, that "deep down nothing ever changes" and that "there is never anything new under the sun"; whereas in truth *everything is constantly changing* and *there is always something new.* Academic criticism would even like to make the public believe that the new techniques will simply be absorbed by the "eternal" novel and will some day serve to perfect some detail of the Balzacian character, of the chronological plot, and of a transcendent humanism.

It is possible that this day will come, as a matter of fact, and even quite soon. But once the New Novel begins "serving some purpose," whether psychological analysis, or the Catholic novel, or socialist realism, this will be the signal to the inventors that a New Novel is seeking to appear, and no one will yet know what it might serve—except literature.

11-75

SELECTED BIBLIOGRAPHY

A. *Works by Robbe-Grillet in French*

1. *Les Gommes*. Paris, Les Editions de Minuit, 1953.
2. *Le Voyeur*. Paris, Les Editions de Minuit, 1955.
3. *La Jalousie*. Paris, Les Editions de Minuit, 1957.
4. *Dans le labyrinthe*. Paris, Les Editions de Minuit, 1959.
5. *L'année dernière à Marienbad*. Paris, Les Editions de Minuit, 1961.
6. *Instantanés*. Paris, Les Editions de Minuit, 1962.
7. *Pour un nouveau roman*. Paris, Les Editions de Minuit, 1963.
8. *La maison de rendez-vous*. Paris, Les Editions de Minuit, 1965.

B. *Works by Robbe-Grillet in translation*

1. *The Erasers*. Translated by Richard Howard. New York, Grove Press, 1964. (Cloth and Evergreen E-392).

2. *The Voyeur*. Translated by Richard Howard. New York, Grove Press, 1958. (Evergreen E-121)
3. *Jealousy*. Translated by Richard Howard. New York, Grove Press, 1959. (Evergreen E-193)
4. *In the Labyrinth*. Translated by Richard Howard. New York, Grove Press, 1960. (Evergreen E-262)
5. *Last Year at Marienbad*. Translated by Richard Howard. New York, Grove Press, 1962. (Evergreen E-320)

C. *Books and articles on Robbe-Grillet*

1. Audry, Collette: "La caméra d'Alain Robbe-Grillet," *La Revue des Lettres Modernes*, nos. 36-38 (1958), pp. 131-140.
2. Barnes, Hazel: "The Ins and Outs of Alain Robbe-Grillet," *Chicago Review*, Vol. XVI, no. 3 (Winter-Spring 1962), pp. 21-42.
3. Barthes, Roland: "Littérature littérale: Alain Robbe-Grillet," *Critique*, nos. 100-101 (septembre-octobre 1955), pp. 820-826.
4. ....: Littérature objective: Alain Robbe-Grillet," *Critique*, nos. 86-87 (juillet-août 1954), pp. 581-591.
5. Berger, Yves: "*Dans le labyrinthe*," *Nouvelle Nouvelle Revue Française*, no. 85 (janvier 1960), pp. 112-118.
6. Blanchot, Maurice: "Notes sur un roman" [on *Le Voyeur*], *Nouvelle Nouvelle Revue Française*, Vol. III, no. 31 (julliet 1955), pp. 105-112.
7. Bonnot, Gérard: "Marienbad ou le parti de

Dieu," *Les Temps Modernes*, no. 187 (decembre 1961), pp. 752-768.

8. Brée, Germaine: "Jalousie: New Blinds or Old?" *Yale French Studies*, no. 24 (1960), pp. 87-91.
9. Champigny, Robert: "In Search of the Pure Récit," *American Society of the Legion of Honor Magazine* (Winter 1956-1957), pp. 331-343.
10. Dort, Bernard: "Sur les romans de Robbe-Grillet," *Les Temps Modernes*, no. 136 (juin 1957), pp. 1989-1999.
11. Friedman, Melvin: "The Neglect of Time," *Books Abroad*, Vol. XXXVI, no. 2 (Spring 1962), pp. 125-130.
12. Goytisolo, Juan: *Problemas de la novela*. [Chapter on Robbe-Grillet]. Barcelona, Seix Barral, 1959.
13. Hahn, Bruno: "Plan du Labyrinthe de Robbe-Grillet," *Les Temps Modernes*, no. 172 (juillet 1960), pp. 150-168.
14. Labarthe, André S.: "Marienbad Année Zéro," *Cahiers du Cinéma*, no. 123 (septembre 1961), pp. 28-31.
15. Labarthe, André and Jacques Rivette: "Entretien avec Resnais et Robbe-Grillet," *Cahiers du Cinéma*, no. 123 (septembre 1961), pp. 1-8.
16. Lefebvre, Maurice: "*La Jalousie*," *Nouvelle Nouvelle Revue Française*, Vol. V, no. 7 (juillet 1957), pp. 146-149.
17. Mauriac, Claude: *L'alittérature contemporaine*. [Chapter on Robbe-Grillet]. Paris, Editions Albin Michel, 1958.
18. Minor, Anne: "*La Jalousie*," *The French Re-*

view, Vol. XXXII (April 1959), pp. 477-479.

19. Morrissette, Bruce: "En relisant Robbe-Grillet," *Critique*, no. 146 (juillet 1959), pp. 579-608.
20. ....: "Oedipus and Existentialism" [on *The Erasers*], *Wisconsin Studies in Contemporary Literature* (Fall 1960), pp. 43-73.
21. ....: "Surfaces et structures dans les romans de Robbe-Grillet," *The French Review*, Vol. XXXI, no. 5 (April 1958), pp. 364-369.
22. ....: *Les romans de Robbe-Grillet*. Paris, Editions de Minuit, 1963. [Contains a bibliography].
23. ....: "Roman et cinéma: le cas de Robbe-Grillet," *Symposium*, Vol. XV, no. 2 (Summer 1961), pp. 85-104.
24. Nadeau, Maurice: "Le nouveau roman," *Critique*, nos. 123-124 (août-septembre 1957), pp. 707-722.
25. Ollier, Claude: "Ce soir à Marienbad," *Nouvelle Nouvelle Revue Française*, Vol. XVIII, no. 106 (octobre 1961) and no. 107 (novembre 1961), pp. 906-912.
26. Peyre, Henri: "Monkeys in a Cage" [on *La Jalousie*], *The New York Times* Sunday Book Review, November 22, 1959.
27. Picon, Gaetan: "Le problème du *Voyeur*," *Mercure de France* (octobre 1955), pp. 20-26.
28. Pingaud, Bernard: "*Dans le labyrinthe* d'Alain Robbe-Grillet," *Les Lettres Nouvelles* (7 octobre 1959), pp. 38-41.

29. ....: *Ecrivains d'aujourd'hui.* [Chapter on Robbe-Grillet]. Paris, Grasset, 1960.

30. ....: "Lecture de *La Jalousie*," *Les Lettres Nouvelles*, no. 50 (juin 1957), pp. 901-906.

31. Rainoird, Manuel: "*Les Gommes* d'Alain Robbe-Grillet," *Nouvelle Nouvelle Revue Française*, Vol. I, no. 5 (juin 1953), pp. 1108-1109.

32. Ricardou, Jean: "Description et Infraconscience chez Robbe-Grillet," *Nouvelle Nouvelle Revue Française*, Vol. VII, no. 11 (novembre 1960), pp. 890-900.

33. Stoltzfus, Ben F.: *Alain Robbe-Grillet and the New French Novel.* With a preface by Harry T. Moore. Carbondale (Ill.), Southern Illinois University Press, 1964. [Contains a bibliography].

34. Weightman, J. C.: "Robbe-Grillet," *Encounter*, Vol. XVIII, no. 3 (March 1962), pp. 30-40. Also in his *The Novelist as Philosopher*, Oxford University Press, 1962.